Better

Jaime Samms

Dreamspinner Press

Published by
Dreamspinner Press
382 NE 191st Street #88329
Miami, FL 33179-3899, USA
http://www.dreamspinnerpress.com/

Better

Cover Art by Anne Cain   annecain.art@gmail.com
Cover Design by Mara McKennen

ISBN: 978-1-61372-342-5

Printed in the United States of America
First Edition
January 2012

eBook edition available
eBook ISBN: 978-1-61372-343-2

This book is for everyone who got through,
found their strength, and made it to a better place,
and to those who helped them do it.

Thanks to Paul G. Bens Jr. for his support way back when this story first began to take shape. It was a long time getting to where it is, and his encouragement was a big stepping stone for me.

Thanks, also, to Ariel for keeping my butt in the seat and always lending an ear when I got stuck.

Chapter
One

TIMES like this, every tiny scar on Jesse's forearms tingled, like they were trying to crawl off his skin. He rubbed at them, trying to calm the discomfort even as his heart rate soared and heat climbed up into his hairline. Those deep blue eyes captured and held his attention.

Well aware he was staring like an idiot, Jesse tore his gaze away from the big blond on the other side of the room and turned back to his work.

"His name is Aadon."

The voice in his ear made Jesse start. "Shh!"

"Just saying."

"Shh-ush!" Jesse scowled at the woman grinning at him across the library checkout counter.

She smiled her knowing, annoying little smile and flipped her book closed. "You are so busted."

"Sarah!"

She leaned close and whispered the next tidbit directly in Jesse's ear. "He's looking over here again."

Jesse shifted his shoulders, shrugging off her nearness. In the close, quiet confines of the library's checkout counter, her breath on his neck was unwelcome. It felt like a hot gust, blowing the debris of old, sharp memories over his skin, and he shuffled a step away. He did glance over, though, just in time to see Aadon's head lower.

Sarah shrugged and hopped off her stool. "Jesse." She snapped her fingers in front of his face. "I'll see you at home?"

"Whose home?" Jesse blinked at her, forcing himself to pay attention.

"Yours. I'll order pizza."

"Again?"

"Yes, again. Only way we can get half vegetarian and half carnivore."

"You and your meat," he muttered.

She leaned across the counter and pecked his cheek. "Puts hair on your chest. You should try it some time."

"Whatever."

She gathered up her books and sauntered out the door.

Jesse managed to keep his eyes on the work of scanning books from the return bin for a whole three minutes more before glancing back at the object of their conversation.

Aadon still sat in the nearest cubicle along the wall, his back to the sea of heavy wooden tables stretched down the center of the room. His head, sporting a glorious mane of blond hair, bent over an open textbook. The view Jesse had of his broad shoulders and long, lean back spoke of an athletic body not dependant on a gym membership for its tone and shape. His profile showed a prominent nose and generous lips, and long, thick lashes gracing eyes Jesse already knew were a clear, vibrant blue. He wished, suddenly, he could chase away the frown that turned those full lips down at the corners and creased his brow into sharp furrows.

He caught himself imagining his own fingers teasing away the frown lines, pictured himself plucking at the down-turned lips with his own until Aadon finally caught his face in a firm grip and kissed him breathless. The thought did catch Jesse's breath and caused his heart to trip over itself inside his chest. He let out a soft curse, sure it was an image he was never going to get out of his head.

For the next half hour, between checking out books and logging those returned, he watched the blond man's head bent over his studies. He couldn't drag his attention away from the big sure hands taking notes and holding the paper cup from which he drank his coffee. Jesse should have stopped him from even bringing the coffee into the library, but admonishing him for something he did himself and setting that kind of double standard wasn't the first impression he wanted to make. Trouble was, he didn't know what kind of impression he *did* want to make. Maybe none at all. That seemed safest. Shaking his head at the thought the gorgeous man would even notice him, Jesse turned his full attention back to his task. Eventually, the soft murmur of voices from the tables and the background hum of the old fluorescent lights made him feel at home again. Beige and staid the library might be, but the smells of book dust and quiet suited him.

He'd managed to convince himself he didn't really care by the time he worked up the nerve to look again, only to find deep blue eyes turned on him, a thoughtful look steady in their depths. Jesse momentarily panicked. What if he and Sarah had been talking too loud? Had the guy heard them discussing him? Shit. Did he know what Jesse was thinking? That imaginary kiss flashed through his mind again, and he flushed hot the way it stirred every nerve ending. Jesse swallowed the sudden, quivering lump in his throat and nodded slightly. *Acknowledge. Be polite. He's not a mind reader. Probably isn't even gay.*

Aadon smiled, baring perfect white teeth and showing dimples.

Jesse froze. Guys did not smile at other guys like that unless…. The lump was back, along with a creeping spread of heat rising up his neck and into his cheeks and curling down his spine to tingle in his groin. He looked away quickly.

"Excuse me?"

A book shushed across the counter, bumping into Jesse's fingers, and he whirled just in time to catch it from spilling over the edge and onto his toes. A man stood at the counter, a few more books in his long-fingered hands. Freckles cascaded down his nose, across his cheeks, and down his bare arms, even sprinkled across the backs of his hands as he spread the array of books in front of him. "Can I sign these out please?"

Heat rose further up Jesse's cheeks.

The guy's gaze flicked over to Jesse's left, where Aadon sat, then back to Jesse, too neutral not to have noticed he'd been obviously spellbound by a stranger. And a male one at that.

"Uhh… sure. Yeah." Jesse sighed. There should be a rewind button for his life. Or at least for this day. He'd have called in sick.

The man just smiled. "Don't worry about it." He pushed a thatch of red hair out of his eyes. "He's worth looking at. My girlfriend is in his ethics class, and she barely takes a note."

Jesse laughed nervously. There was his answer about Beautiful's orientation. He took the guy's student card to scan. *Leo Quinn.* The yellow bar across the top proclaimed him to be in his third year, the same as Jesse, but his campus was the Engineering University, as opposed to the General Arts College Jesse was affiliated with.

"I'd be jealous," Leo was saying, leaning in slightly and winking, "if I didn't know he's firmly in your camp."

"'Scuse me?" Jesse's head shot up in alarm. He found himself once again the focus of those very blue eyes. Aadon was watching him, a slightly shocked look on his face.

The man at the counter waved a hand dismissively, drawing Jesse's horrified attention back to him. "It's all good, dude."

"Right." Trying to hide the blush behind the plastic rim of his coffee cup, Jesse sipped at the cold brew as he handed the card back. He picked up one of the books. At least his hands didn't shake. Carefully, he damped the flash of panic and set the book down again. "That obvious, am I?" He didn't much care if people knew he was gay. He didn't hide it. But this was hardly a conversation he wanted to be having with Aadon watching him so closely.

Leo smiled and leaned closer to Jesse, offering a wink and a huge grin. "Aadon and I go back a long way, and he hasn't fallen for a straight guy since we were thirteen and he tried to get me to pull his taffy."

Jesse almost snorted coffee out his nose. "Pull his taffy? Now there's one I haven't heard before."

Leo grinned and held out his hand. "I'm Leo, by the way."

Jesse pointed at the card still sitting on the counter and nodded. Heavy calluses on Leo's palm made his firm grip seem that much harder. Jesse pulled his hand free quickly. "Jesse."

"Oh, I know."

Jesse blinked in surprise. "You do?" He hid new discomfort by concentrating on checking out Leo's stack of books. The rhythmic beep of the computer scanner served to calm his nerves some with its familiarity. Still. People shouldn't know who he was. He was careful that people didn't know who he was. He'd come to school halfway across the country so people didn't know who he was.

Leo smiled, and Jesse found the expression less than comforting. "I do." He tilted his head in Aadon's direction, tossed a hank of red hair out of his eyes, and grinned. "He's had you under observation for a while now."

"Shithead," Aadon muttered from right behind Leo.

Jesse dropped the book he was holding. "He has? You have?" Shit, shit, *shit!*

"You sound surprised," Aadon drawled, enthralled by Jesse's obvious shock, but not amused at how Leo had put him on the spot. He'd kick his ass for that, later.

"I—" Jesse didn't know what to say, so he said nothing for a moment. When the silence stretched way past awkward, he mumbled: "Not like we're quite in the same league." He squeezed his eyes closed in belated realization that sounded pathetic. "College. Not in the same college," he muttered. Best let Aadon know now he wasn't expecting anything to come from Leo thrusting them into this ridiculously awkward situation.

Leo flicked his eyes from Jesse's face down his body and back up again. "I don't know what league you think you're in, but I promise, even I can see what Aadon sees, so I would hardly count myself out of the game if I were you. Besides, you have that whole"—he waggled his fingers in the air—"mysterious never-seen-with-a-boyfriend thing going on, which is plenty to catch Aadon's attention all by itself."

"Leo! Shut it!"

Leo laughed, picked up his books, and grinned at them both.

Jesse couldn't catch his breath. His chest tightened, and he blindly leaned back on the far counter, away from the other men. How did they know he didn't have a boyfriend? How did they know he even wanted one?

Backing away from the counter, loaded down with books and that huge grin on his face, Leo just shrugged. "All I know?" he said to Jesse. "I plan on seeing a lot more of you before the semester's out."

Aadon smacked Leo on the back of the head as the other man passed. "Asshole."

Leo just smirked at him. "Stop procrastinating, dude."

"Fuck you."

Leo laughed, glanced at Jesse, and snickered even harder before dodging another blow from Aadon. "Later!"

Jesse watched the door swing closed behind him. What the hell was he supposed to do now?

"You all right?" Aadon asked, concern bubbling up at the pale cast to Jesse's features.

Jesse nodded. *Perfect first impression. Have a panic attack at the thought he might talk to you. Excellent.*

"Hello, Aadon." Out of nowhere, Jesse's boss appeared, her sharp tone clipping the words off. "I see you've taken to studying on weekends too, then? This is the third weekend in a row." One of her eyebrows rose above the cold metal rim of her glasses, though she didn't actually look up from the books she was sorting. "I thought you were strictly a weeknight researcher."

"Unlike you, Miss Stathopoulos, lovely as you are, I need my beauty sleep." He nodded in Jesse's direction. "I see you have new help."

Stathopoulos barely acknowledged the flippant flattery. "He's coming along, I suppose. Jesse, dear, go in the back and fetch the new magazines, please."

"Yes, ma'am." Grateful for the offered escape, Jesse hurried off.

"Really, Thea? You going to be Jesse's aunt too, now?"

"Leave him be, Sobrino." She waved her hand in his face even while she was already turning her attention to the books. "Nephew. You, my sobrino make all the pretty ones blush," she muttered.

"Is he all right?" Aadon watched Jesse's hastily retreating back until he disappeared through the door to the back offices before turning his gaze back to his aunt.

The old librarian peered at Aadon over the rims of her glasses. "A panic attack, Sobrino. Or damn near. Do not get in his business unless you mean it. You understand?"

"Since when do you care so very much about your staff, Thea?"

She opened each of Aadon's books, scanning them one at a time, not taking her eyes from the bar codes, except to glance at the computer screen to her right.

"Well?"

"I don't know his story, Aadon. I only know…."

"What?" He leaned over the counter, trying to get his aunt to look up at him. "What do you know, Thea?"

"He's careful about everything, Aadon. A person like that?" She shook her head. "Someone that protective of themselves has been hurt, and you,"— she finally looked at him and poked her scanner in his direction, the bright light in her eye making him flinch—"you don't have a long record of being careful yourself."

"So… what?" Aadon glanced toward the door to the back room, more intrigued than ever. "He's fragile or something?"

"Or something." She sighed and set the books down, finally looking at her nephew for real. "I don't know, Aadon. He's never said anything to me about it, but he reminds me too much of Ricky. Not"—she held up a hand when Aadon would have said something—"the drugs or any of that. He's not gone down the same road your brother has, but maybe he comes from some place similar. Just… he's got walls up, and he isn't about to knock them down or jump over them for just anyone. I can see that much."

Aadon gazed at the closed office door. If anyone knew about watching the world from behind a wall of "careful" and "not worth the risk" it was his aunt. He knew she was telling him not to get involved. He knew she was. But if he was like Ricky, if something had happened to Jesse like what happened to Ricky to make his brother close off, turn to drugs, ruin himself over it, maybe Aadon could help. Maybe, knowing how it *could* go, he could make whatever it was better for Jesse before it got any worse.

Across the counter from him, his aunt shook her head. "How you can be your father's son, I will never know."

Aadon frowned. "What does that mean?"

She had already turned her attention back to completing his scan out. "A smart man would walk away now."

Aadon grinned. "I am the smartest person you ever met, Thea. You've said so yourself."

"And I take it back," she muttered.

Aadon leaned over the desk and kissed her forehead. "No you don't." He gathered up the books she shoved at him. "Don't worry. I promise I won't get my heart broken." With one last look at the sealed door, he flashed another grin and sauntered out, pretending not to hear her last whispered, *Not your heart I'm worried about.* He wasn't an asshole. He had no intention of breaking anything except maybe Leo's head for putting Jesse on the spot like that. But then again… maybe not that, either. Now, at least, the ball was rolling, and he was past the odd paralysis that had kept him from speaking up sooner. This was good. This could be good. He smiled to himself and turned toward Leo's and the free dinner his best friend's girlfriend was sure to have almost on the table by now.

Chapter
Two

"THAT boy," Stathopoulos muttered as she pushed into the tiny, crowded back office.

"What boy?" Jesse asked, looking up from where he was unwrapping the latest edition of *Vogue* for the library shelf. He suspected he knew who she was talking about, but he asked anyway.

"You have to watch a boy like that, Jesse."

"Like what's his name?" He nodded at the door propped open now with a box of books Miss Stathopoulos shoved in front of it with one foot. "Aadon?" As if he could forget the name. Or the blue eyes. Or Aadon's blond hair flopping across his forehead, almost obscuring the way his brow wrinkled with every grin and frown. *Oh, I'm watching.* How could he not watch that?

"You have to be careful around boys like that. You never know what they are after," Stathopoulos admonished, shaking her head, a troubled look on her face.

Jesse knew what he wanted Aadon to be after, but he said nothing. That was a precarious thought. Precarious because he had not thought it about any guy in such a long time. Precarious because for the first time since he'd moved here, even if the thought made his heart stop with fear, he still wanted to pursue it.

"Boys like that...." She stared at Jesse a moment longer, as if there was something else she wanted to say.

"What about him?" She had Jesse curious now.

"Just be careful, Jesse. You never know what you might end up in."

She shook her head again and wandered off with a cart of books headed for the stacks.

Jesse wanted to stick his tongue out at her back, childish as it was. For the first time in how long he was actually interested in a guy and not freaking out about it, and she had to pour disapproval all over the feeling. Why? Because they were both guys? Jesse grimaced. He hoped not. People like that never cared to change their attitudes. He wanted to tell her—every time she commented—he *was* a boy like that. But he needed this job. His rent was already overdue, and his hours were sketchy to begin with. He saw no point alienating her. He just waved away the lingering stench of her perfume and pulled more plastic wrapping off the magazines.

AADON left the library humming, an armload of books he didn't need weighing down his limbs, but not his mood.

He hadn't been able to miss the whispers between Jesse and the girl Jesse was with, or the quick glances in his direction. He'd definitely caught the way Jesse blushed each time those shuttered brown eyes met his. Aadon had to admit that particular shade of pink was a complete turn on. He couldn't help but wonder if the tendency to blush so prettily was accompanied by a tendency to defer. The idea that the guy might be single, gay, *and* lean toward submissive was one Aadon found impossible to get out of his head.

He just wished he had been able to hear what they had been saying. He hadn't had the same problem when Leo had approached Jesse. He'd managed to overhear every pointed thing his best friend had said to the shy stranger. Later, he'd kick Leo's ass for that. Still. It was nice to know for sure that two of his three criteria were indeed met. Jesse was single and gay. He smiled to himself. Sometimes, submissive was something a guy didn't know about himself until it was pointed out to him.

Aadon could do that. And if Jesse didn't bend that way, that would be okay too. It wasn't a hard limit for Aadon. There was still something very seductively vulnerable about the man that Aadon couldn't get out of his head.

He'd been watching Jesse since the beginning of the semester, about a month, now, and not only was it intriguing that he never seemed to go on a date, there was a kind of innocent charm about him that drew Aadon's attention like a flame might draw a moth. Aadon chose to end the comparison there because everyone knew how that ended for the moth. And besides, Jesse didn't seem dangerous. Just interesting, in a quiet, oblivious sort of way, which Leo had confirmed with his not-so-subtle probing today.

Another smile flitted across Aadon's face. The expression felt so unfamiliar lately, and that observation drove it away almost instantly. The books felt heavier, and the sun dipped behind a cloud. There was every chance that no matter how interested he was in Jesse, the interest wouldn't be returned beyond the first date. Most guys, when they got a good glimpse of the life behind Aadon's careful front, had no real interest in the amount of baggage he had hidden in his closet. There was no reason to assume Jesse would be any different.

"Idiot," he admonished himself quietly as he crossed the street and fumbled for his car keys. "You don't have to make your life about Ricky."

Isn't that what Perry had told him? "Just forget your screwed up life and your screwed up brother and fuck me already."

If Aadon hadn't already told himself he was through with the occasional fucking Perry offered, that little gem would have done the trick. Even with his wrists bound behind his back and his ass in the air, Perry could be a class "A" jerk. He got off on the bondage, and when Aadon really wanted a good, mindless fuck, Perry was a good partner. When Aadon wanted a bit more docility, a chance to really take charge and take care of someone, well, Perry had no interest in that sort of submission, even once surmising, out loud, Aadon only wanted to pretend to care for someone to make up for Ricky. Which had just pissed Aadon off royally. Not only was it not true, it was downright presumptuous of Perry to assume he knew either Aadon or Ricky's situation well enough to say it. More and more these days, Aadon simply found that mindlessness wasn't enough. He wanted an actual relationship, with an actual person who wasn't an ass. A relationship that didn't revolve around easy sex.

Tossing his load of books on the passenger seat next to him, Aadon let out an explosive sigh. Perry was not worth the time or energy it took to get worked up over him. Ricky... well, Ricky wasn't going anywhere, and that situation wasn't changing any time soon. He glanced at his watch and made a note of the date. One week from Ricky's next psych appointment. He could call his father and ask him to go, but the argument and the stress of worrying if he actually did or not wasn't worth having the weekend free.

He did, however, call the clinic and change the appointment from Monday morning to Sunday afternoon. Ricky's new doctor was more than willing to meet on a weekend if she didn't have to meet with their father.

Adamos Dounias was not an easy man to talk to, even when you were giving him news he wanted to hear. Receiving yet another report that his eldest son was not responding to his treatment, or that he'd once again turned violent in the face of a seemingly innocent gesture from another patient, was never news Mr. Dounias ever wanted to hear.

Hanging up the phone, Aadon caught himself letting out another sigh and instead, called to mind the memory of Jesse's shy but interested glance from over the librarian's shoulder. He stole a glance of his own at the mountain of books he'd signed out just to get a chance to talk to Jesse and found the tune he'd been humming. Sunday afternoon would come soon enough. In the meantime, he would pluck every tidbit of information he could from Leo's head and figure out a way to ask Jesse on a date

What was the worst that could happen? They'd go out, have a nice dinner, maybe dance a bit, and if that was all that came of it, it was better than Perry. Mind made up, he pulled out of the parking lot and pointed his car down the street toward the house Leo shared with his girlfriend and her cousins.

"HEY." Leanne was just pulling into her driveway as Aadon got out of his car. "I guess you're here to see Leo. What'd he do now?"

"Only tried to embarrass the crap out of me."

She smiled wickedly. "He did say he was going to talk to that guy you've been eyeing once and for all. And I must say"—she opened the front door and ushered him inside—"you don't usually moon quite so long before making your move. So what's up with this guy? Leo!" She dumped her purse and keys and kicked off her shoes. "Addy's here!"

"Really, Lee?" Aadon complained. He'd known both Leo and Leanne about as long as he could remember, but that didn't mean they had to still use that old nickname.

"Of course, sugar. You staying for supper? Krissy's making that thing she does." She whirled her hand in the air, and gave a little shrug. "And Leo just made bread, by the smell."

"You are spoiled rotten, Lee, you know that."

"So stay and share in the spoils, yeah?"

Aadon shrugged. He never refused Leo's fresh baking or Krissy's cooking.

"Hey, Addy." Leo tossed off an unholy grin and snapped the kitchen towel he was holding when Aadon made a lunge for him. The material landed a stinging snap across Aadon's thigh, and he yelped. "Hey, you swung first."

"And you deserve it," Aadon griped, rubbing a palm over the sting. "I cannot believe you talked to him."

Leo turned back toward the kitchen, talking over his shoulder as Aadon followed. "I cannot believe you've been mooning for over a month. What is it about this guy, anyway?"

"I do not moon," Aadon said, flopping into a chair at the table. "And there's nothing special about him."

"Oh, I think there is." Leo winked in Aadon's direction. "He's got the hots for you, for one thing. Did you see the way he was looking at you?"

"Ya think?" Aadon straightened and let the lid of the sugar bowl he'd been fiddling with fall back with a clink.

"Oh yeah. I mean, as far as a guy like that gets the hots for anyone."

"What do you mean, 'guy like that'?" Aadon's brow furrowed, and he went back to spinning the lid on the sugar bowl.

"I mean"—Leo grabbed the entire bowl and set it on the counter out of Aadon's reach—"he's no Perry fucking Sunshine."

Aadon laughed. "Perry Sunshine?"

"Oh, didn't Lee tell you? He's the new spokesperson for Sunshine Sandwiches and"—he waved a hand in the air—"whatever."

"Spokesperson? You mean he wears that stupid foam sun and stands on the corner handing out fliers?"

"Apparently, it's all part of his program," Leanne interjected from where she was standing at the counter peeling carrots.

"I thought he was in marketing." Aadon couldn't quite picture the Perry he knew parading around in yellow tights and a foam billboard. Trying just made him want to giggle.

"Oh, he is. The research class Krissy's in had a shakedown. The new prof was not impressed by the papers people handed in last week, apparently. She handed out assignments based on what she thought the flaws in each paper were. Krissy'll be cold calling some cell phone company's client list next week trying to up-sell digital packages, or something."

"How is any of this supposed to help them graduate?"

"No idea."

"Still," Aadon mused. "Perry as Mr. Sunshine. Might be something to see."

"Hopefully," Leo said, turning to face him, "only to get that jerk out of your system once and for all. Because he is a jerk, and this Jesse guy"—he gave a tiny shrug—"he seems nice."

"Nice."

"Decent. Shy, maybe, and a little not so aware of how hot he is, but yeah. Nice." He turned back to the bread he was tipping out of the pans. "And nice is good, Aadon." He glanced up to where Leanne was smiling at him, and he smiled back. "Nice lasts. You should give it a try."

"Well shit." Aadon slumped into his chair.

"What?"

"Here I was going to be all up in your face for interfering, and kick your ass or something, and you go all... *nice* on me." He made a face.

Leo shrugged again, but smiled. "Self-preservation, my friend. I am not an idiot."

"Says you."

But on his way home, Aadon had to admit, to himself if no one else, that Leo's approval went a long way toward convincing him it was time to make a move. Shy or not, Jesse was a good-looking guy, and surely he wasn't going to stay single for long. He drove home, once again humming, and with his mind made up. He could spend the week finishing the paper that was due on Monday, and on Friday night he'd go to the library and take the plunge. How hard could it be to ask a guy out anyway?

THAT week, Jesse got more studying done than he had in the entire previous semester. He went to the library every night, books under his arm for cover, but never saw Aadon once. It meant he knew what he was doing Friday on his Anthro test, but not even catching a glimpse of Aadon disappointed him just the same. And maybe, it distanced him from the idea that either Aadon or Leo had any interest in—or even knew about—his past. Maybe a simple flirtation was just that. Simple.

Disappointing that it hadn't amounted to anything, but even still, the idea he *was* disappointed was a nice alternative to the constant lump of agitation and tension he'd lived with for so long. It made him think maybe, *maybe* he could do this again. With Aadon, or with some other guy, but either way, it was a yank out of the closet he'd tried to stuff himself back into. It was a relief to find he wasn't as scared as he thought he'd be.

So on Friday, rather than getting up, shaving, showering, and dressing practically on his way out the door, late for work, he was up just past dawn. He did shave and shower, then spent the next half hour staring at the contents of his closet in dismay. He had to pick something, though. He couldn't show up with a threadbare Eeyore towel wrapped around his waist, so he pulled on black jeans and a long-sleeved Death Cab T-shirt, decided the dark tones were too stark against his pale skin, and reached for the blue jeans and a cotton sweater that was the exact right golden brown to match his eyes. Then he spent an hour on his hair, wet it down twice, and it was wet again when Sarah knocked and let herself into his apartment.

"What are you doing?" She watched from the bathroom doorway, peering over the pink ceramic rim of her coffee mug as he fussed.

"Getting ready for work, what does it look like?"

"It looks like you're having a nervous breakdown." She came into the room and sat down behind him, perched on the edge of the tub.

His shoulders slumped, and he let the hairbrush clatter into the sink. "I am."

"Stop trying so hard, sweetie. You're fine. He's been watching for a month now, and you never did anything special to attract his attention."

Jesse peered at her through the mirror. "You sure? I look okay?" He wondered if she could read his other, unasked question in the slump of his shoulders. *Is he just playing? Does he know?* "Maybe he doesn't even—"

"You look fine." She stood and pulled the hair out of his face. "You look perfect. If he doesn't like you for what you have to offer, forget it." She kissed his cheek and drew back to give him a warm smile. "Jesse, if he's fucking around, I'll skin him, okay? But I saw him watching you when you weren't watching him. I honestly don't think he is. I think he really likes you."

"Then where was he all week?"

"Uhh?" She shrugged. "His life? Maybe he was doing that."

"Right." Jesse flushed and slumped against the sink again. "I'm an idiot."

"You're nervous." She smiled at his reflection, and he met her eye, seeking the mocking bite she was so good at. There was just patience there, and understanding. "This is a big thing, right? Aadon, or not Aadon. This"— she indicated his attire, his bathroom still in disarray from his morning preparations—"getting out there again. Jesse, this is scary. And good. You need this." She grinned. "I'm proud of you, bonehead, now fix your hair, and get a move on before Stathopoulos has your nuts in a sling and has you making up for being late with extra weekend shifts."

"Okay." With a deep breath, he squared his shoulders. "Have to do this some time, right? And I mean… look at him." He grinned. "Worth a shot." He left the bathroom and went to the door, pulling on his sneakers and grabbing his bag. "Let's go."

She stood just outside the bathroom door.

"What?" he demanded, the door already pulled half-open.

"You're not really going to wear those shoes, are you?"

"Umm." He looked down at his feet. "No?"

"No."

She pushed her mug into his hand and left him standing there while she disappeared into his room. He heard the sound of his closet door scraping open and her rummaging in the bottom. Peering into her cup, he lamented her sweet tooth. He could smell the sugar, and it kept him from stealing a sip. Finally, she came back with a pair of brown loafers he'd forgotten he owned. "Put these on."

"They're dress shoes."

"And they'll look killer with that outfit."

He tilted his head, unconvinced.

"Trust me."

"Fine, fine." He toed off the sneakers and replaced them with the dress shoes. The polished leather poking out from under his jean cuffs looked smart.

"See? Auntie Sarah knows what she's talking about."

Jesse nodded. "So she does." He shot her a grateful smile. "Thanks."

"You know me." She took back the mug. "Always willing to help you get yourself out there."

His smile thinned a little with the realization he was actively trying to get another man's attention, and her left eye narrowed a tiny fraction.

"Listen, honey, it's not going to be like last time."

"You don't know that."

"Any more than you know it will be. You have to at least try, don't you?"

He nodded. She was right. It was time to try again. It wouldn't be like last time. He shuddered at the memory. Nothing could be as bad as last time.

JESSE waited and watched all day. No Aadon. Maybe he had lost interest after all. He spent the last hour of his shift alone in the deserted library re-shelving books in the stacks, feeling sorry for himself and his blistered feet. He had pushed the last book on Chinese history back into its place when he heard the door open. He glanced at his watch.

"You'd better know what you want," he called. "I'm closing up in ten minutes." He didn't really care if he sounded irritable and bitchy. He felt irritable and bitchy. He'd skipped his lunch break, worried Aadon would come and go while he was out eating, so not only was he hungry, but he felt like an idiot as well, just for caring that much whether or not he saw the man again.

"Oh, I have a pretty good idea what I'm after."

Jesse froze. He'd heard Aadon speak just that once, to the librarian, but it was impossible not to remember the buttery-smooth voice.

"I, um." Jesse wiped suddenly sweaty palms down his jeans and turned.

Aadon leaned against the end of the stack, arms folded across his chest, making his thick biceps bulge and strain the fabric of his cotton shirt. Jesse swallowed and forced his gaze upward, to Aadon's wide, expressive mouth.

Aadon flexed slightly. Not that he was trying to show off. Just that maybe this way, he could contain the wild thud of his heart and not look as flat-out stunned by Jesse's appearance as he felt. This was a different look for Jesse. Not the same long-sleeved T's and jeans, but just that tiny step up. Like he was trying, and that made Aadon a little lightheaded.

Jesse attempted a small up-curve of his lips, trying to relax, and was answered with a wide-open expression that crinkled the skin at the corners of Aadon's eyes. The grin that followed brought out his dimples, and Jesse managed at last to let go of the breath he was holding.

"Well, maybe I can help you find a book...?"

"Not interested in books." Aadon pushed himself upright and glanced at his own wristwatch. "Ten minutes, you say. You hungry?" Let him be hungry, he thought. Because if this was an attempt to make Aadon notice him, it worked. Normally good-looking, sweet, disheveled Jesse was delicious when he tried.

"I, uh." Jesse swallowed, regrouped in hopes he could remember how to complete a sentence, and nodded. "I could eat." Nerves shook his voice, and his palms dampened again. He shouldn't be this nervous. After all, he didn't even know this guy. They might turn out to have nothing in common. Aadon might be just a pretty face who couldn't hold Jesse's attention or interest for more time than it took to eat one meal.

"Okay, then." Aadon pushed his shirtsleeves up. "We can go to the pub on campus."

Jesse's nose turned up automatically. "The only food they have there that isn't meat has been soaking in a vat of grease since noon." He pushed the cart past Aadon to the counter and let it thud against the far wall of the small workspace.

"No deep-fried food, no meat. Got it."

"I'm not a health nut, or anything," Jesse hastily pointed out.

Aadon held up a hand. "Not to worry. My eating habits suck, I know that, but I grew up on Greek cooking. It's a hard habit to break."

"So I guess the Greek place down the street that serves a killer veggie dish is out, then."

"If it's not Mama's I won't touch it. Spoiled, I guess."

"Fair enough."

Jesse tried to think where else they might go that they would both find something on the menu to satisfy them.

"I know a place," Aadon suggested, just before the silence grew awkward. Lord. He could kick himself. Some lawyer he was going to make if just talking to a guy had him this tongue-tied. It had never happened before, and he couldn't figure out what the deal was now.

Except that Jesse took that moment to glance up at him through his lashes, a nervous, expectant expression parting his lips and making his dark eyes glimmer from under long bangs. The appeal hit Aadon in the gut, knocking the wind out of him.

"Uh." *Brilliant.* "Yeah. Just a little hole in the wall, but great food."

"Okay." Jesse nodded slightly. "Just give me a few."

It took the rest of the ten minutes for Jesse to tidy up, turn off the computers, and fish his bag out from under the desk. Aadon watched the way his hands flitted over the computer keys as he worked. The muscles and tendons along the back of his hands flexed as he gripped his bag, and Aadon's mouth watered. He had the sudden urge to reach over and push the sleeves of Jesse's sweater up to reveal the long, corded muscles of his forearms. It was a bit of a weird fetish. He could admit that. Maybe that was one of the things that intrigued Aadon so much about this man. Even in the hottest weather, he could never catch a glimpse of those forearms, so temptingly teased at in the movement of Jesse's agile hands and supple wrists, but never revealed.

Aadon's fingers twitched, and he crossed his arms over his chest, leaned against the counter on one hip, and waited. As Jesse shoved a few things into the backpack, Aadon frantically searched for something to talk about.

"You like working here?" he asked at last.

"Yeah." Jesse glanced at him, smiled slightly, and went back to his packing up. "Worked at the library back home all through high school. Kind of like coming home."

"Really."

Jesse blushed, which sent Aadon's pulse skyward. "Yeah. You ready for that intensity of geek?"

That drew an uncontrolled snort of laughter from Aadon. Jesse was anything but a geek in his eyes. "I'm ready for anything," he confessed, almost feeling on familiar ground with the flirting.

"Huh." Jesse's attention focused narrowly on his bag as he took out his keys and wallet and pushed the bag back under the counter. His blush flew up to his hairline, his gaze remained down. Aadon probably shouldn't find Jesse's nerves so adorable, but he did.

Jesse nodded at the door, glad Aadon took the hint and headed into the outer hallway. Turning off the lights, silencing the hum they made, he quickly followed after Aadon, set the alarm, and let out a deep breath, telling himself to calm the fuck down.

"There," Jesse breathed, relieved his nerves hadn't caused him to punch in the wrong code. It had been changed often enough because of him. Remembering numbers was not his long suit. "Always feel like I'm going to set the thing off myself," he admitted before glancing Aadon's way and managing a smile. "Ready?" He rattled his keys. "Your car or mine? I should warn you, though, mine is just short of a death trap." He fervently hoped Aadon would choose to let Jesse drive.

"We can walk, if you'd prefer."

Did Jesse's fear show through that much? He nodded. "Perfect."

It was. The wind had died down, leaving only a few clouds drifting in lazy tracks across the sky, and the evening sun was warm enough. Jesse's sweater kept him from getting cold but was not so warm he would sweat. The walk wasn't a long one, though Jesse did suddenly wish for more comfortable shoes. What if Aadon wanted to walk again after they ate? He struck Jesse as the kind of guy who liked activity; not quite a jock, but not the bookish type Jesse was.

"It's a nice night," Aadon commented as they walked from the library down the pink gravel path leading to the street. His low, soothing voice drew Jesse back gently.

Jesse nodded, wishing he had more skill at small talk. He could never think of a thing to say.

"You're in Anthropology?" Aadon asked.

Again, Jesse nodded.

"Law." Aadon ran a hand down his chest, and the motion caught Jesse's attention and held it as the hand dropped away to Aadon's side. He didn't know which was more enticing, the man's broad chest or the apparent strength in his big, square hands.

"I know." Jesse blushed when Aadon looked over at him, seeming mildly surprised, and definitely pleased, if the show of dimples was anything to go by. "I pay attention," Jesse mumbled.

"So I see," was all Aadon said, but the tone was enough to tell Jesse he'd been caught staring. Again.

Aadon felt the familiar tingle of excitement all the way to his toes. In settling for Perry, he'd forgotten what a rush it was when everything was new and uncertain.

They turned onto the sidewalk, threading through a knot of students headed toward the dorms just past the library. Coffee shops and bookstores lined the street, with a coin laundry and a craft supply store thrown in for good measure. At this time of day, most of the foot traffic headed back to campus. The two men navigated against the flow for half a block in silence.

Finally free of the crowd, Aadon jostled Jesse's shoulder lightly with his own, though he had to lean a little to accomplish it. The top of Jesse's head came about even with his chin. Just about perfect height, as far as he was concerned. "I didn't think you had noticed," he said. It was only a very slight lie. He shivered, remembering the feel of Jesse's eyes on him in the library, and the tingle spread.

"I had," Jesse replied, his tone casual, his hands stuffed deep in his jeans pockets.

The confession elicited a smile from Aadon and warmed the tingle from that zing of physical excitement to something a little deeper and harder to define.

Jesse glanced sidelong at Aadon, and at last, there was an answering glint in his eyes, as though he knew exactly the things he was doing to Aadon's insides.

Jesse relaxed into his own skin a bit. It felt good, having this effect on another man again. And there was most definitely an effect showing on Aadon's face and in the deep glow in his eyes and the way he leaned in slightly. Rather than making Jesse want to squirm away, it gave him confidence, made him feel a little bit powerful that this big guy was hanging on his words like he wanted to lap them up. "You like law?" he asked, struggling to get the image of Aadon lapping at things out of his head and failing utterly.

Aadon nodded. "I'd have to, to put this much work into it."

"And here I thought you were just coming to the library to see me."

"A happy bonus, that." He was quiet for a minute, and then answered the question more seriously. "Yes, I like law. And it isn't because my father and my uncle are both lawyers. That isn't the reason I decided to try for the bar. There are people in the world who need lawyers who can't afford them."

"Wow."

All that, Jesse thought, *and a big heart too.* Obviously, this was too good to be true, and the other shoe was going to fall any second. No. He wasn't going to think like that. Sarah was right. It wasn't going to be like last time. Jesse wasn't going to let it be like last time. He knew what he was doing now. At least, he knew what not to do.

He glanced at Aadon, flashed a smile, and marveled at the way Aadon's breath caught on the expression, even though the big man tried to hide it with a little grunt as he shunted around Jesse to pull open a shop door.

"Here we are. Leo says they have the best veggie burgers in the city." Aadon yanked the door open as flustered butterflies beat around inside his gut and made it hard to breathe whenever Jesse smiled. That smile was everything: a little bit shy, a little bit sexy, a little bit *knowing* what it did to Aadon.

"It's a big city," Jesse said doubtfully, turning to go inside and letting Aadon off his hook for the moment.

Jesse had walked by this hole in the wall every day on his way to and from classes and never noticed it. Usually, he shied away from fast-food places, and especially fast-food veggie burgers. They typically had nothing to redeem them. Aadon held the door open for him, though, so he could hardly refuse going inside.

It was nothing like what he expected. It certainly was not a fast-food joint. There was a diner counter with stools, but stools that looked comfortable, and the counter had been resurfaced in what looked like actual wood. The floor *was* wood, and on the left, a row of tables covered in white linen and adorned with a rainbow assortment of colored napkins were already mostly filled. Behind the counter, a young man Jesse couldn't help but notice in his tight fluorescent pink T-shirt and white, spiked hair, cleaned and stacked glasses on a tray.

The bartender smiled at Aadon. "Hey, you!" he called, lifting an arm in a flowery wave. His shirt rode up, away from the studded belt he certainly didn't need to hold up the painted-on white jeans to reveal a glittering green gem at his bellybutton. He pointed them to an unoccupied table. "Be right with, sweetie."

Aadon rolled his eyes. "Good thing he's related," he muttered. "Otherwise, I would have to call him out on that." It amused him, bringing people here for the first time. It was never what they expected. Jesse was no exception. His eyes went a bit wide as he looked around, his head swiveling.

"Not what I expected," he murmured.

Aadon grinned. "No one really expects this from the outside."

"I guess not. How long has it been here?"

Aadon shrugged as he nodded toward the table the bartender had pointed out to them. "Since I was in high school, at least." He placed a hand on Jesse's back when it began to seem like his date had taken root in the entrance and guided him toward the table. He tried to figure out if he imagined Jesse flinch away from the touch slightly, or if it was just a start of surprise. At least he moved forward, and when Aadon flattened his palm along the small of Jesse's back he didn't move away.

They pulled out chairs and sat, and Jesse straightened napkins and cutlery in a sudden bout of nervous fidgeting. "And has"—he tipped his head toward the bar—"has he been calling you Sweetie all that time?"

Aadon's brows went up. Jealousy? Already? That warm feeling in his gut lowered slightly at the thought, igniting a spark under Aadon's instinct to protect where he saw vulnerability. "He's been calling me all kinds of names since we could talk." He waited, curious if Jesse really was going to show insecurity, or if he was just curious.

"Oh." Jesse's gaze came up, frank, unavoidable, and almost demanding an answer to the question he wasn't asking.

"He's my cousin," Aadon said, the need to reassure a pressure he couldn't resist. "Me, him, and Leo. The three musketeers."

Jesse's eyebrows went up.

"Or something." Aadon waved a hand. "Don't worry. We never used our swords on each other."

Jesse's mouth fell open slightly, and Aadon grinned.

"That isn't what you were wondering?"

"No!" But he blushed and dipped his head. "Is that really a first date conversation?"

Aadon laughed out loud. "You are the first first date I've ever had who asked if I was knocking on the bartender's door."

"I like to know what I'm getting myself into," Jesse muttered, furious with himself. What kind of jerk asked for a sexual history before the drinks had even been ordered?

Aadon reached across the table to where Jesse was still fiddling with his knife. "I'm not celibate. But I'm not reckless. Good enough?"

Jesse nodded, his eyes fixed on where Aadon's fingers covered his. "Good enough," he whispered. By force of will, he kept his hand where it was, hoping it would show he wasn't all asshole, wasn't all insecure wimp. Wasn't afraid.

For a split second, Aadon was sure Jesse was going to pull free. Then he didn't, though his shoulders rounded, and he looked away, past Aadon's shoulder to the glass wall behind him. Something dark, slightly shadowy had invaded the other man's eyes, and Aadon took his hand back, smiled, and picked up his napkin. He shook it out and smoothed it over his lap as he spoke, hoping to smooth over Jesse's sudden shift of mood, to make it okay, whatever *it* was. "Good," he said, willing Jesse to look at him. "I have no problem setting that issue out on the table. I've had my share of guys, and also, my share of scares. I don't do drunk and spontaneous, and I always protect myself." He gave a little shrug. "No harm in getting that out in the open."

Jesse nodded and at last dragged his gaze back. "Same here. Careful."

Aadon got the feeling there was way more to that than those three words, but he let it go. This was a first date, not a marriage proposal. If Jesse needed that information for whatever reason, it wasn't unreasonable to ask for it. Early, maybe, but now Aadon could see the chinks his aunt had tried to point out to him. Careful was only the very tip of all the things Jesse was, and Aadon had an overwhelming desire to find out what else was under the surface.

Jesse could kick himself. For someone who didn't know how to make small talk, he sure knew how to dig into a guy's private affairs in a hurry. And Aadon hadn't even flinched. Either he was in this for the fast fuck and figured expedience was the way to go, or he actually might be the perfect guy. Jesse wasn't sure which was more intimidating.

He needed a distraction. Talk of Aadon's sex life was not making it easy to concentrate on much else. He could suddenly feel the places Aadon's hands had rested, the pressure on the small of his back and the warm slide of those thick fingers over his. Wavering anticipation seemed to ooze slowly outward from those spots, as though Jesse had already made up his mind where this was going to go. The thought excited and terrified him at once, and he wasn't sure if maybe the terror wasn't part of the excitement.

Blinking back those thoughts and where they might lead, he took another look around the restaurant.

The place was so much more than a simple hole-in-the-wall diner. Only a few of the couples at the tables were mixed. That should have made Jesse feel more at home, but it only made him more nervous. At the back of the room, where he expected to find doors to the kitchen, were huge glass panels, one of them hinged and sporting a long chrome bar at waist height. On the other side, he finally realized, was a full-fledged bar, complete with dance floor and spinning lights, though no one had yet turned them on.

"How cool is this place?" Aadon asked, following his gaze through the glass.

Jesse shrugged. He hadn't been in a bar in a long time. Not that he was in one, now, but even next to a closed one was closer than he'd been since he'd switched schools. He tried hard not to let his nerves show.

Aadon smiled at him. "Don't worry," his date reassured. "There are no go-go cages or anything. It's just a bar. You can go, you can dance, and no one will harass you, if that's what you're worried about."

Jesse nodded and managed a limp smile. Let Aadon think he was worried about people giving them looks. It didn't matter that he'd met his last boyfriend in a place like that, or that it had seemed so benign at the time. Anthony had seemed benign too. Nothing was ever what it seemed, though. He'd found that out the hard way.

"Are you okay?" Aadon leaned a little closer, peering at him. "Jesse?" Aadon sounded suddenly concerned, alerting Jesse he'd been silent too long.

The waiter arriving at their table at just that moment saved him having to find an appropriate, banal response for this practical stranger. However well-meaning the guy might be, he didn't know Aadon and didn't have any intention of sharing the sticky, unpleasant details of his life. He turned a polite smile on the flamboyant waiter and accepted the menu he held out.

"Thanks."

"So what'll it be, hon?"

Jesse managed not to flinch at being called "hon" by a flashy stranger.

Aadon's foot moved under the table, clipping Jesse's, and the waiter grimaced. He gave Aadon a glare and turned high-wattage charm on Jesse. "Mimosa?"

Jesse did flinch at that. "Just whatever is on tap, please." He glanced over the waiter's shoulder. "You do have something on tap?"

"Sure, sure. Straight guys come in here, too, you know." He winked at Jesse. "But you're okay here, sug. No worries."

"I'm not worried," Jesse replied, and immediately regretted it. It sounded so defensive it made even him wince. He glanced over at Aadon, but could see only the top of his blond head. If he'd heard, he pretended he hadn't.

"Aadon?" The waiter swung a hip out in Aadon's direction, coy to the point of dislocation.

Aadon tried to wrestle his burly protective instinct under control before he looked up and Jesse saw it in his face. "Beer's fine, Mike." He was rewarded with a wet tongue darting out from between Mike's lips at him before the bartender sashayed away. "He hates that," Aadon confided, leaning over the table to pull Jesse into his space.

"Hates what?"

"When I call him Mike."

"Is it not his name?"

"Sure it is. Everyone else calls him Sweet Thing." Aadon's lips quirked up sideways, and he rolled his eyes.

The effect on Jesse was immediate. He smiled. His shoulders dropped from the defensive upward slant, and he shifted his feet until one bumped Aadon's under the table. He didn't move it away.

Aadon grinned and winked, soaring at that small victory. "I have no idea where it came from, but he pouts whenever anyone uses his name."

Jesse glanced over at the bar. "Somehow, that's not difficult to imagine. Him pouting, I mean."

"No. Not really, is it?"

"Tell me about him." Jesse watched as Mike pulled the taps to pour their beers.

"Him?" For an instant, Aadon thought he'd read Jesse all wrong. Then the other man turned back, gazed at Aadon, brown eyes alight with interest.

"Yeah, him. The three musketeers. Long time for all three of you to still be so close." Jesse leaned his arms on the table, and this time it was Aadon being drawn in. "I'd like to hear about it."

"Uh."

Jesse grinned. Finally. Aadon stared at him in that parted lips, glazed sort of way that Jesse knew meant he couldn't look away. And knowing he'd caused it helped Jesse relax into the moment.

He didn't mind one bit listening to Aadon's butter-cream voice sliding over the stories of his childhood with his cousin and best friend. He talked with his hands, describing the oak tree in his backyard that housed their clubhouse with grand gestures that almost had them both wearing their drinks. And when he talked about his mother, his hands curled in toward himself, his voice softened, like he was protecting each word, each memory.

"Sounds like she loved being the center of that little world," Jesse observed.

"Den mother, caterer, and nurse." Aadon smiled. "Yeah."

There was more. Jesse could feel it like he could feel a chill breeze drift over his back every time someone opened the door to the fall night. But Aadon didn't go there. His childhood, it seemed, ended about the time he turned twelve, if Jesse was judging things right.

"Then high school," Aadon said, leaning back in his chair. "Sweet Thing appeared, Leo… went all hippie and—" He shrugged. "I had to get in here, right?" Jesse assumed Aadon meant the university. Aadon smiled, tried to make it sound normal, but Jesse could see the sad leaking out around the edges. Sad that filled up gaping holes in his childhood Aadon had chosen to leave out of the story.

Not that Jesse could call that kettle black. He had his own holes, didn't he? And they weren't going to get filled up because one guy was nice on a first date.

By that time, cousin Sweet Thing had brought them both another round and their meals, and it was okay to let the conversation go before it had to become about what they weren't telling each other, and that was good. Jesse could almost be thankful to the guy for the reprieve.

In the end, it turned out Leo knew a good veggie burger when he tasted one. The meal left Jesse considerably more relaxed than when they'd arrived. He almost thought about ordering a third beer when the lights behind the wall of glass came on, strobing red and green and blue through the diner.

The minute the strobe lights came on, the relaxed air evaporated. Jesse's fingers curled around the edges of their table, and Aadon feared he might pass out, he was so pale.

Gently, Aadon covered Jesse's straining hand with his own. "You all right?"

Jesse nodded, though his gaze flicked from Aadon's face to the flashing lights beyond the glass door, and his attention caught there, like a butterfly in a net, his lashes fluttering rapidly. Aadon squeezed his fingers, trying to bring him back.

"Jesse?"

A blast of sound overrode the thumping rhythm of the bass beat as a group of young men opened the door to enter the bar. Jesse flinched, shook himself, and fixed his gaze on Aadon's fingers closed securely around his. The music faded away again as the door swung shut, but it left him in a cold sweat.

"I'll get the check." Aadon patted his hand and pushed his chair away from their table. "Give me two minutes, and we can go."

Jesse concentrated on regulating his breathing. Aadon hadn't asked what was wrong. He didn't make a big deal of it. He just went to the counter, paid the bill, and walked Jesse out the door.

Autumn air curled around them, crisp, clean, full of the stillness between one moment and the next.

The silence stretched.

Finally, Jesse had to say something. "Listen, I—"

"It's fine." Aadon turned that smile on him. "I'm not much of a dancer anyway."

That had to be a lie, and Jesse called him on it.

"Okay, so I like to dance. But if you don't—"

"I used to," Jesse blurted. He hadn't been dancing in a long time and hadn't expected to say anything to Aadon about it. "I used to go dancing all the time."

"But?"

Jesse shrugged. *But what?* His last boyfriend had been a go-go boy—a handsome, fiery, controlling man whose memory made the thought of dancing into something that turned Jesse's stomach, made his palms sweat, and pissed him off because he had loved it so very much, and now….

"I don't anymore." That sounded too final. "At least, I haven't in a long time." He was ruining everything. He had to relax, and the more he told himself that, the harder it was to do.

"There are other things to do besides dance," Aadon pointed out, determined to help Jesse recover from whatever it was the loud music and flashing lights had hammered him with.

And damn it all if Aadon didn't sound perfectly reasonable about that. Jesse looked over and was surprised to see Aadon still smiling at him. Maybe he hadn't ruined everything.

"There's an old movie theatre on King," Aadon offered. "It plays movies from the thirties and forties all night. We could check that out."

"You like old movies." Odd that this bit of information didn't come as a surprise.

Aadon grimaced. "I know. All this"—he indicated his own body with his hands—"and I'm just a big geek on the inside." He turned puppy eyes on Jesse. "So will you go to the movies with me?"

Jesse laughed. The man was outrageously confident and self-effacing at the same time. It couldn't be real, and yet Jesse was almost inclined to think it genuine. Why else would he not be running for the hills after Jesse's display in the restaurant? He couldn't resist. And he had nothing to worry about, he told himself. The movie theatre was a block away, and it was a public place. A dark public place, sure, but they wouldn't be the only ones there.

"Yes." He smiled around drawing a deep, fortifying breath and nodded. "Let's go to the movies."

Chapter
Three

"SO?"

Jesse sipped iced coffee and serenely stared at his book without answering Sarah's inquiry. He wasn't reading, and Sarah likely knew that, but he waited for her to speak again anyway. She went back to her paper and continued to write and hum to herself. Finally, he looked over at her. She was so much better at this than he was.

"So, what?" he asked at last, knowing he was dying to tell her, and that she knew that.

She grinned at her writing a little longer before glancing up at him through her eyelashes. "So, you went out last night."

"Maybe."

"I called. You never don't answer your phone. Where did you go?"

"Just out."

"With?"

He smiled, knowing she could tell, just from that.

"And?"

He shrugged. "And what?"

"And, how was it?"

"It was…." He tilted his head, considering. "Good."

"Where did he take you?"

Jesse frowned. "He didn't take me anywhere. We went for burgers. And to a movie. A really, really, bad, gawdawful movie." A grin swept across his face. "It was fun."

It *had* been fun, once he relaxed a little. Once he talked himself into believing Aadon wasn't going to ambush him with anything he didn't want. In fact, he'd been the perfect gentleman. He'd been perfect, period. Too perfect. He knew exactly what Sarah was going to say.

"And he didn't...."

"Didn't what?" The conversation just got a lot less interesting. His voice dropped about three degrees, and she heard it, judging from the way her face went still.

"He didn't try anything?" She set her pen down.

"No." Jesse closed his book, all pretence of reading or playing this cat and mouse information game gone. Why couldn't she just settle for "I had fun" and let that be enough? Why did she have to poke at the rest?

"I was just wondering." She fingered the edges of her paper and twisted the straw in her drink. "I wondered, you know, because you're so skittish."

"I'm not skittish!" He hadn't meant to yell at her. She just watched him as he stood and paced over to the fridge, opened it, closed it, and leaned on the counter. "Okay. So I'm a little skittish. But I have good reason to be."

"Of course you do. I wasn't implying that you didn't. It's just, I mean, it's a big thing, Jess, dating again after."

"I don't want to talk about it," he warned.

"Well, maybe you should. You know you never did. Maybe it would help."

"I don't need your help, Sarah."

"Fine." She gathered up her things and started shoving them into her backpack. "But what about when he tries to kiss you? What about when he reaches out to touch you, or wants to take you dancing? Are you going to tell him then?"

"He doesn't need to know."

"If you're going to get serious about him, he does, Jess. This is important."

"We went on one date. Would you give it a rest?"

"Are you going on another?"

Jesse shrugged, noncommittal. He hoped so. He wanted to. He didn't want to dredge up all the things Sarah was pointing out. He didn't want to date anyone who needed to know any of that. "I don't know."

"For you, that's serious. Tell him. Or talk to someone. If not me, then someone."

"Every time I go on a date do we have to have this conversation? Because I could tape it. Put it on playback."

"Jesse, do not get mad at me for worrying about you. I just want what's best for you."

"You, Sarah, do not know anything about this," he snarled, pointing a finger in her face and curling a lip. "Or what's best for me. I'm fine. Just stay out of my business."

"Remind me of that the next time you call in the middle of the night because you can't sleep, and you can't get that shit out of your head." Her lips snapped shut, twisted, and her nostrils flared. "I love you, baby, but you are not fine."

He let her bang out the door. She was frustrated with him. They'd had that particular discussion before, but it had been a while. She meant well, he knew, but he just wasn't ready. He might never be ready. Idly, he ran his fingers over one forearm, mentally feeling the leftover marks there. It wasn't anyone's business but his, and it didn't need to shape his life. He was still lost in thought, trying not to think at all and failing miserably, when the phone dragged him away from the unpleasant memories.

He groped for it. "Hello?"

"Hey." There was a pause. "You all right?"

"Yeah." He sounded short and tried to modify his tone. "I'm fine, Aadon. I was just thinking." He grimaced.

"About me, I hope?"

No, definitely not about him. About someone who might, conceivably, be the very opposite of him in every way. "Um." He cleared his throat. "Yeah."

"Liar."

It was said jokingly, and Jesse couldn't help the smile that turned his lips.

"I was telling Sarah about last night," he conceded, leaving out the lecture and the fight and hoping Aadon wouldn't notice the omission.

"Did you tell her how bad the movie was?"

Jesse chuckled. "I did."

"Well, I want to make it up to you."

Jesse sank to the floor to lean against the cabinets. "Oh?"

"Let me make you dinner."

"Umm." Jesse panicked. It was too soon. He should never have accepted the first invitation. He couldn't do this, couldn't be alone in an apartment with this strange, too perfect man. Sarah was right, and he hated it. "Listen, Aadon, I had a great time last night, but—"

Aadon didn't give him a chance to brush the invitation off. He didn't know what Jesse's hang-up was or even if he wanted to know, but he did recognize his own need to make whatever it was better, to see Jesse relaxed like he had been once they'd left the bar last night.

"Listen," he hedged, fumbling for a way to make the idea less intimidating to Jesse. "I invited Leo and his girlfriend too. Do you think your friend Sarah would like to come?" He waited, oddly hopeful Jesse would say yes. Even with the extra wheels, Aadon wanted to see him again.

Jesse's pounding heart slowed somewhat. "Pardon?"

"Oh. Is that not her name? I thought—"

"No, that's her name. Sorry. I—"

"You thought it was going to be more intimate than that."

Jesse swallowed, nodded, realized Aadon couldn't see it, but Aadon was talking again, sparing him the need to talk through the near hyperventilation.

"It was, but you're obviously not comfortable with that," Aadon was saying.

There was a pause, and Jesse could imagine the other man giving his tiny, self-effacing shrug.

"Not to worry. I understand."

Did he? Really? Jesse doubted it, but the fact that Aadon was willing to accommodate something Jesse didn't even want to think about, much less explain to him, was too much to just ignore. "I want to come," Jesse blurted, despite himself. "I'm sure Sarah would love to meet you."

There was a smile in Aadon's voice as he agreed. "Perfect."

He gave the address, and Jesse hung up the phone feeling completely drained. It took a little while to call down the hall to Sarah's room. When she answered, she sounded tired, wary, still pissed off. But she had answered, and for that, Jesse was grateful.

"Want to go out tonight?"

Chapter
F o u r

"YOU didn't tell me I would be a third wheel," she whispered fiercely at him when the others had all disappeared for a minute.

"Fifth," Jesse corrected her around the ice he'd sucked out of his glass. Okay, so she was still pissed, but she needed to let it go already.

She growled at him and smiled at Aadon who came back from the kitchen just then with another drink for her. "Thank you."

"I would have invited another person," Aadon told her apologetically as he handed glasses of wine to Leo and his date. "But I wasn't sure if I should ask Allison or Kevin, and Jesse here wasn't giving me any hints."

"It's fine," Sarah said sweetly, even as she glared at Jesse. "I'm currently not dating. Period. I couldn't make up my mind, so I figured I'd wait until someone turned up, and no one has, so...." She shrugged and held up her drink. "A few more of these and I won't much care."

"Well, then I suppose I should get dinner on the table before you don't care about that either. Leo, you want to get the table ready for me, please?"

Aadon wondered at the woman's hostility as he wandered back toward the kitchen. She reminded him of a pit bull, and at the moment, it seemed Jesse was her bone. She obviously knew he was gay, so Aadon couldn't figure out the possessiveness. Logic told him, as nice as Jesse looked, as sweet as his vulnerability made him, the girl and the issues he didn't want to admit he had were maybe more trouble than he was worth. But then Aadon felt the prickle of eyes on his back and glanced over his shoulder. Jesse was watching him, biting his lower lip like that, and the way he broke into a blushing smile when he realized Aadon saw him checking out his ass.... It had been a long time since that fire in Aadon's gut burned so hot. He hadn't even realized how close Perry had come to putting it out completely. Maybe all Jesse needed was to have his own fire relit and carefully fanned to life again. Aadon wondered if he could do that without either of them getting burned. He didn't know, but for chrissake, Jesse was nibbling on his lip again, and fuck if Aadon didn't think it was worth finding out.

Blinking away the distraction, Aadon turned his attention to his best friend, at the moment busy giggling drunkenly with Leanne who just rolled her eyes at her boyfriend and shook her head.

"Hey, Leo?"

"Yeah, yeah." Leo rose, muttered something under his breath about slave labor, but took Leanne's hand, led her off to the dining area, and began rooting through drawers for place mats and cutlery.

Aadon turned back toward the kitchen. Jesse was busy watching him go when Sarah's sharp elbow dug into his side. He looked at her, irritated, but she merely pointed to the kitchen.

"Did you forget how to do this or what? Go in there and help him!"

Jesse made a face at her, refrained from pointing out he really didn't know how to do this in the first place, but he did get up and go to the kitchen door. He leaned against the frame and just watched Aadon's supple fingers gingerly pull tinfoil off something that smelled like roasted meat. Beside him on the counter, a casserole dish with shitake mushrooms and rice steamed and made Jesse's mouth water. Other pots simmered on the stove, and a huge salad bowl balanced precariously in the opening between kitchen and living room. The scene immediately reminded him of his mother's kitchen and the chaos that reined there when she was deep in the throes of readying a holiday meal for him and his uncles and cousins.

He cleared his throat. "Um. Can I help?"

Aadon glanced up, then back to his work.

Jesse got distracted by Aadon's fingers again when Aadon popped them into his mouth to lick the juices off. He didn't at first notice that Aadon was watching him. When he did, he turned pink.

Aadon only smiled. "Now that certainly helps." He abandoned his task and sauntered closer to Jesse. "I was beginning to think I really was wasting my time."

He was close now, and Jesse could smell his cologne. It was a nice smell.

"No, not wasting time."

"Would it be a waste of time for me to ask for a kiss?"

Jesse swallowed and found he really didn't have a voice. He shook his head, and even he didn't know what he meant by it. But if he was honest, and with Aadon's chest mere inches from his, there was precious little room for anything but honesty, he had to admit he'd been thinking about this all evening. So when Aadon leaned close, he let himself be kissed. It wasn't what he feared. Aadon tasted a bit like the meat juices he'd just licked from his fingers, but it was only one facet. He also tasted like the dark wine they'd been drinking, a salty residue from the appetizers, and under it all, there was something that Jesse knew was just Aadon, and it was something he wanted more of.

"Hey! Aadon!" Leo called from the other room, and Jesse heard his girlfriend say something to him, which was followed by a grunt from Leo. "Aadon," he called again after a second, "we're starving in here, man!"

Aadon was already pulling away. Jesse sighed and licked the last traces of that something from his lips. He went to the sink, washed his hands, and stood close enough to the other man he could feel Aadon's heat.

"What can I do?"

Aadon handed Jesse ingredients for salad dressing and watched as Jesse competently began mixing, every once in a while licking his lips and smiling a soft little smile.

Clearly the man had no idea he was a walking wet dream, and Aadon found, more and more, he did not want to wake up.

ALMOST two hours had passed after dinner when Sarah started eyeing Jesse, clearly ready to be heading home. Jesse would have thought he'd be ready by that time, too, but Aadon hadn't stopped smiling at him all night. Their one short kiss seemed to confirm something for him because he was more animated than Jesse had yet seen him. And more attentive. It made Jesse feel powerful somehow, to have made such an impression.

In the end, it was Leo who finally acknowledged Sarah's ever-more-blatant cues and stood, reeling just a little from the wine. Leanne allowed him to lean on her as she too stood and turned him to the door.

"We've stayed so late, Aadon. I hope you don't have anything too early tomorrow," she said, laughing at Leo's comic stumbling.

"Nope." Aadon grinned. "Sunday's my day off. No studying, no research, no papers." His smile broadened. "No office work. Just going to laze as much as I can manage in one day." He turned to Jesse. "What about you? You working tomorrow?"

"No. Day off for me too."

He normally would have made an excuse, but the suggestion in Aadon's voice was too much to resist through the amount of wine he'd drunk. He might change his mind in the morning, but when Aadon donned his coat and shoes as Jesse readied to walk Sarah home, he thought he probably wouldn't.

Sarah looked at him, suddenly too sober for his liking. He chose to ignore the warning in her eyes. He couldn't hide from life forever, and it had been more than two years. Most of the scars had faded. Soaked in a little bit of liquid courage, the memories would be easier to deal with, if they even surfaced. Besides, Aadon was proving himself nothing like the last guy, and hadn't she been the one to tell him to give this a chance?

The streets were quiet outside Aadon's building. They said good-bye to Leo and Leanne at Leanne's car and strolled, three wide, down the sidewalk toward the rowdier downtown. Jesse let Aadon slip his bulk between himself and Sarah. He wasn't interested in any more of her quiet disapproval. She had encouraged this, after all. He was just following through on the logical next step. And he wanted it. Just because before now, he'd never met a guy he wanted to invite to spend the night didn't mean he wasn't ready. It just meant guys like Aadon were rare.

"So you two live in the same building?" Aadon's question, directed right down at Jesse, snapped his attention from that line of thought. Aadon smiled, and Jesse found himself a little giddy. He didn't feel like deciding if that was the fault of the wine or Aadon's spectacular dimples.

"Yeah. Down the hall from each other, actually," Sarah answered. She peered around Aadon at Jesse and stuck out her tongue. "But I found the place. He followed me."

"I always follow her. She's the big sister I never had."

"And you need a big sister? To what? Keep you out of trouble?" Aadon asked, a clear note of teasing in his voice.

"She's always looking out for me." It was all the concession she was going to get that Jesse knew she was concerned.

"Somebody has to." Once again, she peered round Aadon to glare at him, but the sharpness seemed to have softened. Maybe she understood Jesse really was ready.

"I might volunteer for that job," Aadon said, glancing at Jesse but quickly turning to Sarah. "Give you a break."

Sarah hooked her arm into Aadon's. "I'll let you know."

"Is there a test?"

"Of course."

Aadon chuckled.

Most of the rest of the walk was taken up by Aadon quizzing Sarah on her life and classes and her making pointed comments leading back to Jesse.

Jesse managed to avoid rolling his eyes too often, though he was a little worried at the rate she was going, she would raise Aadon's suspicion. He didn't want to field questions Sarah might cause the big blond to ask about his past. Not tonight. So he deflected her comments and kept the conversation focused on her.

Aadon mostly watched Jesse, wondered, but kept his curiosity to himself. He knew better than anyone, some information a guy had to be free to volunteer. He wasn't going to pry.

It was a pleasant trip, and Jesse found himself longing to link his own arm through Aadon's as Sarah had done. He didn't know if Aadon would appreciate that much of a public display, however, so he refrained, preferring not to do anything that might upset his date.

They were turning onto their block when Jesse's toe found a crack in the sidewalk, and he stumbled, jolting into Aadon, almost flipping onto his face. He would have been embarrassed, but Aadon simply caught him around the shoulders, tucked him in close under his arm, and kept walking. After a few steps, Jesse slipped an arm around his waist. He felt Sarah's fingers in his a moment later. She squeezed his hand and let him go. It surprised him how much that small show of acceptance set his mind at ease.

She didn't linger over good-byes at her door when they finally arrived, and soon, Jesse was leading Aadon down the ugly purple paisley carpet to his door. They were only a few steps away when Jesse stumbled again, this time over the lump in the carpet that only seemed to be there when he was drunk.

Aadon caught him and held him for a moment, close against his body.

Jesse took a deep breath of aftershave, soap, and maleness and thought he must be quivering in Aadon's grip because every nerve tingled. He was far less drunk, suddenly, than he had been a minute ago and torn between looking up into Aadon's face and closing his eyes to lean against him. It flashed through his mind how very different this was from what he remembered, but he quickly shoved the thought away. No remembering. Just now.

"You seem to have a bit of a clumsy streak," Aadon observed.

Jesse shrugged slightly. "Maybe." *If it'll get me closer to you,* Jesse placed a palm against Aadon's chest and closed his eyes, *I can be freakin' Dick Van Dyke.*

A heartbeat of silence pounded between them, and Jesse swallowed, lifted his chin, and blinked his eyes open.

"This is you?" Aadon asked, pointing with his free hand to the door behind Jesse.

"Uh." Jesse pulled himself together and straightened. "Yeah."

"I think your phone is ringing."

Jesse had thought that was the sound of own nerves jangling in his head. He turned and looked at the heavy wood door. "Yeah." The ring of his phone filtered faintly from inside, and he fumbled in his pocket for his keys. "My mother just doesn't get time zones," he muttered as he slid the square-headed gold key into the slot and twisted.

The sound of the ringing increased immediately as the door swung open, and Jesse lurched across the recliner for the receiver. He twisted as he slid sideways into the chair and brought the phone to his ear.

"Hi, Mom." Pointing to the fridge, he made a drinking motion, and Aadon nodded.

Jesse watched as he slid out of his coat and shoes and opened the refrigerator. Illuminated in the only light in the room, Aadon's muscled frame was making it hard for Jesse to concentrate on his mother's voice on the other end of the line.

"Sorry, Mom. Say that again?" He sat up and swung his legs to the floor.

"I said, I talked to the lawyer today."

"Why?" Jesse absently took the water bottle Aadon handed him, his attention now fully on his conversation. "Did he call you?"

"Yes, Jesse. He wants to talk to you."

"About what?" The warmth Aadon had kindled in Jesse's gut cooled, souring the wine and making him queasy.

"About what happened."

"I told him what happened. Why do I have to go over it all again? I thought they said Anthony took the deal." A cold lump had formed in the pit of Jesse's stomach. Of all times for this to come up again, why now? Why, just when he thought it was finally over? In his hand the water bottle crumpled, and cold liquid spilled over his fingers.

"Apparently, he got a new lawyer who told him if he had evidence that you and he were in a relationship, it could change his case. He's looking to sue that last lawyer for incompetence or some such. He thinks he can get a lighter sentence."

"Everyone knows we were in a relationship, Mom. It isn't like we kept it a secret." Jesse glanced at Aadon who was watching him, concerned.

"It's the kind of relationship that matters, according to the lawyer."

The cold lump grew to constrict Jesse's breathing. "What do you mean?" He was suddenly, acutely aware of Aadon sitting on the arm of the chair, silent, listening to his every word.

"I—"

"Mom, I told you everything. We talked about this." He got up because he couldn't sit so close to Aadon, couldn't feel him looming over his shoulder while he talked about this. "What is the lawyer saying?"

"He said Anthony told his council you liked…." She hesitated, clearly hoping Jesse would finish the thought for her, but with Aadon in the room, he couldn't. He waited, because even though he was fairly certain he knew what was coming, he had to be sure. "That you liked him to tie you up," she said, the words spilling out fast, almost indecipherable. Jesse knew Aadon couldn't hear her, but he blushed.

"That was different."

He should have known it had been too easy. He'd been a fool to take up with Anthony in the first place and fool to give in to his demands. The fact that he'd let the man do those things to him hadn't meant he'd liked it. At least, not at first. When he'd started to see the allure, Anthony had pushed and pushed until it didn't matter if Jesse said no, or what Jesse wanted, and that was when he'd finally realized he had to stop it.

It hadn't been an easy call, and Anthony hadn't been gentle about saying good-bye. That final scene had landed Jesse in the hospital, Anthony in jail, and brought lawyers in on both sides. At the time, it had been a clear enough case of battery, and a deal to drop some of the charges had got Anthony out of his life. Now, all the ugly secrets were crawling out of the closet, and Jesse had nowhere to hide.

"I don't care what he says, Mom," he lowered his voice and turned his back on Aadon. "I didn't ask him to beat me up."

"Is someone there with you?"

"Yes."

"Sarah?"

"No."

"Who?"

"Mom, focus. What is the lawyer saying? Is Anthony trying to buck all the charges?"

"He says it was just rough sex, that it got a little out of hand and you were embarrassed. He says he doesn't deserve to be in jail. The lawyer wants to talk to you again, get your side of the story."

"My side. I told him everything there was to tell already. I don't want to." He set down the bottle before he spilled more and pinched the bridge of his nose between thumb and finger. Aware his voice had risen again, aware of the note of panic that brought out those sharp edges, he tried to temper it. "I don't see the point in going through it all again."

"The point is, if you don't he gets away with it."

At what point did Anthony's punishment become Jesse's agony? He didn't have the strength to go through that night again. It had been terrifying the first time, painful to tell it all to a stranger, and damn near impossible to explain it to his mother. Now, when he finally thought it was behind him, they wanted him to tell the story again. He wasn't sure he could. He thought maybe he didn't care whether Anthony got away scot-free or not, so long as he didn't have to relive it ever again.

"I can't, Mom."

"Jesse."

"Mom, just…. I can't."

He hung up on her protests and stood very still. The room was spinning around him, and he didn't really think it had as much to do with the wine as with his own distress. He could feel Aadon behind him—breathing, waiting, just being there, and all his reasons for not ever bringing a man into this apartment came rushing back on him, burying him, making it impossible for him to turn.

"Is everything all right?" Aadon asked at last, when the silence had become a thing in the room with them. It was obvious from the timbre of his voice that he knew the answer.

"Aadon, I—"

"I should go."

There was a rustle of sound, and Jesse spun. Aadon was pulling on his coat. He glanced up, and it struck Jesse. This was not the man he hated, not the one who had hurt him, not anyone he needed to fear.

"You—"

The phone ringing cut off Jesse's thought. He looked at the illuminated screen and frowned. Gently, he placed it on the table beside the recliner.

"Answer it, Jesse."

"I can't talk to her about this right now."

He couldn't explain why. Her concern, her placid calm concern, was soothing when he was in the same room with her but infuriating when he was half a country away and in need of a reassuring hand. The ringing jangled, and he grimaced.

"She'll be worried."

"She'll be fine."

Aadon shook his head and picked up the phone himself. The beep of the call button was loud over Jesse's pursed-lipped silence.

"Jesse Turbul's residence."

On the other end of the phone, a clear, stern feminine voice said something Aadon was too distracted by Jesse's hunched form to actually hear.

"Yes, ma'am," he replied, hoping it was the right response. He glanced at Jesse, apology in his eyes, he hoped. He didn't know what was going on, exactly, but the snippets of conversation he'd overheard gave him enough of an idea that all the skittish nerves Jesse had shown so far suddenly made sense.

"He doesn't want to talk." Jesse's mother wasn't asking. Apparently, she knew her son well.

"That's what he said, yes," Aadon agreed, because at the moment, that's all he knew for certain, other than the overwhelming urge to pull Jesse close and make the world leave him alone.

"Is he all right?"

"No, I wouldn't say that," Aadon said carefully.

"Who am I talking to?"

"Aadon. Aadon Dounias."

"And who are you?" Not angry, exactly. But stern. Protective.

"I'm his friend." Aadon nodded at Jesse, trying to reassure them both he was a friend. That Jesse was safe from whatever had him so spooked, that nothing bad was going to happen. Lord knew he had enough experience in soothing spooked nerves and calming irrational fear. The whole situation brought to mind his brother's delicate balance between fragile calm and stark raving terrified the next person who touched him was going to pin him down and take every bit of humanity he had left.

"You don't know what's going on, do you?" she asked.

"No, ma'am, I don't."

A sigh. "He has to tell you. I can't. It isn't… my place." Aadon could hear her struggle with her need to protect her son and her inability to do so. He imagined he could hear her asking him to do it for her, and he nodded again just as she asked him to make sure someone stayed with Jesse.

"I can stay." Jesse's eyes went wide. "If he wants," Aadon added soothingly, dropping the hand he had halfway raised to reach for Jesse.

"Do you know Sarah? She lives down the hall."

"Yes, I do."

"Ask her…."

"I'll do that."

"Don't leave him alone. Please."

"No, I won't. I promise."

Finally, Aadon hung up and passed Jesse the phone. He pretended not to notice the way Jesse's hand shook as he accepted it.

"What did she make you promise?" Jesse's voice was barely above a whisper. One arm wrapped around his middle, and once again, Aadon was struck with the desire to pull him close and keep the rest of the world away.

"Not to leave you alone," he said, keeping his distance, watching carefully. "She's worried."

"I'm fine." There was a waver in his voice, though, and only a complete idiot or someone needing not to get involved would believe him. Jesse dragged his gaze up from the carpet to look at Aadon, to see the complete panic and need for escape in the other man's expression.

Clear blue eyes gazed back at him. Aadon's lips were turned down in a slight frown. His brow was creased, wavy little lines puckering the smooth skin. "You're not fine," he said gently, taking a small step closer. "What do you need? Should I go get Sarah?"

"No. She'll be sleeping." He didn't want to bring her into this. He wanted the whole thing to go away. He wanted to go back half an hour and not answer his phone. He wanted this to be the night he finally put this mess behind him. He really didn't want to prove Sarah right.

"You need someone." Aadon wasn't giving up. Wasn't leaving him alone.

Jesse blinked at the tall man, bit his lip. Aadon wasn't leaving. Why? "You're here." He wasn't sure why he said it, why he asked. Aadon didn't need to get involved either. He'd be better off walking away now, but he hadn't.

"I may not be the one you need spending the night." It was a reasonable thing to say, and he was probably right. It meant Aadon probably had some idea of what Jesse had said to his mom on the phone, that he knew, on some level, what the problem was. And he wasn't running for the hills, he wasn't mocking. He was just standing there, worried, calm, trying to help.

A wave of dizzy gratitude washed through Jesse, and he wobbled.

Two quick strides brought Aadon close enough to grab Jesse's elbow, hold him up. He kept his touch carefully neutral, ready to let go, more than ready to hold on. "Whatever this is, Jesse, I don't want to make it more difficult for you. Just tell me what you want. That's what I'll do."

It couldn't possibly be that simple. The hand Aadon extended to keep him steady was warm, light, and comforting. Jesse wanted so much to close the last little bit of distance and sink into the comfort. He knew if he asked Aadon to leave, the other man would. The apartment would be empty.

Nothing would be able to hurt Jesse, and he'd be safe enough in the cocoon of aloneness he'd cultivated for himself. If Jesse told him, "I want you to stay," would he actually do it? Just because Jesse asked, would he really do it?

Swallowing the little pride he had left, Jesse lifted his chin and met Aadon's gaze. "I want to tell you." He was going to say "but," however, once the words were out, he found he meant them. If Aadon wanted to know what was going on, he would tell him. He just didn't know where to start.

Here was something Aadon hadn't expected. Jesse's back straightened. He looked Aadon in the eye and offered about the only thing Aadon really wanted. Trust. And suddenly, the weight of it all, the worry and fear dropped away from his own heart, and he nodded. This was good. But Jesse was shaken, a little drunk, and this was not the time for true confession, for stupid sex, or anything other than sleeping it all off and starting fresh at the beginning.

"There's plenty of time for that," Aadon decided aloud. "Tomorrow, or the next day. Right now, you need to sleep off the wine and not say anything you don't mean, not do something you'll regret." Aadon kicked off the shoe he'd put on and took off his coat again. "Do you have an extra blanket? I'll sleep on the couch."

Jesse nodded. Part of him was enormously relieved Aadon hadn't demanded the explanation. Part of him was disappointed he didn't seem to want one. But he wasn't leaving, and that was good. Jesse focused on the simple task of preparing his guest a place to sleep. He went to the closet in the short hall leading to his bedroom and talked himself through it.

It wasn't like he didn't have friends, like he'd never had someone crashing on his couch after too many drinks at a bar, or studying well past when the buses stopped running. He rummaged past the towels and facecloths, behind the poorly folded sheets to the heavy afghan at the bottom of the pile. Bringing it back to the main room, he handed it to Aadon. They stood facing one another in the light of a lamp Aadon had turned on. For an awkward minute, neither of them spoke.

"You're sure about this?" Aadon draped the blanket over one arm.

Jesse nodded.

"I can still get Sarah. I'm sure she wouldn't mind."

"No. She wouldn't. But I don't want her. I don't want…." He hesitated. He had been about to say he didn't want her harping that he should have listened to her and talked to someone. He merely shrugged. "She puts up with enough from me. I'll let her sleep. Tomorrow I'll call her."

Aadon nodded and went to the couch where he spread the blanket over the worn upholstery. "Fair enough."

He sat and looked back over his shoulder to where Jesse was still standing in the middle of the room. "I know I don't know what's going on, exactly, Jesse, but I can make a fair guess. If it means anything for me to say it, I won't move from this couch until you come out. Close the door, lock it if you want. It won't hurt my feelings."

A bright flash of vertigo swept through Jesse. So he knew. At least, he knew enough to make a fair guess. So why was he still here? Why did he still look so calm and concerned and why hadn't he beaten a hasty retreat like any normal guy would? And why did Jesse still want him so bad? Wasn't that just a stupid, horrible, dangerous idea?

"Is it weird," Jesse asked quietly, "that I'd rather you slept in the bed with me? That I want you closer?"

"Not weird. But not smart. And you aren't in any condition to make a smart choice about that right now. Go to sleep. We'll talk in the morning. If you want."

JESSE didn't actually sleep for a long while. He knew Aadon was still there, just beyond his half-closed door. He wondered if the other man slept, or if he lay there rethinking what a stupid idea it was to get involved with someone obviously completely freaked out by life.

When morning came, would he have had enough time to think it through and realize he didn't want anything to do with him? Jesse wouldn't blame him, but he knew it would hurt. It was best he didn't hope for too much. Rolling over in the dark, he watched the wall across from the window as a neon sign somewhere outside blinked off and on, the blue light splashing across the white paint in a soothing, predictable pattern. Everything in life should be that easy to deal with, he thought. Everything should be. Nothing was.

Chapter
Five

MORNING light wasn't enough to wake him. The alarm clock he should have turned off the night before shrilled through an unpleasant dream he managed to forget by the time he'd pulled himself up out of cotton-headed sleep. He moaned around his headache and, for a blessed few minutes, managed to forget that his life, once again, had dipped into that dim, ugly place where he couldn't see far enough to know it would pass. Then a noise from the washroom, the toilet flushing, brought him upright with a painfully spinning head. The phone rang, but only once. A deep voice spoke, and a moment later there was a soft knock on his door.

"Jesse?" He didn't answer right away. "It's your mom. Should I tell her you're still sleeping?"

"No." Jesse swung his legs to the floor, groped for a pair of jeans, and went to the door. Aadon was standing in just his jeans, his chest and feet bare, and holding the phone. Jesse swallowed hard, took the receiver, and retreated back into his room.

"Mom?"

"Hi, honey." There was a pause. Jesse waited. He knew what she was going to ask without really asking. "That young man is still there." Which translated as "Did you sleep with him?"

"No."

"Honey, you have to be careful."

"I know, Mom. I am. He slept on the couch, okay?"

"I worry."

"Well, don't."

"Jesse, I have to. I'm your mother." Another pause would be followed by some variation on "How are you holding up," which would be code for "have you picked up a new batch of razor blades from the pharmacy?"

He headed her off.

"I know." He sat on the bed. "I'm sorry. I just woke up. I haven't even had coffee yet, and my head hurts. And I know what you're worried about," he said, a little more quietly. He didn't want to risk Aadon overhearing. "I am not going to… turn stupid again." He'd almost said it out loud. Almost. They both knew the scars on his arms were self-inflicted. Neither of them had ever said so out loud. Maybe the day he would actually be healed would be the day he could say, "I used to cut myself, but I don't anymore," out loud. She didn't say anything in reply, so he moved past it. "And Mom—"

"Yes?" It was like she heard but didn't hear. He didn't know if it bothered him that she didn't acknowledge it.

Jesse sighed and let it go. "Tell the lawyer he has everything there is. There's nothing new to tell. If Anthony appeals, then he appeals. I don't want to do this anymore."

"And if he gets out of jail and gets away with what he did?"

"Then let him."

"Jesse—"

"Mom. I'm done. I'm tired, and I'm sorry. I know you want there to be some sort of divine justice on this, but it isn't worth my life going tits up to keep him in jail. He's out of my life, and that's all that matters to me, okay?"

"Jesse, I don't think it is okay at all."

"Well, it isn't your life, Mom."

"Jesse, just—"

"I have to go. I have company." He hung up. He didn't like cutting her off, but he wasn't up to arguing about it. He was never up to arguing over how crappy the justice system was or how it let people get away with things they should never get away with. He mostly didn't like to defend how he had let Anthony get away with things he shouldn't have let him get away with or think how the man had taken something he might have actually enjoyed and twisted it into something that now terrified him.

"Jesse?" Aadon's voice cut through his thoughts. "There's coffee."

"Um."

He stood, looked around for a shirt, and found Aadon was standing in the doorway watching him. Jesse fell back a few feet before his brain caught up and stopped him. It didn't stop him crossing his arms over his chest to try and hide.

Aadon backed up too and waved one of the coffee cups he was holding back toward the other room. "I'll just—"

"It's okay." Jesse let his arms fall and willed himself to not touch the scars. He'd said he would tell Aadon what was going on, and he would. If he wanted the guy, and he did, eventually, he'd have to explain the scars. He couldn't always have sex with his shirt on.

Aadon's eyes flicked down and back up to rest on his face. Jesse's nerves thrummed. His breath came too uneven, and he was sure Aadon could see him shaking.

"I'll wait out here."

"You can come in."

There was a pause as they sorted out what the other had said.

"Jesse, it's fine."

"No. You might as well."

He motioned for Aadon to enter the room. It was hard to let him see the scars as he reached for his coffee, hard not to yank his arm back when Aadon looked.

"I didn't know how you take it," Aadon said, sticking firmly to neutral territory and trying to work out if he was surprised at the mess of Jesse's arms. He understood self-destructive tendencies. Hadn't Ricky given him a crash course in that? He understood the kinds of things a boyfriend could do to someone vulnerable and wanting so much to trust as Jesse was, to make him that self-destructive. His gut heaved. He held it in, willed it not to show on his face, made himself hold out the cup of coffee without the rage shaking it out all over the carpet.

"Black is fine," Jesse whispered, accepting the drink and using it to warm his chilled fingers.

More silence. Jesse thought he should say something, but it seemed pretty self-explanatory. And he wanted to know if Aadon would do as even his mother did and pretend to be oblivious.

"That's why she didn't want me to leave you alone?"

No pretending, then. Jesse nodded. "It's…. When…. I just." He stopped, closed his mouth, and shook his head. "I should find a shirt."

"Yeah. Sure." Aadon glanced around the room, fighting to control the anger at how Jesse had to be hurting and knowing he couldn't do anything about it. Helpless was so not his thing. His gaze fell on the bedside table, the clock, Jesse's cell phone, and his mind flashed bright crimson at him. Ricky. He'd changed the appointment to Sunday. Today. Now. He had forty-five minutes to make the hour drive to Ricky's clinic and meet with his doctor.

"Shit."

Not waiting for Jesse to finish with getting dressed, he returned to the living room to find his own clothes. If he missed this meeting, Ricky would lose his spot in the shelter he lived in. He needed that spot. That safety. If he wasn't yet showing signs of getting better there, it was the one place they'd found that at least he wasn't getting worse.

Jesse heard Aadon's retreat and made himself not look back. That was that. Now he knew exactly how much it took to drive even a guy as nice as Aadon out the door. He squelched the disappointment and put his mug down to dig through a dresser drawer for the black shirt he'd decided against once before. Pulling it over his head, pushing his arms through the sleeves, felt good. He had his armor back. Facing the world was easier when no one could tell what a mess he was. He turned, but Aadon had already left the room.

Jesse sighed and told himself he hadn't really expected anything else. Picking up his mug, he went out into the main room. Aadon was stuffing his foot into his shoe. He already had his coat on. He really hadn't expected anything else. Still, the bottom dropped out of Jesse's gut.

Aadon looked up as he reached for the doorknob. "I have to go." He pointed to the door with his other hand.

"Sure." Jesse clung desperately to the numb. "Whatever."

Aadon winced at the dull look in Jesse's eyes. Anger would be better. Or disinterest. Not this… blank. Like Ricky. Blank. Aadon pursed his lips. Like Ricky, who was his brother and needed him, and if he had time to explain properly, he would, but Ricky was not a running-out-the-door-late story. He was a lifetime of fuck up and pain, and Aadon couldn't let him down. "No, really, Jesse, I mean it. I just remembered." How lame that sounded. Aadon wasn't idiot enough to think this looked like anything other than a dash for freedom.

"Yeah. I get it," Jesse said, moving toward him.

"Jesse—"

"It's fine." Anger, finally, but directed anywhere but at Aadon, like he was afraid to use it.

Jesse pulled the door open, buried his fury. How stupid did the guy think he was? Just get the fuck out and leave him the fuck alone. He held onto the anger, wrapped it around himself tight because it was the best protection he had against the pain, and unleashing it would only lead to worse things. "I'll see you around."

"I'll call you, Jesse. I mean it." God, Aadon wanted to touch him, explain, but one touch would lead to more time than he had right now to fix this. "I will call you. I swear."

Jesse held the door open, said nothing, glared at the floor. Get. The fuck. Out.

Aadon could read the expression. No matter what he did now, someone was going to be damaged. In a worst-case scenario, Jesse would get over a perceived rejection. Ricky could not go through another move, to another facility, new doctors, new orderlies, strangers, changes, all the shit that went with being dependant on the rest of the world to do his thinking for him because all that was left of him was a bundle of nerves and fear.

Furious with himself for dropping both balls, Aadon ducked past Jesse and jogged down the hallway.

"Sure you'll call."

Jesse closed the door quietly behind him, poured his coffee down the sink, and went back to bed.

DRESSING didn't seem like much of a priority the rest of the day. When Sarah called, he begged a headache to get her off the phone.

"Come on, Jesse. I know he spent the night. I saw him walking away from the building this morning. Spill."

"No." He hung up.

A minute later, the phone rang again. He didn't even check the caller ID but buried the headset under the sofa cushions and turned up the TV. He wasn't interested in another conversation that led anywhere near men. The phone rang three or four more times. He didn't bother to see who it was.

AADON cursed as he ran home, fumed as he fumbled with his keys to get inside, get his car keys, wash the memory of Jesse's lumpy couch off his skin with a splash of water over his face. He called Jesse's number as he climbed in his car and started the engine. At least he could explain, even if he couldn't go back right this second and beg his forgiveness.

He got voice mail and left a message. "I know you're pissed. I know. I get it. Believe me, I get it. This is not about you. Not about the cutting, I promise. I'll explain, but not to your voice mail. Call me back. Please."

A car horn honked, a flare of sound blasting past his window as Aadon veered frantically back to his own side of the road.

"Perfect. Get your stupid fucking ass killed, Dounias. Shithead." He tossed the phone onto the passenger seat, scrubbed a hand roughly over his face and through his hair, and forced his full attention onto the road and the drive.

He arrived most of a half hour late and ran through the hallways to the doctor's office just in time to see the orderlies arriving to collect Ricky and bring him back to his room. He heard the low, soothing tone of the doctor's voice as he rushed up.

"… sorry, Ricky. I don't know why he didn't show." Heavy sigh. "I wish the rules—"

"I'm here!" Aadon skidded to a halt just at the office door, and Ricky, on the other side, jumped, big blue eyes flashing up at him, a shock of straw-blond hair slapping across his face as he jerked back.

Aadon backed down, lowered his voice, smiled a small, careful smile at his older brother. "Hey, Ricky. Sorry I'm late, bro." He gently patted Ricky's shoulder. "Sorry." A quick glance over Ricky's slumped shoulder gave him a view of Dr. Stephanie Carol's relieved features. "Doc, I'm so sorry. Something…." He pursed his lips. Jesse was not a "something came up" kind of excuse.

"I had something real important to take care of," he said instead, reflecting bitterly on the inside how horribly he'd actually failed to take care of Jesse at all.

She smiled and ushered them both back into her office, waving the orderlies away. "Don't worry about it, Aadon. You're here now, and this is good. We have a lot to talk about." She patted Ricky's shoulder as he shuffled past her, and he glanced at her, offering a small smile in return. "Good news, too, isn't it, Ricky?"

His smile grew by one tiny increment, and he nodded. "Yeah," he said, so softly Aadon barely heard. But he had said something. One word, maybe, but an actual, honest-to-God response to a question directed at him, and he made eye contact when he did.

Aadon breathed out a sigh and let that small miracle ease his mind. If Ricky could find his way back through the morass, even that small way, surely Jesse could.

"SO." DR. CAROL shifted her weight, effectively blocking Aadon's exit from her office as they both watched Ricky, docile and apparently content, follow an orderly back to his room. "Want to talk about it, Aadon?"

"Sorry?" Aadon blinked at her, his head full of the image of his brother sitting calmly, watching him, actually *seeing* him, nodding when the doctor asked him a question, smiling when Aadon said something to him, and generally being responsive and alert. It had been months since Aadon had seen him doing this well.

She turned, drawing him back to the moment with her careful scrutiny. "You're never late, honey. And you've been distracted and... worried for the full hour. What is it? Because I know"—and here she smiled wide—"it isn't to do with Ricky. He's doing wonderfully."

Aadon made a wry face. Trust her and her tiny bifocals perched on the end of her pert little nose to notice something was wrong. "He is doing really well," Aadon hedged. "I don't know how to thank you."

Her brown eyes crinkled around the corners with another smile that plumped up her already plump cheeks, and Aadon couldn't help but be reminded, once again, of his mother. His mother before anxiety pills and weight loss and depression. Before she gave up. His mother who couldn't—wouldn't—have anything more to do with her eldest son, or even Aadon, if he insisted on still trying to protect Ricky. For that split second, he wished, fuck, he wished she *was* his mother. He sank back onto the couch he'd been sitting on earlier as they had gone over Ricky's evaluation.

He sat there, slumped against the back of the couch, staring at his hands, picking at imagined calluses, weighing what to say. Jesse's problems weren't his problems. Hell, he didn't even really know what his problems were, exactly, though he could make an educated guess.

"Talk to me, Aadon." Dr. Carol sat next to him and laid a kind, small hand on his knee. "I know you aren't his only family, but you are Ricky's main support system, and I need to know you're okay. For his sake."

"I am," he assured her, glancing up and meeting her eye for the fraction of the second that half truth would let him. "I'm fine. It isn't really... mine, you know?"

She lifted one thinly plucked brow. "No. I don't know until you tell me."

Aadon frowned and focused his attention back to his hands. "Did Ricky ever tell you? What happened, I mean. What really happened to him. To... wreck him. Before the drugs and shit hollowed him out and fried his brain."

"Aadon."

"I know, I know. Don't talk about him like that. I'm sorry. It's just...." His chest squeezed tight, bands of steel pressuring all the air out of him. "I barely remember, you know? When he was... happy. Normal. I was just a kid. No idea." His eyes stung, and he blinked that back because he couldn't go there. "I want to," he confessed, a secret, tiny confession only she could know. "I want to remember. To have at least that." He drew in a ragged breath. "You would think I was over this, right? I'll never have—" *A brother.* Not the way he should. Not the way Ricky deserved.

"I know the details, yes," she admitted, her hand remaining on Aadon's knee where she'd laid it. "Not from him. I doubt he even remembers most of it himself, and frankly, I think that's best. He should never have to take that part of his life back, Aadon. Some people, they can deal with the kind of trauma he suffered. Some people can't."

"Ricky couldn't."

"Ricky didn't have the tools then, and doesn't really have the faculties now."

"It isn't fair, you know," Aadon mumbled, marbles of grief rolling around on his tongue, making his words thick and indistinct. "He was just a kid."

"No." She gave his knee a tiny rub. "And it isn't fair that he didn't have support, or that you don't."

"I do—" Aadon clamped his mouth shut. "It isn't their fault, you know. They don't get it."

"Being raped?" she asked, and Aadon flinched. "Or being gay?"

"I thought we were talking about Ricky."

"You tell me what we're talking about."

Aadon sighed. She always did this. Made him say everything out loud. "They don't get that he wasn't strong enough to say no to that creep. That he didn't even realize he should have said no, or that he let it go on and on… and that he never got mad."

"You don't think everything that happened after had anything to do with anger?"

"Sure it did. But in my family, getting mad means getting even. Making it so the other person suffers." Aadon tried hard to imagine his gentle brother purposely causing anyone to suffer and shook his head. The only person Ricky had ever harmed was himself. And what if Jesse was headed down this same trail? What if Aadon running out of his apartment this morning like a crazed maniac was enough to give him that final push?

He lifted his head at last and fixed Dr. Carol with a hopeful stare. "If I… would you… I mean, I don't know if *he* would, but if I could get him to, would you…."

Sterile office silence greeted that clusterfuck of a request.

"Some lawyer I'm going to make," he muttered at himself and drew in a deep breath. "If I brought a friend here, maybe, because he needed to talk, would you… I mean, you've done such a great job with Ricky, and…."

A small, patient smile creased Dr. Carol's face into that kind, professional mask she rarely used around him. "*If* your friend wants to talk, certainly, Aadon, you know I will listen. But he has to want to. You know that." She fixed him with a stern but not angry glare. "I can't help anyone who won't talk to me. That's just the way it works."

He nodded. This was her, no longer talking about a theoretical friend, but telling him she wasn't satisfied with this little impromptu session. She was worried. He tried to reassure her with a smile, full on dimples and all. "I know. Thanks, Doc. I'll—" He shrugged and hauled himself to his feet. "I'll, you know." *Think about that.*

"Just remember," she warned him, getting to her feet and following him to the door. "I can help Ricky only so far. You're his brother. I need to know *you're* okay."

Aadon nodded, wanting to tell her he was, knowing she wouldn't believe the half lie anyway, and so he just nodded.

"I'll see you in a week."

"A week?" He stopped in the hallway. "Ricky's evals are only once a month."

"They are." Her face was all no-nonsense firmness. "But I will see *you* in one week. I'll have Janice call on Friday afternoon to remind you." She closed the door gently in his face.

Aadon wandered down the hall in a bit of a daze and spent the ride home alternately freaking over this new development and calling Jesse at every stop light. Neither one of those activities netted him any peace of mind. Jesse didn't answer his phone, and Doc Carol's worried expression as she let him out of the office only reinforced his own sense of being slightly out of his depth.

It was almost dark by the time he pulled up to his building, exhausted and wound into a tight knot of anxiety. His brother's psychiatrist—his crazy, hollowed-out, messed up brother's psychiatrist—had just made him an appointment to come back to her office for a one-on-one session of his own. What. The. Fuck.

Chapter
Six

SARAH knocked on Jesse's door sometime after the evening news, but he didn't let her in. She came back later with pizza, which she had to leave outside his door since he wouldn't answer her muffled inquiries. When he was sure she was gone, he opened the door, retrieved the pizza, and retreated back inside. Settling on the couch with a depressing movie and pizza didn't make him feel any better, but it saved him having to talk to anyone. He fell asleep there, and knocking on his door woke him sometime long after the sun had passed noon.

"Jess?" There was more knocking. "Jess? Baby, please let me in. I'm getting a little scared."

"Coming."

He opened the door, and Sarah came in with two huge, steaming ceramic mugs. She didn't even hand him one but put them both on the counter and took his hand. Turning it palm up, she pushed his sleeve out of the way and ran light fingers down his forearm. That's what he liked about her. No beating around the bush. He pulled his hand free and picked up the coffee she'd brought, handed her one, and watched her fold herself onto his sofa, making herself at home.

Lifting the cup to her lips so she could peer at him over it, she waited.

He clicked through the channels with the sound down.

"You can surf all day. You know it won't bother me."

A quick glance showed him she had lowered her mug but was still watching him.

"If I tell you what happened, will you go away and leave me alone?"

"You know I will never go away, Jesse." She took another sip. "Did he? Go away, I mean?"

Jesse nodded.

"Why?"

Jesse shrugged, but his hand ran a fast rhythm over his forearm, and even though she pointedly watched that distracted motion, he couldn't make himself stop. "Guess he just decided he wasn't that interested after all." He knew she wasn't going to buy so simple an explanation. "My mom called."

"And?"

"Anthony has a new lawyer."

"So?"

"He's suing the old one and appealing his sentence." He sighed, but Sarah rose and came to squeeze into the chair beside him. "When we settled the first time, it was about that one time. One night. One." He drew a breath and shuddered. "Now he's suing his lawyer for incompetence for not basing the entire case on the history of our relationship."

"I'm not sure I follow."

"Everything we did together is going to be fair game, Sarah. Everything."

"So?"

"So?" Jesse squirmed to the edge of the chair where she couldn't see his face. "So. I'm not interested in my sex life being a matter of public record. No one needs to know that I—" He snapped his mouth shut. "It isn't anyone's business."

"So you like subbing." Her hand ran smooth, unhelpful circles over his back. "So do I. It isn't an invitation for anyone to smack you around."

"Thank you." Jesse slammed his mug down on the table and watched it splash over the rim onto the already stained surface, then couldn't stand to be there, squashed into the chair next to her, all that mass of *other person* so close. "Because I want everyone to know that wasn't the only time it happened." Both hands scraped through his hair, stopped there, handfuls of it gripping and pulling, like the pain of that could erase the rest.

"It wasn't?"

"You know it wasn't."

"What does any of this have to do with Aadon? Did you tell him?"

"Not really." Jesse let go of his hair, sank into one of the kitchen chairs. His arms rested across the table, and he ran a thumb down the inside of his right forearm. "According to Leo, he wanted to know why I've never had a boyfriend. He satisfied his curiosity, and that's all he was interested in. So what? It's not like I expected a whole lot. Who wants this much baggage?"

"Stop that." Sarah had risen from her comfortable seat and came to stand beside him. She placed a hand over his, stopping the rhythmic rubbing. "You had a bad few months after it happened. You did some stupid things. It's behind you. You will find someone who isn't worried about baggage. We all have it."

"Sure."

There was a knock at the door, cutting off any more placating from her. Jesse groaned.

"It's okay, sweetie." She patted his shoulder. "I'll make whoever it is go away."

She went to the door and opened it a fraction.

"Hi."

The low, liquid voice sent a shiver down Jesse's spine. His hand started to move again, up and down his arm. He couldn't feel the tiny scars through the fabric, but he knew they were there.

Sarah just stood with the door half-closed and said nothing.

"Can I come in?"

"Why? What do you want?" Sarah's voice was far from welcoming.

"I just wanted to see he was okay. I had to kind of run out yesterday, and—"

"He doesn't want company," Sarah cut him off.

"Did he tell you what's going on?"

"He told me you took off out of here yesterday like your tail was on fire."

"His mother called." Aadon's voice rose a tiny fraction, hardening and turning frosty around the edges. "He didn't give me any details, but whatever it was, it shook him up, and he wouldn't answer the phone yesterday. I was worried."

"Maybe he just didn't want to take your calls."

"Maybe I'd like him to tell me that himself."

"Maybe the two of you should stop bickering over me like I wasn't here." Jesse rose from the table to face them. "Let him in, Sarah."

She stood back and held the door open, but her expression was dark, and her eyes glittered.

"Hi." Aadon stood just inside the doorway. He looked awkward in tailored pants and a dress shirt, his jacket hanging open and his hands clenching and unclenching at his sides.

"Hey." Jesse managed a quick glimpse at his face, but his gaze quickly dropped to the floor just at the toes of Aadon's shoes.

"I'm sorry. I know it was odd yesterday. I didn't explain."

"No need."

"There is. The way I took off. It was rude."

"Forget it. I gave you an opening and you took it." He shrugged. "No harm, no foul. I don't blame you, really."

"Jesse, shut up and let me explain."

Jesse clenched his teeth.

"I did have somewhere to be. There was a meeting. I couldn't miss it."

"And you couldn't just say?"

"Maybe, with everything, I didn't think you needed to deal with my shit too."

"What are you talking about?"

"Look." Aadon took a few steps forward, shuffling his expensive loafers across the ceramic tile of the entrance. "It's a long, involved story." He lifted a shoulder, and his lips quirked in a little self-deprecating half-grin. "My nice, white-bread family is completely screwed up, and you can't get to know me without hearing the whole sordid tale, but it doesn't have to be right this second, does it?"

"I think it does," Sarah said.

"Sarah." Jesse shot her a look.

"I'm just saying."

"Well, don't." Jesse appreciated her protectiveness, but not the teeth behind it that she seemed quite willing to sink into Aadon's jugular. The poor guy looked completely shell-shocked, and Jesse moved slightly to put a bit more presence between him and Sarah. "I can say perfectly well whatever I want to say for myself. At least I've learned that much."

"Are you sure?" She sounded dubious.

"I'm sure." He pulled open the door. "You can go." He pointed out into the hallway. "I'll bring your mugs back later."

"Because I can stay."

"Oh, I know you can, but you aren't going to. Out."

"Call me if you need anything."

"Out."

"Fine." She shot Aadon one more look.

Jesse couldn't decide if it was less hostile or not. He closed the door behind her.

"Quite the guard dog."

"She's really just one of those little yappy poodles."

Aadon chuckled. "Sometimes, that's all you need."

"I wish I'd had her around years ago," Jesse conceded. "She would have spared me a lot of trouble."

"You wouldn't have listened to her."

"Probably not."

Jesse led Aadon into the apartment and sat on the recliner, pulling his feet up under him. He wasn't sure why he'd let the other man in. Maybe because Sarah had yapped, and he was tired of hiding behind her. Maybe because spending another day like yesterday was too much to even contemplate, and he hoped Aadon actually had a good reason for taking off. Maybe because Aadon was just that gorgeous, that perfect, and he felt... safe around the bigger man who stirred things in him that hadn't been stirred in a long, long time.

Aadon followed him across the room a little more slowly, kicking off his shoes with a sigh and shrugging out of his suit jacket. He folded it neatly and hung it over the back of a kitchen chair before sitting on another, giving Jesse whatever space he needed to feel comfortable.

"You do believe me, don't you?" he asked, fearing that he'd already scuttled this relationship beyond salvaging.

"About yesterday?" Jesse shrugged. "It doesn't matter if you were freaked. Most people are. Most people who know, anyway."

"I take it not very many do."

"Just Sarah. Mom." Jesse looked up and caught Aadon's gaze. "You. And I'm not quite sure why I told you."

"They looked like old scars."

"They are. And they aren't. Something…." Jesse searched for words for a minute but came up with nothing really suitable. "Happened. I handled it badly." He lifted his arms slightly from where they rested on his knees. "This was a less than helpful solution. Some days, I can look back on it and wonder what the hell I was thinking. Other days, it's not that easy."

"Yesterday was one of the other days?"

"Yesterday was one of the other days."

"And today?"

Jesse sighed. "It might be a little early to tell." He glanced at the window over the kitchen sink and followed the deep golden rays of late afternoon sun across the floor. It wasn't a good sign he'd slept the entire day away. He hadn't done that in a long time, either.

"You know you don't have to tell me anything you don't want to," Aadon was saying.

"It's like what you just said, though, isn't it? If you want to get to know me, you have to hear the whole thing. I would like to say it doesn't matter, but—"

"But maybe it doesn't matter today."

In the end, they didn't share. They sat on the couch and watched old movies, ate popcorn and drank cola until they were both bloated and the sun was going down. Finally, Aadon rose to leave but offered to take Jesse out for dinner. The emotional energy to leave the safety of the apartment was too much for Jesse to muster, so Aadon went alone. He surprised Jesse by coming back an hour later, changed into jeans and carrying take out.

"That was a quick change," Jesse commented, holding the door open for him and taking the tray with two cartons of milk and two steaming cups of coffee that smelled like vanilla and caramel.

"Actually, I had the clothes in the car," he admitted. The bags rattled as he plopped them onto the coffee table. "I hope you like Chinese. Meatless is a little tougher to come by than I would have thought." He paused, looking at the blue and white milk cartons. "Oh. Do you drink milk?"

"Does a body good." Jesse smiled. "Tell me you got this from the place down the street. They have the best veggie stir-fry in town, and their rice is never sticky."

"I did."

"Good."

Jesse brought plates from the kitchen, the clatter of dishes and the warm aromas of sauces soothing his nerves like all the hiding the day before hadn't managed to do. He sat down beside Aadon on the couch. They were close enough the hairs on Jesse's arm stood on end when their shirtsleeves brushed. It was closer than they'd gotten all day, and Jesse realized how careful Aadon had been with him.

Now, Aadon glanced over, measuring Jesse's mood by studying his face and waiting for him to speak first. Jesse had no idea how to break this silence without a confession he wasn't sure he was ready for. He concentrated instead on manipulating the chopsticks and veggies. It was a bit of a relief to discover how hungry he was under the stress and misery. The food helped even out the rough edges of his nerves. In the end, it was Aadon who spoke first.

"About yesterday."

"You don't have to explain. It was a bit much. I just…. I don't know why I showed you."

"Why I left had nothing to do with that." The self-mocking grin flashed across his expressive features. "You are a lot braver than I am, Jesse. I ran out of here without an explanation because I was being selfish."

Jesse waited until the moment of explanation stretched thin and dangerous. He watched Aadon study his plate in a show of self-consciousness that did more to endear the man to Jesse than all of his previous perfection had managed.

"You don't have to tell me anything, Aadon."

"Yes. You deserve some explanation."

"You explained. You had somewhere to be. If you want to tell me the rest, there will be time." Jesse put his plate down and turned, pulling a leg up onto the couch to better face Aadon. Now was the time to give him an out for real, knowing he could handle it if Aadon decided to walk. "If there isn't going to be another opportunity, then maybe you shouldn't tell me at all."

"I had a meeting I couldn't miss," Aadon said, not looking up, sounding like this was something he had rehearsed.

"Okay." Jesse let him go at his own pace. Whatever it was, it was important enough to Aadon to make it hard. It wasn't like Jesse didn't know that feeling. Intimately.

Aadon pulled in a deep breath and looked up. "My older brother is in Havenside." He said it fast, like yanking off a Band-Aid.

"The halfway place?" This surprised Jesse a bit. Aadon gave all the signs of coming from a wealthy, happy family. That he had a brother with drug problems severe enough to require rehabilitation didn't fit with the image Jesse had been constructing in his mind.

"It isn't halfway to anywhere," Aadon replied, his voice gritty and bitter. "It's assisted living. He put so much crap in his system during high school, by the time they flushed it all out, there wasn't much of him left. He couldn't look after himself any more. Now someone has to meet with him and his counselor every month or they kick him out. Dad's finished with him, and Mom just can't face it alone any more. That leaves me."

He'd delivered the entire speech staring at his plate while he twirled his chopsticks between his fingers. He shrugged. "Been going to these meetings on my own for five years now. Since I turned eighteen. He's ten years older than me. I don't hardly even know him, but he's my brother. It isn't the kind of happy families story you want to share with a whole lot of other people."

"I guess not."

"And yesterday, that was the first time in five years I ever came close to not being there for him, even if he has no idea who I am most of the time."

"Sorry I dumped my shit on you." It was all Jesse could think to say.

"I don't mind." Aadon reached with a free hand to pat Jesse's knee. Instinctively, Jesse dropped his foot to the floor to avoid the touch, and for a split second, Aadon's hand hung in the air before he slid it under his plate and began pushing the food around with the wooden utensils.

"I'm sorry." Jesse slumped back against the cushions. "It isn't you."

"You don't want to be touched right now. I get it." He put his plate down finally and looked back over his shoulder at Jesse. "Whoever did that to you, he shouldn't get away with it."

"I don't want my life to keep being about what happened. I just want to put it behind me. Forget about it." Jesse sighed. Suddenly, he felt like he would float away. All that hiding and secrecy, and there it was, out there, and Aadon was still looking at him, watching him, waiting for him to keep going. The whole world hadn't stopped because someone knew he had this thing that had happened to him and that it made him nervous and jumpy sometimes.

"That was what the phone call was about," he said, bravely moving past the moment of revelation and pretending this wasn't the biggest thing in his life. "Anthony got a new lawyer. Someone to tell him there's a way to convince the world what he did was okay."

"But it wasn't." Aadon wasn't really asking a question. Even though he didn't know the details, there was enough evidence for him to draw a few conclusions. What he concluded only made him want, more than ever, to make things right for Jesse again, like they would never be all right for Ricky.

Jesse glanced up. Maybe he wouldn't have to spell the whole thing out in all the humiliating details. "No," he said. Simple. True. Oh, so painfully true. "It wasn't."

The room wrapped around them for a few minutes, enveloping each in his own thoughts. Warm lamplight and the soft popping and rumbling of the old water heaters under the windows made the place safe. Aadon's presence wasn't a threat. He fit in the room, another comforting presence Jesse was almost afraid to count on.

"If he appeals and you don't come forward to tell your story—"

"I told my story already," Jesse interrupted. "I showed them the bruises and the casts." He paused, and when he spoke again, his voice dropped, the anger not enough to compensate for the humiliation. "They have the rape kit. They don't need to hear it all again."

"You don't want to tell it again."

"No. I don't. Why is that such a crime?" He couldn't stop the horrible anger or contain it enough to keep it from lashing across Aadon's concern.

But the bigger man didn't flinch or snarl back. He didn't even look away. "It isn't." It was Aadon's turn to shift positions, sitting cross-legged beside Jesse, facing him so there was no way Jesse could hide. "But why would you let him tell his version and not make sure it was the truth?"

"We were together a long time. I'm sure whatever he says will be true of our relationship at some point. He can make his case without having to lie."

"Not lying and telling the whole truth are not the same thing at all."

Jesse studied Aadon's face. The man was trying to help, he knew. He couldn't be angry at him for wanting to understand. He'd already invested enough of his own emotional baggage to prove he wasn't just curious, but that didn't mean he was here for the long haul or that Jesse could trust him with the uglier details of his and Anthony's relationship. "Maybe I don't want the whole truth out there." God, please don't let him ask what that meant.

Aadon turned that over in his mind for all of six seconds. Coupled with the pleading look on Jesse's face that he understand, that he not ask and make Jesse admit to anything else right now, he knew. Jesse had surrendered much more to this asshole, Anthony, than just his body. He'd trusted him with fuck only knew how much of himself, and rather than respect the strength it took to give that kind of trust, to be that helpless to another person, Anthony had used him. Hurt him. Turned something beautiful into Jesse's worst nightmare.

No wonder he didn't want to go through all that again.

"Look." Aadon fingered the strings trailing from the cuff of his jeans. How could he possibly make this right? How could he explain that what Anthony had done had been a horrible breach of trust, that Jesse hadn't deserved it? God. Surely by now, he knew he hadn't deserved it.

Drawing in a deep breath, Aadon squared his shoulders and drew on every bit of knowledge he had about what it meant to be responsible for that much of a person. "I don't know anything about what you and this guy did when he wasn't beating you up and forcing you." He looked up again, and Jesse couldn't look away from the intensity of his gaze. "You don't have to tell me. That's private. It's yours. But I know enough about the scene to make a fair guess that he didn't get what it was you were doing. If he ever used your submission against you, whether or not you liked any of it, he wasn't treating you like a partner. He was controlling you, and that isn't what it's about."

How the fuck did he know? Jesse hadn't mentioned anything about submission or anything like that. And yet Aadon's gaze was steady, sure, daring him to contradict what he had surmised. He couldn't lie right to his face. He couldn't deny it, and he couldn't quite make himself say it out loud.

Jesse got up and paced across the room, unable to resist the urge to rub at the scars under his shirtsleeves. He turned at the far end of the room to face the sofa and Aadon's placid calm. Still, he leaned on the end of the wall near the entrance with his arms crossed tightly over his chest, his shoulders up tight and stiff, and his back pressed hard against the cold wall. "How would you know what any of it was about?"

For a long minute, Aadon just looked at him, a slight frown on his face. "I know you don't know anything about me." His frown deepened. "But you can trust me."

"That's what Anthony said."

"I'm not Anthony."

"I don't know if I'm ready."

"Then you're not."

Aadon got up, every motion fluid and softly non-threatening. He picked up their plates and carried them to the kitchen, dumping the contents into the trash and setting the dishes in the sink. Silently, he packed up the food and put it away in the refrigerator, threw away the soiled napkins and empty containers, and washed his hands under steaming water. Jesse watched him, too tightly wound to help or act, as though this was just the end of another date.

At last, Aadon stood in the kitchen doorway, the space of a few feet and a gulf of uncertainty between them. He smiled, this act, as every other, completely benign. "I'm not going anywhere, though I should, with all your issues."

Jesse pushed himself away from the wall, a spark of anger giving him the strength to break his shell at last. It brought him a step closer, within reach of comfort, within reach of being hurt, but Aadon only held up a hand.

"But I'm not going to because I want to help you. I want to show you how this is supposed to work."

"How what's supposed to work?" Jesse's heart fluttered a wild, out of control staccato, and he knew his face flushed.

"A relationship where you can be vulnerable with another person and not worry they'll use it against you." Aadon took a small step forward, then another. "Submitting doesn't give your partner the right to do whatever they want."

Jesse frowned, fear a heavy lump in his throat he couldn't quite swallow around, leaving him too weak to move, too cowed to even step back. Aadon's aftershave drifted around them, permeating the air, adding its heavy scent to the underlying smell Jesse had observed and appreciated once, just a few nights before.

"You're in control," Aadon said gently. "Just say what you want."

"Too close," Jesse whispered, wondering where the fearlessness that had let him kiss this man had disappeared to.

Immediately, Aadon stepped back, removing himself to the kitchen doorway and leaning on the frame.

"I just want to not feel this," Jesse said after a minute, examining his own shaking hand, glaring like that would be enough to make the fear dissolve and the tremors cease.

"It takes time," Aadon said.

"I feel safe around you." Jesse looked up at him with a faint smile. "Most of the time."

"You have to take your own life back, Jesse. No one can do it for you."

Jesse slumped back against the wall. "If I tell them everything, how I let him—"

He hesitated, but Aadon only waited, watching him patiently. "I let him do things, Aadon. I even." He blushed, the heat of embarrassment rushing up under his hair. "I liked it sometimes, when he wasn't… when he didn't hurt me."

Jesse sighed and let himself slide down until he was sitting on the floor, leaning on the wall with his knees safely up close to his head. It made his emotional wobbles a little easier to bear. "If I tell them I willingly let him put me in that position, where I had no power to stop him, they're going to say—"

"What?" Aadon's voice dropped the word, like a heavy blow, into the middle of Jesse's mumblings, making Jesse look up. "That you deserved it?" He crouched to better peer into Jesse's face. "No one deserves to get hit. No one deserves to be raped."

"It was just part of his game."

For a split second, Aadon looked so angry, Jesse thought he would lash out himself, and he had nowhere to go. The wall at his back stopped any retreat. Aadon was too close for him to move. He sank down, trying to hide behind his raised knees.

Black rage shook Aadon to his core. A game. For the first time in his life, he understood the anger that made a person want to hurt someone, want to take revenge and wrap it around another human being's neck until they choked on it.

Jesse just stared at him, eyes big and dark, face slack, too close to the blankness he so often saw in Ricky. Aadon shoved relentlessly at the anger until it was under control again. The moment passed. Tense muscles relaxed, the storm of fury cleared enough to let him speak, at least, though it remained in the low grate of his voice. "That's a sick game."

"I didn't know," Jesse said quickly. "I was a kid, barely out of high school. I was hardly even used to dating other men, and he was gorgeous and a little dangerous." He shrugged. "A lot dangerous. But I didn't know that until it was too late."

He cleared his throat, trying to find the right way to explain how he'd let things get so bad. He picked absently at the metal bar bridging the gap between the ceramic entrance and the kitchen's linoleum and didn't notice Aadon move until he could once again smell the man's aftershave. He didn't dare look up, but he let Aadon still his restless fingers by putting a hand over his. He stared down at their hands and managed to tell the rest of the story without falling apart. How he had tried to move out while Anthony was gone. He skimmed over the beating. Most of it, he didn't remember anyway, and the flashes that did come back to him sparked an unreasoning terror, putting him back in that place where he was too small, too bruised, too hurt to fight back. He finished with the barest facts in a subdued voice.

"He raped me and just left me there—broken wrist, broken ribs." He shivered with remembered cold. "Took me hours to get it together enough to call 911. I was still in the hospital when they arrested him. I didn't see him again until he came to court to answer the charges." Jesse turned his hand over to grip Aadon's fingers. "I never want to see him again. I never want to think about it again."

"Then don't." Aadon settled beside him, leaning against the wall so their shoulders touched, offering only the comfort Jesse wanted.

"Will you stay?" Jesse asked, surprised at the idea he'd rather trust in Aadon's gentle good will than be alone in the dark remembering the long, freezing night of aching muscles and broken bones Anthony had left him with.

Aadon kissed the top of his head softly. "On the couch. But I have an early class."

"Okay."

Still, Aadon made no move to get up. He wasn't inclined to rush Jesse through the process of putting himself back together. Hell, he didn't want to rush himself. He felt as weak and helpless as Jesse looked, only Jesse needed him to be strong, so he sat with him, held his hand, breathed with him, and just tried to exist through all the shit that was too hard to think about.

When they finally rose, both of them a little stiff from sitting so long on the cold floor, only the small lamp by the sofa and a sliver of light from under the bedroom door illuminated the space. Somehow, the near dark gave Jesse a little bit of courage, a tiny blanket of safety, and he reached up a hand and touched Aadon's face.

"I'm not so helpless as I was then, you know. I can fight back now."

"I hope I never give you a reason to," Aadon said honestly. Gently, he took Jesse's hand from his face. Holding his wrist in a loose grip, he pulled it down to the small of Jesse's back and held it there. Because when everything had been said, and there was no energy left to feel anything, or explain it, or find the words, he still wanted the guy. To protect him, to teach him, just to hold him and show him it could be okay to trust again, and this was something they would both understand. He hoped.

He looked into Jesse's eyes, glinting in the near darkness, and it felt like he held a trapped bird. His head told him to let go. His heart told him if he just held on long enough, carefully enough, that bird would sing for him.

Jesse's heart thudded a staccato rhythm against Aadon's chest. Something like fear, but not, skated up and down his spine, and he leaned a little closer to Aadon to see if it would go away or take hold. It slowed, heated, made his skin tingle.

Aadon smiled and leaned close. "Kiss me, Jesse."

It wasn't a request. Rising up onto his toes he gently touched his lips to Aadon's, automatically doing as he'd been told, hard experience telling him it would be better than resisting. Aadon's tongue flicked against his lips, and he gasped, his spine going rigid in response, his heart beating painfully hard. He twisted his wrist a tiny bit in Aadon's grip, felt Aadon's fingers loosen, ready to let him go. When Aadon tried to pull him a little closer, he resisted and was instantly released.

He stepped back, dizzy, breathing harder than one little kiss warranted, bewildered at the sudden freedom.

"What?" He blinked at Aadon, the dim light working against him now, making it hard to see the other man's features. "What did I do?"

"Believe me." Aadon cleared his throat, easing a bit of the huskiness from his voice. "When you're ready to, I would love to explore that side of you a little more." He took a deep breath and stepped outside of Jesse's space. "But not tonight."

"What did I do wrong?" Jesse asked, a mixture of relief and disappointment gurgling in his stomach and making his heart flutter frantically.

"Jesse...." Aadon's head tipped back, his eyes closed, and the big man took a few long, slow breaths before he lowered his head again and took Jesse's hand. He pulled it between them, pressed Jesse's palm to his very hard cock and sighed. "You didn't do a thing wrong, baby, I swear. But this is a big deal, and I can feel you shaking. I'm the one who could do something very wrong if I rush things." He released Jesse's hand only to cup his face in both of his. He lifted Jesse's face, a show of tenderness in his touch and his eyes and in the kiss he bestowed on Jesse's lips. "Please trust me."

Jesse nodded within the confines of Aadon's warm, dry palms. "I do." He did.

For a long moment, Aadon searched his eyes. "I know. And that's... dangerous. For both of us. There's no rush to get into this. Not before we know each other better. I need to know your limits, and that"—he caressed Jesse's lips with one thumb—"that will require you telling me everything."

Jesse sucked in a hard breath that caught in his throat. His eyes went wide, and he couldn't control the impulse to pull away. For only the barest of instants, Aadon held him, and that was enough. Like a steel trap slamming shut, his mind closed, his heart ripped a new painful beat up his throat, and he yanked away.

Aadon stepped back, hands out to either side of himself and a concerned look on his face. "You're not ready."

Jesse shook his head. "No." He wasn't. That was glaringly obvious. "You must think I'm a complete fool."

Aadon shook his head. "I think you're frightened, and reasonably so. And I think you can get through this. You've survived this long. You can get past this. And I'll help, if I can, but I won't push you. I won't let you push yourself. The hard truth is, right now, you have a hard limit of zero tolerance. Nothing wrong with that. But we both have to respect it, and let it move back at its own pace. That might take a while."

"And when you get bored waiting for me to not be a basket case?"

"I don't think you're a basket case." Aadon smiled, one of those wide, open expressions that deepened his dimples and lit up his eyes. Even in the dimness, Jesse could see the honesty in it. "I think you're something special. Someone I want to get to know better. If I *were* your Dom"—his eyes went a little darker, his expression taking on a deeper warmth and sternness—"the very first thing I would ask of you would be to remember that."

"Remember what?" Jesse asked, fascinated by the way Aadon's gaze pulled him in, held him without even the tiniest hint of threat.

"That you're special. Important to me and worth my every effort."

Jesse tilted his head slightly, taking that in. Had Anthony ever said such a thing to him? Lots of times, he had asserted his dominance and ownership. Had he ever said Jesse was special to him?

"I think it's probably time we both got some sleep," Aadon suggested. "Not that I wouldn't be perfectly happy to stay up all night in your company, but I have an early class, and you probably have stuff going on tomorrow. I'm going to go out on a limb and say you maybe haven't had a very restful couple of days." Honesty compelled him to admit, at least to himself, that he hadn't, either, and he was exhausted.

Jesse nodded. On one level, he felt as though he'd just been sent to bed like a wayward child. On the other, he felt a warm glow of appreciation for the idea that Aadon cared enough to notice how wrung out he was. One thing he knew he wanted before he left the other man to the mercies of his lumpy couch. "Do I get a goodnight kiss, at least?"

Both Aadon's eyebrows shot up, vanishing under the thick fringe of his bangs.

Jesse swallowed hard. "Please?"

"Oh for God's sake." Aadon held out both arms to Jesse. "Could you even *be* any more adorable?"

He couldn't help it. Jesse grinned wide and stepped into the circle of Aadon's embrace. "If I tried, probably."

"Well don't try," Aadon snarled, affection honeying his words. "It'll kill me."

"Death by cute."

"Horrible way to go."

Jesse snickered, and when Aadon's arms folded around him, he sank comfortably against his chest. "My lethal charm. To be used only in the event of dire emergency," he promised.

"And not every time you think you need a kiss?" Aadon arched away a bit so he could see Jesse's face.

"Well...."

To stop him answering that, Aadon covered Jesse's lips with his own. It wasn't a half-measure of a kiss. For all the tenderness in the touch of his fingers under Jesse's chin and the gentle pressure of his mouth, it was as deep and promising a kiss as Jesse could ask for.

FOR a long time after he'd handed Aadon sheets and blankets and headed to his own bed, he lay there, behind the safety of a half-closed door and prowled through the evening's events. He could still feel Aadon's hard chest against his. He could smell the other man on his shirt, feel his lips, and wonder what it might feel like to hear his voice whispering gentle commands in his ear, and the thought didn't terrify him. For the first time in a very long time, he could imagine a future when he wouldn't smile from behind that wall of fear at a world he didn't actually live in. He'd grown so used to the fear, to the knowledge small things, like dancing, kissing, comfort, were not a part of his life. The idea he might enjoy them again was a little baffling and a little intoxicating at the same time. He hadn't been willing to take the risk in so long, but Aadon made so many things seem possible. Just his presence in the next room made a sound sleep, free of dreams, a reality.

Chapter
S e v e n

JESSE woke not remembering having fallen asleep, but the smell of coffee brewing and the sound of the shower running drifted down the hallway. He burrowed under the covers until just his eyes remained uncovered and indulged in thoughts of a very naked, very handsome, wet man only a few feet down the hall. Those thoughts led to his awareness that there was nothing wrong with his libido, at least. Maybe he wasn't ready to act on the thoughts yet, but he could see a time coming when he could, and the world looked a little more pleasant from this new perspective. For once, he let himself believe it would last.

Standing at the kitchen counter, pouring coffee and allowing the idea of sharing his space distract him, Jesse only peripherally heard Aadon pad down the hallway from the bathroom. When he did look up, it was to see the other man tiptoeing across the living room, a sheepish look on his face.

"Forgot my bag out here."

Jesse set his cup down carefully and licked his lips. "Your towel's slipping."

"What?" Aadon's hand flew down to grip the flimsy knot at his waist. He shook his head. "Brat."

Jesse just grinned and sipped his coffee. "Don't stand there half-naked much longer, or I'll make sure it slips."

Aadon picked up his bag, but instead of heading back to the bathroom, he sauntered over to the counter. Though he remained on the other side of it from Jesse, it wasn't a barrier to him leaning over and planting a sweet, deep kiss backed by a lot of tongue.

"Wow." Jesse's grin faded to slack-lipped contentment, and Aadon traced the outline of his reddened lips with a finger.

"That," he said approvingly, "is so tempting."

Jesse blinked at him as it slowly dawned on him what Aadon meant. "Me? After—" He bit his lip. *Last night.* He didn't say it, but the question rang in the air anyway.

"After you listened to my excuses and let me get away with acting like an idiot?" Aadon smiled. "Even more than ever."

Jesse frowned at him. "After I spilled my guts all over you," he corrected. "Don't brush it off."

"Okay." Aadon dropped his bag and rounded the counter. "After you told me everything, I'm just happy to still be here, to feel like you trust me that much when you have no reason to and every reason not to." He placed both hands on Jesse's hips and drew him close. "Can I kiss you again?"

Jesse nodded, breathing the fresh-washed scent of him deep and gazing up at him. "You'd better, I think."

Aadon didn't need to be told twice. He bent and gave Jesse a kiss he'd intended to be a slow, calm and relatively chaste one. Then Jesse melted into him, gripped his towel at his hips in clinging fingers, and parted his lips under Aadon's. The kiss just went on and on. Aadon slid a hand up to cup Jesse's head, to dig his fingers through the thick thatch of dark hair and hold him steady. Jesse's slim form molded firmly against Aadon, and the world went away.

"A-hem." A clatter of ceramic made Aadon jump. Jesse's fingers dug into the skin at his waist, and he gasped. "No more mugs at mine," Sarah explained as they both turned to where she was digging mugs out of the kitchen sink. "Sorry." The flash of her eyes didn't match the apology even a little, and Aadon backed out of Jesse's arms.

"Hey, Sarah." Jesse's cheeks flamed. "You could have called."

"Since when?" Her chin thrust out, and she glared.

Aadon stepped a step closer to Jesse, instinct moving him to put his bulk between his guy and this she-demon.

"Here." Jesse reached for the last mug in the sink. He rinsed it and poured coffee and what seemed like a half-gallon of honey into it. "Drink, Brodzilla."

Sarah put the other mugs down and took the offering. She barely took her gaze off Aadon, though, and jutted her chin at him as soon as she'd sipped from the steaming brew. "What's he doing here?"

"I—"

"He kept me company last night." Jesse moved to lean on the counter, effectively putting himself between them. "I needed not to be alone."

"Huh." She wasn't giving up the belligerence easily.

Jesse's voice lowered, and he leaned forward. "Be nice or go home, Sarah."

She slid her robe-clad self onto one of the tall stools on the other side of the counter. "Thank you for the coffee."

"Sarah...."

"I should—" Aadon picked up his duffel bag and hefted it. "Be right back." He made his escape into the bathroom and closed the door behind him.

"What the fuck, Sarah," Jesse snarled, the moment the bathroom door clicked shut.

"He's the reason you checked out for two days." She sipped her coffee and glared. "I don't have to like him for that."

"He explained, and I believe him. He had something he had to take care of, and—"

"And what?"

"And." Jesse shrugged. "We talked."

Very gently, she set her mug down. "About?"

"Everything," Jesse said softly. "He knows everything, just like you wanted. I told him about Anthony. He knows...." He rubbed his arms. "He knows about the cutting. Everything. So you can calm the hell down because I told him everything, and he didn't run out the door or ignore it or anything else. He just listened." Jesse didn't think this was the time to explain what else Aadon had done last night, or how his heart thudded hard and fast every time he imagined himself sanding there with his hand pinned at his back and Aadon's lips taking his. He got a little thrill of adrenaline just thinking about it. It wasn't any of her business.

She studied him for a minute through the steam rising from her mug. "I worry, Jesse."

He smiled. "I know you do, and I love you for it. I know it looked bad. I know I had a little meltdown, but…. " He took a deep breath. "It's okay. I trust him. Please just try and give him the benefit of the doubt."

"If he hurts you—"

"He won't."

"I bet you thought that about Anthony too."

Jesse shifted his weight, trying to remember a time when he would have said the same about Anthony. He licked his lips and met her eye. "I—not like this, Sarah. I didn't know anything when I was with Anthony. I was a stupid kid, and if I'd known anything, even how to listen to my own gut, I would have left him a lot sooner than I did. But I didn't, and I got hurt, and that's—"

"If you say it's your own fault, I'll skin you," she warned.

"I was stupid. I made a mistake. This is different." He offered a tentative smile. "I feel it, Sarah. He isn't anything like Anthony."

Her eyes narrowed. "Is he a Dom?"

Jesse's skin heated from that tingling place in his gut that imagined himself at Aadon's mercy to the roots of his hair.

"Jesse, be careful. Please."

He nodded. "I will be."

"I want to be happy for you, baby," she said, her voice slightly strangled and her hazel eyes shimmering too much. "I do."

"Then be happy. I'm not a kid any more. I can do this. I have to do this. If you don't trust him, trust me." He stood a little straighter and crossed his arms over his chest. "I learned my lesson. I am *not* going through that again. Not for anything."

She nodded, stood, even picked up her coffee, but she didn't look very convinced. "I'm just down the hall," she said at last. "On speed dial."

"I know."

Letting out a heavy sigh, she finally headed for the door. "Don't forget it."

"I won't." He held the door for her as she slipped into her fluffy pink slippers. "I promise. Now go get dressed and don't skip class."

"Yes, Dad."

"I mean it!" he called after her. "Don't fart the entire semester away, chicky!"

"Yeah, yeah!" She waved over her shoulder without turning around, and Jesse sighed a little huff of relief. Maybe she'd let it go. Hopefully, she'd relax a little and not be so hostile to Aadon. He didn't think he could stand to lose her over this. She'd been his rock when he'd moved here, and he did love her. But he couldn't hide from everything forever. He wanted his life back.

"All right?" Aadon asked from the end of the hallway as Jesse let the door swing closed.

"Yeah." He smiled. "Yeah, I think so. She just needs to get used to the idea."

"I don't want to come between—"

"Stop it. She's my problem, not yours. I'll deal with her."

"She's just being protective." Aadon had crossed the room, and now he dropped his duffel at Jesse's feet and swept an arm around Jesse's waist. "A fluffy, pink little bull dog, she is."

Jesse grinned up at him. "She is. Just give her time."

"And what about you? Do you need time? Or can I see you again tonight?"

"You'd better." Jesse settled, comfortable in the circle of Aadon's arms, and rested his hands on the taller man's biceps. "I'll bring a couple movies home from the library. We can order in."

"Sounds like a perfect plan." And it did. Aadon wasn't really interested in pressuring Jesse to face public scrutiny or any of the many triggers he undoubtedly had left over from Anthony. He wanted to go slow, figure out what it was about dance floors and flashing lights that made Jesse break into a cold sweat. He wanted to know what else his new boyfriend would rather avoid than face. Eventually, maybe they'd face those things together, but for now, he was willing to go as slow as Jesse needed.

"You going to kiss me or just stand there staring?" Jesse asked, snapping him back from his thoughts.

Aadon focused on the delicate pink infusing Jesse's cheeks and grinned. "Oh, yeah. I'm going to kiss you. As often as I can, believe me."

"Goo—mmfh."

Now *that* was a sound Aadon could get used to.

Chapter
Eight

AADON felt like a dutiful son, knocking on Dr. Carol's door Monday evening. He knew this was past her regular office hours, but this was the time her secretary had told him to arrive, so here he was. She hadn't said anything about billing him for this session. He wasn't used to the idea that one of these doctors would seriously care enough to give up personal time just to help him.

She wasn't dressed in her long white coat and sensible blouse/skirt variation, as he was used to seeing her. She had on jeans and a T-shirt with the face of some country music singer in a ten-gallon Stetson splashed across the front. Just like a regular person. She was even in her stocking feet and had a pen tucked behind her ear.

"Hi." Aadon shoved his hands into his jean pockets.

"Hello, Aadon." She stepped back and held the door open for him. "Come in, please."

"Thanks, Doc."

"Coffee?" She motioned to the little alcove where she kept a Bodum and electric kettle sitting on top of a small bar fridge.

"Nah." He waved a hand. "I'm good."

"Would you mind plugging in the kettle?" She smiled at him and shrugged. "I admit, I could use it."

"Sure." He did as asked, speaking over his shoulder as he figured out how to turn the thing on. "You know, if it's too late, if you're tired—"

"Nice try. Come sit."

All he could do was nod and capitulate. He'd come all this way. No point in not at least hearing what she had to say.

"So." She settled into the deep armchair across from him, her feet curled under her, and peered at him. "Last time you were here, you seemed worried about something. Or, someone?"

Aadon nodded. How much of what he now knew about Jesse's past did he have a right to tell her? It wasn't his story, and yet....

"Everything you tell me is completely confidential, Aadon. You know that."

"But it isn't really my story to tell."

"However, I can look at you and see that you've taken on the burden of it anyway. Is it safe to assume this has to do with the friend you mentioned last week?"

"Yeah." Aadon leaned forward, balancing his elbows on his knees and studying the random whorls of contours in the carpet. "He's got some heavy shit in his past—oh!" He clamped his mouth shut and glanced up at her. "Sorry."

A soft chuckle met his apology. "Don't worry. Just talk. I'm here to listen."

Aadon nodded. "Stuff... happened. To him. He thinks it's his fault, in a way. Because he didn't know how to handle it."

"Like Ricky?" Her voice was tight with concern and what he'd come to recognize as her professional anger. He knew her well enough to know she was a strong advocate for abused kids, and that was probably why she had gone to such lengths to help Ricky. Even if he wasn't a kid now, he had been when it happened, and in a lot of ways, he was still stuck back there.

"Not exactly. He was older. Old enough to consent, but not experienced enough to understand what he was consenting to, or who he was... giving that to. The guy...." Aadon shook his head, unable to find a word to describe what he thought of Anthony.

"I understand the details aren't yours to share, Aadon. Let's just agree that I understand he was assaulted, that he's not okay with it, and neither are you." She leaned forward, the rustle of the movement drawing Aadon's attention to him again. "Is he safe now?"

Aadon nodded. "Yeah. This was a few years ago. That guy's under lock and key. It isn't that."

"Good. Then it's you I want to talk about. What are you feeling?"

"Angry." That was easy enough. He wasn't too blind to see the similarities in Jesse's trauma to Ricky's. He understood that feeling, deep in his gut, that he wanted someone to pay for it; to hurt the way the people he cared about were hurting. And he wanted to make it right for them. "I want…." He watched his own hands curl into tight fists, watched as though they belonged to the monster inside that was no better than the fuck-ups who'd done the initial damage. Lashing back didn't make it better. Letting Jesse or Ricky see that monster only frightened them more. But it was so hard to contain it.

"You want?" Dr. Carol prompted.

"I want… to…." *Hurt someone.* How did that make him any different, any better, than Martin, for molesting Ricky, or Anthony, for what he did to Jesse? It took a tremendous force of will to open his hands, but he managed it. Besides, Anthony was in jail, and Martin was far beyond anyone's reach to hurt now, and the fact he'd faced the same treatment in prison that he'd dished out, that he'd not been able to handle it, still didn't soothe Aadon's fury. "I want not to feel like Martin got off easy. I want to be able to say no one should be driven to take his own life, or suffer through what he did in there, but I don't feel it, Doc. What kind of monster am I that I think he deserved it? That I think it wasn't enough punishment for him?"

"All that makes you, Aadon, is very, very human."

"I feel like a monster. Like some crazed maniac." His hands were fists again, and he forced his fingers to straighten. "I want to hurt them. Ricky and Jesse, they don't. They don't care what happens to these creeps. Why does it matter to me, more than it matters to them? They're the ones it happened to. I want to, and I can't, and it's so… *frustrating!*"

"You feel helpless."

Aadon didn't like that word. He glared at her, but she didn't flinch. "I can't fix it. I can't make it better."

"No," she agreed. "You can't."

"How the hell is that supposed to help?" he snarled.

Behind him, the kettle boiled, sending a shrill whistle through the room. The psychiatrist lifted one eyebrow, and reluctantly, Aadon rose and went to fill the Bodum and pour the water.

The task took a few minutes, forced him to concentrate on that instead it the anger boiling into a sick mass of acid in his gut, and by the time he carried a tray with coffee pot, mugs, and cream and sugar back to the table in front of the couch, he at least didn't feel the burning anger to strangle anyone.

"And that's how it's done, Aadon," she said, leaning forward so she could pour coffee into both mugs.

"'Scuse me?"

"That's how you diffuse that anger. You focus on life. On here. Now. You do what needs to be done in this moment. You live." She handed him his mug and sat back again with her own. "You don't want to feel helpless? Then you do everything in your power, right now, to take care of them now. You can't change what happened in the past. You can't predict what will happen in the future, how they will get past their own feelings and barriers. You can only be there for them now, even if that means making them coffee, holding their hand. Loving them." She sipped her steaming brew, studying him over the rim of her cup. "I assume you do love this man."

"Jesse. His name's Jesse." Aadon slumped back into the couch. "I just met him. I don't know." His thoughts drifted to that kiss, to Jesse crouched on his kitchen floor, and the overwhelming need to take that pain in his eyes away. "I think. Maybe."

He was silent a few minutes. "I shouldn't."

"Shouldn't what? Love him? Why?"

"What if…." Aadon dragged his gaze up to look at her, hoping she would give him the right answer, tell him what to do. "What if I'm not good for him? What if I'm not what he needs? I don't want to hurt him more. I want him to be happy. I want…." He thought back to their first date, to the walk between restaurant and movie theatre, when Jesse had talked, nonstop, about old movies, and they'd argued if Cary Grant really was the quintessential leading man. "I want the smile, that one that lights him up, I want it to always be there. To be real all the time, not just once in a while when he lets his guard down."

"But you have seen him with his guard down."

"Yeah." Aadon smiled at the memory of Jesse gazing up at him, teasing him for instance that the actor was all that. It was a warm memory. Not the same heat as when Jesse melted against him, received his kiss like it was the only thing in the universe that mattered. That was a different heat altogether. It was special, and terrifying, and what if he didn't deserve that?

"Aadon, honey, I don't think you give yourself enough credit. If he can let his guard down, even a little bit, around you, then that can only be good for him."

"But if I hurt him, if I do the wrong thing…."

"What wrong thing could you possible do? If you care about him this much?"

Aadon swallowed a mouthful of burning coffee and glared at the floor. Did he dare talk about the way Jesse practically oozed submission? About how much he wanted to be the person who accepted that gift and took care of the man? But that skirted too close to telling her details about Jesse and what had happened that weren't his details to divulge.

"It's… complicated," he said at last.

"You'd be surprised how even the most complicated things boil down to a few, very simple truths, Aadon."

"Such as?"

She only shook her head. "I can tell you, but you won't really believe me. You won't understand until you actually feel it, live it, figure it out for yourself, where you live."

Aadon heaved a sigh. "That's not very helpful."

"Okay, so tell me something. When you walked in here tonight, how did you feel?"

"I told you. Angry. Nervous, I guess. I didn't know why you wanted me here, without Ricky."

"And I told you. I'm counting on you to be there for your brother. We both know you're it. If your parents ever do come around, it won't be in a way he needs. That's their issue to deal with, and unlike you, neither of them took my offer. You're here, talking to me, and that tells me a great deal about what you will and won't do for your brother."

"You don't think I'm messed up?"

"It's a messed up situation. Ricky will never be the man he could have been if this hadn't happened to him. Perhaps, because they knew him better before, your parents can't seem to get past that. They want their son back, and they can't have that. It will never be. Ricky is who he is, and you—" She smiled. "—you come here once a month to meet with me, you come on weekends to see him, you don't ask him to be anything but what he is."

"It isn't like I want him to be like this. I would love to have a brother...." Aadon frowned. A brother who what? Who looked at him with trust and understanding? He had that. Ricky trusted Aadon, and if he didn't get everything about the world around him, he did get that Aadon came to see him, to visit, and be just with him, because he wanted to be there and no other reason. He understood that much, and their time together was simple. The most uncomplicated thing in Aadon's life. Ricky wanted to see him, and he wanted to be there. That's all it was and all it needed to be. It made them both happy.

"A brother who?"

Aadon chuckled. "Very tricky, Doc."

"Not being tricky. Tell me what you're thinking."

"I love my brother. I like seeing him happy. I like visiting him. He doesn't need to be any other way. It doesn't matter, as long as he's happy."

"Happy patients are healing patients, Aadon. Every day I work with him, I see a little more, not what he was, but who he's becoming. Little pieces, glimpses. And it isn't going to be easy, because he does have a lot to deal with, and learning to wield the tools he needs to do so won't be as easy for him as it is for most. A lot he buried under the drugs and the self-destruction is going to hurt all over again when it comes to the surface, but maybe, if we find enough pieces, we can help him remake himself. However it is he wants to be."

"You think there's any other way for him to be?"

"He's been a shell a long time. He's been allowed to hide inside that shell, and maybe that's all he could handle all this time. No one can force him out, but I see a day coming when he might choose to start breaking it open, and who knows what kind of man will emerge?" She set her cup down, reached across and took Aadon's, setting it on the table too, so she could hold both his hands in hers. "If he does do this thing I think maybe he can do, you need to be fiercely strong, because you could see a glimmer of potential, you could want very badly for him to get better, and that might not be possible. It might be too much. It might break him completely, permanently. And you have to be prepared for that."

"So, you're saying there's hope, but that I shouldn't get my hopes up."

Her smile, this time was a little sad, a little knowing. "I've seen it before, this potential for breakthroughs that never come, or that come, and prove to the person they just don't want to do it. That it's easier to take the medication and stay inside where nothing can touch them and they don't have to hurt. I want you to see what could happen, to understand what it will be like for him. I hope for this for him, Aadon, but only if it's going to be better than what he has now. And I want to know you're ready to deal with whatever happens."

"That's why this extra session."

"Partly. I'm trained, Aadon. I know the signs of stress. I can see you cracking, and I don't want that for you."

Aadon pulled his hands free from hers. Touched that her concern included him and wasn't only about the ramifications for her patient, he gave a small nod of assent. "So, okay. Yeah. There's stress. But you even said. The only way to do this is one small thing at a time, right?"

"Usually."

"Do you think…?"

Dr. Carol waited, watching him carefully, maybe with a bit of amusement turning her brown eyes soft under the twinkle.

"I mean, if I need to talk again."

"You know my door is always open, Aadon. Always."

"I appreciate that, Doc. Thanks."

At least, on the ride home through the fog and misting rain, Aadon didn't feel quite so out of his depth any more. Just knowing he had someone to talk to was a huge help. And he could take her advice and move slowly, one small thing at a time. Hopefully, being around Jesse, wanting the other man as much as he did, would not be extreme torture. Mild discomfort, he could endure. He just hoped Jesse would understand and not always be throwing his lethal puppy eyes at him every time he turned around. There was nothing wrong with a simple date now and then. Once they knew exactly what was going to happen with Anthony, they could figure the rest out.

Chapter
Nine

SOFT thudding interrupted Jesse's already sketchy concentration, and he looked up at the door to his apartment. He knew who the soft, cautious knock belonged to and debated answering it. Aadon did everything softly around him now. Since *That Night,* everything had turned tentative between them, and it had begun to get on Jesse's nerves.

It didn't help that a few nights ago, they'd been sharing a rare, intimate moment on the couch when Sarah had come barreling into his apartment, overexcited about something Jesse didn't even remember now. It had taken over an hour for Aadon to peel Jesse off the ceiling and drag the story out of him, one reluctant word at a time. Anthony had often come home at odd times, surprising Jesse, keeping him off balance, never sure when he was going to have to get on his knees, spread his legs. Now, he could look on Anthony's tactics and know them for the manipulative control schemes they were. At the time, he'd just done what was necessary and lived on pins and needles in between. Sarah's grand entrance that night had triggered a panic Jesse couldn't control and brought out Aadon's overprotective coddling.

Jesse wasn't the fragile flower Aadon seemed to think, despite those infrequent reminders of his past, and the constant solicitation was beginning to chafe. Catching himself rubbing a thumb over his inner forearm, he stopped and picked up his pen.

The knock came again, followed by Aadon's muffled voice. "Jesse?" A pause followed, then, "You're not at work because you have a class now, but you're not there, either. Where else would you go?" Another pause followed by Aadon's voice turning down a notch in an effort to disguise the ruffled feathers of worry. "Open the door. Please."

With a sigh, Jesse put on his game face and got up from the table. Unlatching the chain, he opened the door and stepped back to let Aadon enter.

"Hey." He went back to his seat at the table and cleared some of the books to give Aadon a place to set the coffee cups he carried. "How did you know I skipped class?"

"Saw Sarah at the coffee shop. She asked me if I'd seen you today." Aadon studied Jesse's face carefully, alert for any of the tell-tale signs of stress or uncertainty he'd learned to recognize.

"So? She didn't go either. Go harass her." Jesse picked his pen up, put the lid on, and tossed it back on the table. He began to tidy his papers using short, sharp gestures.

"But she never goes to class, so that's hardly unusual." Aadon pulled a cup from the cardboard tray and handed it to Jesse, forcing him to stop fidgeting. "You don't skip."

"How would you know?"

Aadon smiled and slurped foamed milk off the top of his drink. "I pay attention."

"If I didn't know you're benign, that would be creepy." He didn't mention that he thought Aadon paid too much attention. He didn't want to argue, he didn't want to appear ungrateful that Aadon was attentive and concerned and careful. He didn't want to think he didn't have any control over where their relationship went or didn't go. That was too much like....

Anthony.

Jesse slammed the door on that thought and forced a smile, trying to relax into his seat. "I have a paper due." He pointed to the spread of books and papers. "I'm not hiding out, so don't worry."

Not like last time.

"No. I didn't think that."

"Sure."

"Does it bother you so much that I worry?"

"No." Jesse sat up straighter, put his cup down and took Aadon's from him. "I like that you care." He took Aadon's hand and stood. "Just, maybe you could show it a little more...." He grinned and lifted an eyebrow suggestively.

Aadon stayed seated, and Jesse had to give a little tug.

"Come on. I've worked all afternoon." He tried putting some twinkle in his smile. "I want to relax."

"Watch some TV?" Aadon stood and deftly slid his hand free, taking his coffee to the couch and picking up the remote. He clicked the television on and surfed through a few channels.

Jesse followed more slowly. "I actually had something else in mind."

"I know." Aadon watched him from the arm of the couch, his blue eyes steady and unsmiling but not unkind.

"Oh." Suddenly unsure, Jesse stuffed his hands in his pockets.

Aadon clicked the set off again and turned to face Jesse more fully. "It isn't that I don't want to."

"But?"

"What's the rush?"

Jesse swiftly discarded a dozen vulgar answers and settled on a shrug, trying to make his voice casual. "Why wait? It's not like I'm a blushing virgin or anything." He moved close to Aadon, pulled his hands free of his pockets and gripped the sides of Aadon's shirt in both fists so he couldn't back away. "Kiss me. Please?"

Aadon did, carefully at first, but Jesse wanted more.

He cajoled a little with his tongue, and Aadon obliged, pulling him close, turning the tables by slipping an arm around his waist and holding him tight. Jesse moaned, a tiny sound under Aadon's firm kiss, and Aadon's hand raked up through the hair on the back of Jesse's head, tugging at it just enough to send a tingle rushing down Jesse's spine. Aadon demanded without words he tip his head back and expose his throat.

For a moment, Jesse got lost between the conflicting urges to surrender or to free himself from Aadon's grip. Aadon must have sensed his instant of hesitation, because before he could make up his mind, Aadon freed him.

He staggered a step back, the support of Aadon's arm suddenly gone.

"Sorry." Aadon blushed and wiped his mouth. "Sorry, Jesse."

"Did I complain?" Jesse moved close again, but before he managed to reclaim his kiss, the phone rang, giving Aadon the perfect excuse to move out of reach. Jesse sighed and picked up the receiver. "Hello?"

"Hi, honey."

Jesse flicked a look at Aadon to roll his eyes, but the other man had already moved out of earshot.

"What is it, Mom?" He knew by her slight pause he hadn't tempered his irritation enough.

Taking his cue from Aadon's quick retreat to the kitchen, Jesse went to the table and picked up his coffee. There would be no reclaiming of kisses tonight. He could tell by the way Aadon's face smoothed over as the distance between them increased from a few inches to an entire room. He leaned on the edge of the table, resigned. "What's up?"

"Mr. Nivens came by the house today."

"Since when do lawyers make house calls?" Jesse glanced at Aadon, this time receiving a sympathetic frown. "I thought we'd settled this."

"He was in the neighborhood. And he explained everything about Anthony's case."

"Mom." Jesse put down his coffee again and slumped into his chair. "I don't care about his case. It isn't anything to do with me anymore. Besides, he took that deal, so whatever he does, it won't get him out of jail. He as much as admitted what he did."

During a long pause on the other end of the line, Jesse listened to paper shuffling and his mother muttering to herself. "Ah." She said at last. "Here. According to Steve—"

"Steve?"

"Mr. Nivens."

"You're on a first name basis now?"

"According to Mr. Nivens," his mother repeated, a little more sharply, "if Anthony wins this suit against his previous lawyer, he actually does have grounds to appeal his sentence, at least, if not his conviction."

Jesse closed his eyes, combating a sickening spinning sensation. Aadon's hand on his, fingers lightly curling around his own, drew his attention to the unconscious, habitual rubbing of his forearm. He pulled free and smiled, a little weakly, at the other man. "He won't likely win this lawsuit anyway, will he?"

"Apparently, if he argues the evidence just right, he stands a very good chance of winning."

"That's bullshit."

Aadon's firm hand on Jesse's shoulder stopped the spinning, and he reached up to touch the warmth and strength being offered.

"I just thought you would want to know where things stand," his mother explained, sympathy and not a little worry oozing from her voice, even over the phone lines. All that caring didn't disguise her own anger. Jesse thought maybe she was more pissed than he was at the prospect of Anthony finding any kind of leniency for his actions.

"I can't do anything about it anyway," Jesse pointed out. "I can't stop him from filing."

"You can tell your side."

"Dammit, Mother—"

"Don't swear at me, Jesse Tyler." Her voice softened. "I know how hard you find it to talk about this, but, honey—"

"I'll think about it." He pinched the bridge of his nose between thumb and forefinger, willing her to calm down. She was rarely agitated enough to use his middle name. It was his father's, and she only invoked *him* when she was severely disappointed. Like she was calling back the ghost of her dead soldier husband to guilt their son into line. "I'm sorry."

"I know, honey." She waited, but he really didn't have much else to say. "I'll send you some phone numbers. You might find you need to talk to someone about this. Just to get some advice."

"I said I'd think about it."

"You don't have a lot of time to think, Jesse. Mr. Nivens has mailed you copies of everything you need to read to get up to speed. As soon as you get it, look it over, and please, please call me."

"I will." He touched the end button on the phone, and it beeped in his ear. Gently, he rested the phone on the table.

"You okay?" Aadon took his hand again, and his fingers tightened around Jesse's.

Jesse nodded, glanced at Aadon's concerned face, and shook his head. "I don't know."

"I should probably get going."

"You could stay," Jesse suggested, knowing the answer he'd get before he finished asking the question.

"Jesse."

"I know." Jesse stood, walking to the door with Aadon. "My couch is deadly."

Aadon stopped and turned to him, taking his face in his hands and gently kissing him. "There will be a better time for this, I promise." Pulling away a bit, he smiled. "You sure you're all right?"

"Yeah." With a firm grip, Jesse took Aadon's hands away from his face. "I'm fine." He handed Aadon his coffee and pulled the door open. "We're still on for tomorrow, right?"

"Of course." Another quick peck landed on Jesse's cheek. "I'll come by around eight, and hopefully, this movie doesn't suck as bad as the first one."

Jesse managed to smile at that. "I can hardly wait."

The door closed softly, and Jesse stood a long minute, his gaze tracing over the pattern of the wood grain. It sickened him that Anthony might get away with everything, but bringing it all up again only delayed getting on with his life, and he desperately wanted to get on. Aadon wouldn't wait around forever.

JESSE met Aadon at the little diner where they'd had their first date. It was closer to nine, and Aadon had called to say he'd be late, though he didn't say why, and Jesse had offered to meet him at their destination, since it was almost midway between their apartments.

A Friday night crowd packed the little diner, and the flashing lights on the other side of the glass wall already lit up the simple, busy dining area. The white tablecloths spun with colored light, and the dark wood made the place look more shadowy than usual. Jesse stopped just inside the door to look around.

"We can go somewhere else, if you want," Aadon suggested immediately, his hand coming to rest comfortingly on the small of Jesse's back. He remembered his companion's reactions to the spinning lights the first time they'd come and couldn't quite figure out why Jesse had suggested they come back here.

Jesse shook his head, determined not to let a few unsettling memories get the better of him, for once. "No. This is fine." He pointed. "There's a table over there."

They threaded their way through the occupied tables to the end of the long bench near the glass wall where a tiny table for two huddled in the inconspicuous corner. Jesse slid onto the bench, and Aadon took the chair opposite. Within minutes, Mike came sashaying up to them, two beers in hand. He raised one eyebrow, and both men nodded, so he set the drinks and menus down, winked at Jesse, and swayed off.

"So." Aadon picked up his menu and gazed at Jesse over the laminated cardboard. "What do you want to do after we eat? Still up to taking our chances with the old movies? We can pick up the late, late show if we take our time over dinner."

Jesse glanced to his left through the glass beside him. He managed to keep his voice steady as he replied. "Or we could dance."

Aadon set down his menu, needing to really see Jesse's face. "I thought you didn't dance."

"I haven't in a while." Jesse, determined not to make a big deal out of it, picked up his own menu. He flipped it to the back and read the wine offerings, suggesting something light to go with his meal. Aadon shrugged agreement, but didn't resume his perusal of the menu. Jesse squared his shoulders. "Just because I haven't danced in a few years doesn't mean I've forgotten how."

"Are you—"

Slapping his menu down on the table to cut off Aadon's question, Jesse glared. "If you ask me if I'm sure about something one more time, I swear. I wouldn't suggest it if I didn't want to do it." His pulse pounded too loudly in his ears, making a rushing noise over which he found it hard to hear Aadon's calming reason.

"All right." Aadon pushed his menu away and sipped his beer. He was suddenly too queasy to eat. Jesse was way too adamant about this; a sure sign he wasn't sure about it at all. Only Aadon didn't think anything he said would dissuade his boyfriend. "I just don't want you pushing yourself."

"Aadon, listen to me." Jesse hauled back on his emotions, struggling for a calmer tone, unsure he managed to put Aadon at ease at all. "I had a bad experience. It didn't kill me, and I'm not going to stop living because of it. I know you aren't him, all right? Please stop treating me as though you're afraid I might break. I won't." For a long minute, he endured Aadon's scrutiny. "I won't."

"I worry," Aadon admitted. He shouldn't have to apologize for that. All he had to do was look at his older brother to understand what happened to a person who didn't deal with his issues, didn't have someone he could turn to when he needed. Aadon was not going to let that happen to Jesse because he was too preoccupied with how the other man left him half-hard with want just by being in the same room with him. "What can I say? These things have a way of sneaking up on you when you least expect it."

"How would you know?" Jesse asked. "Has it ever happened to you?"

"Well, no, but—"

"Then don't try and tell me you know anything about how it feels. You don't. I know what I'm ready for and what I'm not, and I promise, if I feel the least bit uncomfortable, you'll be the first to know."

Aadon sat back in his chair.

Belatedly, Jesse reached for the hand Aadon had wrapped around his beer. "I appreciate your patience. Really, I do, but I would appreciate it more if you stopped trying to get in my head and just let me set my own pace. Maybe just once in a while it would be nice to know you'd rather get into my pants."

"You're right."

Jesse blinked. "I am?"

Aadon sat forward with a little shrug, pulled his hand free, and picked up his menu. "I don't know what it's like. I shouldn't have presumed."

Invitations didn't get more open than that, but every instinct screamed at Aadon that Jesse was trying too hard. It didn't help that every touch of the man's fingers on his skin set him on fire. The memory of Jesse melting into him, surrendering instantly, was too fresh. Even months old, it was too fresh. He wanted that. But Jesse had no idea he was even offering it. It was sheer instinct to obey—to stay safe—that he capitulated so easily, not a conscious will to let Aadon have him, and that wasn't good or right. Aadon would be worse than Anthony if he took advantage of it.

"You're mad."

Jesse's soft accusation was like cold water in his face, and he almost sputtered.

"No, I'm not." He kept his gaze on the menu, desperate not to let the sweet, cajoling side Jesse had get to him.

Jesse watched his date for a while, waiting for the blond head to lift. Only when Mike came to the table a few minutes later did Aadon look up. He glanced at Jesse, turned to Mike and placed his order, waited until Jesse had ordered and Mike had left before quietly excusing himself from the table. Jesse waited a long time, much longer than it would take for Aadon to use the facilities, before following him.

The heavy restroom door swung open on silent hinges, and the peculiar smell of a bathroom trying too hard not to smell like a bathroom engulfed him. Jesse drew in a silent breath and stepped inside.

Aadon leaned on the counter by the sinks, his back to the mirror.

"I'm sorry." Jesse tried to make the apology light, tried to see into Aadon's shrouded eyes.

Finally, Aadon looked at him. "Why?"

"I got a little defensive." He held up his hand, finger and thumb an inch apart, sheepish smile on his face.

Aadon stifled a groan. How could he be so fiery one minute, and this… adorable the next and not know how crazy it made him? He pushed himself off the sink and closed his hand around Jesse's fingers, closing the space and kissing the fingertips. "Maybe that's the point. As long as you feel you have to defend yourself around me, I have to be careful." He closed his eyes, kept his lips pressed to his warm fingers.

God this was hard. He wasn't doing Jesse any good, wanting him this bad, knowing he couldn't—shouldn't—and knowing he wouldn't be able to resist much longer. He shouldn't still even be with him. It was too much. He just wasn't what Jesse needed.

Jesse felt the churning sensation in the pit of his stomach even before Aadon spoke again and yanked his hand free, mouth open, ready to fill the void before Aadon could speak. Before he could say what Jesse knew he was about to say. He was too slow.

Aadon took his face in both hands, tilting it up and looking into his eyes. "As long as I have to be that careful, this can't work."

"But—"

"Because I don't want to be careful, Jesse," Aadon went on, overriding his faint protest, passing a thumb over Jesse's lips and backing him up against a stall.

"Then don't." The words warbled out past Jesse's pulse fluttering in his throat. He swallowed hard. "Don't be careful." Aadon's toned body pressed his against the cold metal. The rush of fear and excitement mingled, and he knew he'd lost the ability to tell which was which. He didn't know if he cared.

"If I'm not, I could do more damage than Anthony ever did." Aadon's palm caressed his cheek, his fingers slid into Jesse's hair, and he kissed; a light strike of his lips and tongue, there and gone too quickly to capture, but expertly bringing him back down to where he could almost breathe normally. The rush faded, and Jesse wanted it back.

He gripped the front of Aadon's shirt, preventing him from moving away. "You're not anything like Anthony, and I'm not who I was then." He never would have demanded Anthony answer his desire like this. Kissing Aadon firmly, not hard or angry, just without compromise, Jesse closed his eyes, willed the other man to understand. He needed this so desperately. Needed to know he was wanted, desired. Needed to know Aadon could look on him as a man and not a shattered thing.

A soft groan welled in Aadon's throat and spilled out into Jesse's kiss. It was so good. So sweet, and held so much conviction. It was, finally, too much to resist. He answered it, tongue stroke for tongue stroke, slowly wresting control of the kiss from Jesse as he pinned him between his hard body and the cold metal of the bathroom stall. His big hands cupped Jesse's head, his body an immovable weight against him, soaking in Jesse's heat and desire, keeping him still and contained.

Jesse couldn't breathe, couldn't think, and his fingers tightened to fists in Aadon's shirt. This was exactly the kind of mindless surrender he'd always craved. Exactly what Anthony had never once given him. Because Anthony had never asked for it the way Aadon was doing with his firm, gentle touches and his warm hands, possessive, but not hard or hurtful. Jesse let go of that last bit of control and felt his head impact the stall wall with a soft thud. His hands relaxed, his body heated and melted to conform with Aadon's, and he opened that last little bit to feel Aadon's tongue sweep in and possess him.

The kiss left them both panting and Jesse trembling.

"This is definitely going to be better than that crappy movie," Jesse murmured in a wafer-thin voice, amazed he could speak at all. The only part of him that wasn't boneless and soft was his dick, and it pressed against Aadon's thigh, unashamedly iron-like and demanding.

Aadon pulled him close, chuckling, brushing a hand through his hair with soft, gentling strokes. "Kiss me like that again, and the night will be over before it even starts," he admitted. He held Jesse's head against his shoulder, reveling in the other man's lassitude. He'd once thought Perry's willingness to be tied up was something special, sexy and hot. It was not this. Nothing was like this.

Jesse's tingling excitement eased at the praise. He sighed into Aadon's embrace, and this time, he let the uncertainty quivering around the edges go, along with the arousal. He clung to Aadon a minute more, though.

They went back to the table, sat, ate, talked, but Jesse barely remembered the taste of the food or the topic of conversation. Every brush of Aadon's gaze across his face stirred him, every soft laugh and teasing smile turned him a little bit sideways inside. He couldn't eat fast enough. He practically pulled Aadon out the door. All thoughts of wasting time on a dance floor or movie theatre vanished.

They stumbled back to Jesse's apartment, wine-scented breath white in the cold night air, and tripped up the stairs to his door. Jesse stumbled on the lump in the carpet and found himself sandwiched between his door and Aadon. He grinned.

"Seems we've been here before," Aadon said. His breath wafted across Jesse's face, smelling of wine and anticipation.

"Yeah." Jesse squirmed around, struggling to get his key in the door. "And this time, we're not stopping." He got the door open and tumbled inside, pulling Aadon after him. He took the time to yank the phone cord out of the wall before dragging Aadon down the hall to the bedroom.

They only made it as far as the door before Jesse turned and pushed Aadon against the wall, tugging his shirt free of his jeans and pulling it up over his head.

"Jesse."

"Shut up." Jesse kept him from speaking with kisses, hungry for this now that he had it within reach. It had been so long. Aadon wasn't Anthony. He didn't have anything to fear. His fingers found Aadon's belt and unbuckled it.

Aadon grabbed his hands, pulling them up before he managed to get at the buttons. Gently, he shoved Jesse away. "Jesse."

"What?" He glared at Aadon, panting, twisting his wrists to free his hands.

Aadon brought them down to his sides but didn't release him. "Slow down," he demanded.

"No." Jesse stopped trying to escape his hold. Truth be told, those big hands around his wrists anchored him to now, to what was happening, kept him in the room with Aadon, rather than letting him float away to some other place where sex was a series of vague sensations that didn't matter. He liked this better. Meeting Aadon's eye, he lifted his chin. "I don't want to stop."

Aadon stepped away from the wall, forcing Jesse to retreat backward across the floor. He tripped over the discarded shirt and landed with a soft thump on the bed. Aadon kneeled, one knee beside him, bending close and nuzzling at his neck. "We aren't stopping. But we have all night. What's the hurry?"

Relieved Aadon wasn't putting him off again, Jesse resumed undressing him, his movements calmer, less frantic and fumbling. In moments, they were both naked and stretched out across the bed. Aadon's lips teased, brushing over his, touching his chin, his collarbone, traveling further, until Jesse gripped the bedspread in both fists, lifting his knees, spreading his legs in anticipation. He couldn't help squirming in delight at the sensations Aadon sent through him with just the touch of tongue and lips.

Jesse let out a tiny little moan as Aadon licked up the length of his erection, and abruptly, Aadon stopped. Jesse glanced down to find Aadon looking at him.

"Sorry." Jesse pushed up on his elbows to see Aadon's face better, to read his expression and figure out what he should be doing. "I didn't mean to make any noise."

Aadon felt the beginnings of a frown and smoothed it away. He didn't know why Jesse would apologize for making noise. That small sound had set fire to his blood, awakened everything in him he'd suppressed with Perry. He wanted to hear it again, louder, with more pleading need behind it. Why Jesse would apologize for it was something Aadon didn't want to think about here, now.

Suddenly uneasy at the look that passed over Aadon's face, Jesse tried to sit up, but Aadon crawled back up, pinning him gently beneath his weight.

"Make as much noise as you want," Aadon reassured, feeling a twinge of anger that Anthony had twisted so much of Jesse into knots he couldn't even joy the simplicity of a blow job.

"Really?"

Aadon smiled, but instead of replying, he turned his attention back to what he'd been doing. He needed to reassure Jesse, and letting him see any sort of anger, no matter who it was directed at, or worry in his eyes would not do that. He concentrated all his attention on the smooth skin under his lips and forced his mind away from thoughts about what could possibly have been done to him that Jesse didn't want to voice his pleasure.

His efforts were rewarded as he glided his tongue in a long, flat streak over the crease between Jesse's thigh and hip.

Jesse flopped back with a long, soft moan. For a few minutes, he managed only gasping breaths and pitiful little sounds. It had been so long. He remembered this, though. The sensation of someone's mouth on him, teasing him, tempting him to move, to lift his hips, to reach down and guide. He gripped the sheets again, in tight fists, and willed himself to stillness as that vague disquiet began to distance him from what Aadon was doing.

He wasn't sure when the act blended into the memories of it, or when he lost his connection to the man in bed with him. All he knew was touching wasn't allowed. Touching the man who sucked him off would only bring punishment, even though he knew, on some level, that wasn't true, he couldn't get his mind around how things had changed…. He squeezed his eyes closed and concentrated on remaining utterly still, quiet, safe, reminding himself, again and again, this was Aadon. This was okay.

It was hard, though. So hard. It had never felt quite this good before. Or, rather, he didn't remember it feeling this good. He glanced down to watch Aadon's mouth work, his lips, stretched and shiny around him, and wanted, almost more than he could control, to reach down and tangle his fingers in the thick hair tickling against his thighs.

"Please." The plea came out before he'd realized it had formed in his thoughts.

Aadon looked up, gently releasing him. "Please what?"

"I—"

Jesse swallowed, pushed back the fear that hammered ruthlessly against his ribcage and managed a smile that only trembled slightly. Aadon regarded him from the depth of blue eyes turned dark and deep with desire.

"Can I touch you?" The question came out a small, hesitant whisper, and Aadon merely looked at him for a few seconds, unsure what to make of the request. Wasn't the whole point of lovemaking to touch? How deeply had Jesse really been hurt he didn't remember that basic fact?

Jesse wanted to take it back, sudden panic growing that he shouldn't have asked at all, but Aadon finally spoke.

"I wish you would." He picked up one of Jesse's hands, uncurling his fingers from their death-grip on the sheets and laid it against his cheek. "Better?" He refused to flinch at the chill in Jesse's fingertips, but instead, turned his head so he could kiss the soft palm.

Jesse ran fingers through the hair drifting down over Aadon's eyes and nodded. "Better." Still a whisper. Still so uncertain. This was new, odd, and yet he knew in his head it shouldn't be. His body certainly didn't have any qualms about what Aadon was doing. It was everything inside, still tied up in Anthony's tight, impossible knots that wouldn't let him believe it could be real, even when it was right here, patiently waiting for him to catch up.

He managed a smile. He couldn't admit he wasn't there, yet. He couldn't bear to give up the tenderness or desire in Aadon's gaze, so he closed off that bit of him still bound to someone else's bed, someone else's old, broken vision of what love was, and pressed his palm firmly to the man who wanted him. "Very much better."

"Good." Aadon shifted to a more comfortable position and tilted his head to one side. "Can I finish?"

Jesse nodded and stammered out a reply. "I—I wish you wou… yeah. Ahh." Once again, he dropped his head back to the pillow as Aadon resumed, chuckling around Jesse's cock and making him shiver.

It didn't take long after that. In fact, in an embarrassingly short space of time, heat and tension surged through Jesse, ripping apart the fabric of what was now and what was past. A shout of almost-agony clogged in his throat and struggled out in a thin groan as Aadon came off him and stroked him to completion. His release warmed the cold, sweat-slicked skin of his belly, and he stared at the faraway ceiling trying to place himself in space and time.

Aadon waited patiently for him to come back down, stroking his side and hip with a gentle touch that reassured him as he blinked back to reality.

"S-sorry." He smiled, but couldn't quite look Aadon in the eye. "Guess it's been a long time."

Aadon had pulled himself up the bed and now lay half across him. He touched Jesse's face tenderly with the backs of his knuckles and kissed his cheek. "That's okay. I'm a little out of practice."

"Didn't notice." After a minute, Jesse focused more fully on his face. "Thanks."

Aadon just shrugged.

"What about you?" He put a hand on Aadon's chest, feeling the heavy heartbeat under his palm.

Aadon took the hand and pushed it down between them, closing Jesse's fingers around him and guiding his hand up and down his erection in a few demanding strokes before he let go. "Keep doing that." He gripped Jesse's hips in tight fingers, thrust himself into Jesse's fist with slow, deliberate concentration, his gaze burning through Jesse and searing his confidence. "More." Aadon clenched his teeth and shoved Jesse onto his back, grinding down into his fist and against his hips.

Jesse lifted his head, desperate for more intimate contact, and found Aadon's jaw with his lips, traveling up over his scratchy chin to firm lips that answered his quest with hunger and urgency.

Aadon quickly took control of the kiss, just as he controlled the rhythm of Jesse's strokes.

Pinned, his hand and mouth used for Aadon's gratification, Jesse forced himself to skirt the fear and remember what it was about that control that turned him on.

And then Aadon was burying his face against Jesse's neck, making needy, desperate sounds muffled against skin. "Tighter." He panted the word into Jesse's throat and Jesse complied.

Aadon dug his fingers into the thin layer of flesh over Jesse's hipbones, hammering against him and pulling him close with an arm around his waist. He needed more. Needed—He tightened his arm, crushing Jesse to him so he didn't give in to the desire to take what Jesse wasn't ready to give. But that fist wasn't tight enough. All the skin contact in the world could not make up for the tight heat he wanted.

"Faster," he demanded, wrapping the other arm around Jesse's shoulders, making it almost impossible for Jesse to move at all, let alone give him the friction he was demanding. He just thrust his hips harder, concentrating on the sweat-slick heat between them, on the sharp rise and fall of Jesse's chest and the crashing of their hips together. He could feel every tense, stiff muscle of Jesse's body, and part of him screamed to stop, to slow down, but that hungry beast who wanted this guy so much had already taken over.

Jesse did his best, but the crush of Aadon's body, the tight bands of his arms around him, didn't give him much room to move. He closed his eyes, focused on hanging on, breathed in the scent of this man, and clamped down on his mind's struggle to go elsewhere. He had to stay here, with Aadon, prove he could do this, that it wasn't the terrifying monster of his nightmares eating him alive. It was his lover, the one he wanted to please, to bring pleasure to, and it was okay. It had to be okay.

A low rumbling growl escaped Aadon, and he came without warning, filling the space between them with more hot, sticky fluid, bruising Jesse with his grip. Another snarl, deep in his throat, and Jesse felt the flat of Aadon's teeth against his collarbone.

He couldn't stop the whimper that escaped, had no control over the flinch at the feel of teeth on his skin. Caught in the tight embrace, though, there was no place to flinch to. He gasped, lungs working, frantic for air his tightening chest couldn't give him. He hadn't quite worked up to a full-blown panic attack when Aadon went as suddenly limp against him as he had been frighteningly possessive just seconds before.

Aadon's breath caught in his throat, and a shiver ran the length of his lean body. Jesse slipped his hand from between them, wiping it surreptitiously on the sheets before he wrapped his arm around Aadon and willed his own heart to slow down and his breathing to even out. He didn't quite trust himself to speak, so he just held Aadon and waited, cradling the bigger man close against him, too uncertain to let him see his face or the fear he'd felt at his unexpected ferocity.

When he thought he could ask with some semblance of calm, he whispered against Aadon's hair, "You okay?"

Aadon only nodded without even lifting his head, and for a while, they lay in silence. Eventually, Aadon uncurled from his tight knot, but he kept his face averted. "Sorry."

"For what?" Jesse kept his tone deliberately light, even though he could still feel the places Aadon's fingers had gripped him.

"Guess it's been a while for me too." Finally, Aadon looked at him. "I didn't mean to scare you."

"You didn't," Jesse lied. Aadon called him on the lie, and he shrugged. "I knew you wouldn't hurt me," he said, and he meant it. He knew what imminent danger felt like, and as fierce as Aadon's orgasm had been, its intensity hadn't felt threatening. The threat had all been in his head, in the past, and he desperately wanted it to stay there.

He ran a thumb lightly over Aadon's bottom lip where it looked a little bruised, as though he'd bitten down hard on it, then reached up to kiss it lightly. "I'm not afraid of you," he whispered. Finally, he got the smile he'd hoped for, even if it looked a tiny bit strained around the corners.

"You are an extraordinary thing, Jesse Tyler Turbul."

"A sticky, extraordinary thing," Jesse corrected. "Shower?"

"Yes." Aadon clambered out of bed and stepped into the tiny cubicle first, and Jesse hastily changed the sheets while he waited. When Aadon finished and came out with a towel around his waist, Jesse thought he might make it up for another go, but Aadon's subdued expression changed his mind.

"What's wrong?"

Aadon leaned on the bathroom door and crossed his arms over his chest. "I don't know if I can do this."

"What?" Jesse sat on the bed, his stomach suddenly dropping, legs too shaky to hold him up. "Do what?" Every nerve ending tingled with impending disaster.

Aadon came into the room and sat beside him. "I think I'm in love with you." He didn't look at Jesse when he said it, though, just at his own hands and the wrinkled skin on his fingertips.

"I don't see the problem there." Jesse wanted to touch him, to take one of the big hands in his and reassure him, but thought better of it. Everything had gone so much better than he had hoped, and now this.

Aadon smiled and finally lifted his head to gaze at Jesse. "That's what gets you into trouble. I've spent a fair amount of time in the scene, and found enough damaged people out there. I didn't want to play with any of them. I have enough of that with my own family."

"And I'm damaged."

"Yes. But at the same time, you're perfect." For a few seconds, Aadon closed his eyes, seeming to gather his thoughts. He started talking again without opening them, but Jesse didn't need to see into his eyes to hear the sorrow in his voice. His face had gone slightly pale. In his lap, his hands continued their fevered exploration of the wrinkled fingertips. "I told you about my brother in rehab."

"Yes."

"Well, he didn't just pick up a bottle one day. He had reasons." Finally, Aadon opened his eyes. "I was a baby. I had no idea what had happened to him until I was much older, and even then, I didn't know the extent until I was the one talking to his doctors. Apparently, in high school, he was a smart kid. Smart enough Dad enrolled him into an enhanced program where he went to the college for classes once a week. A grad student there took him under his wing. No one even had a clue what this guy did to him until it was too late. He turned into a different person. Then he started using, and…." Aadon glanced up at Jesse and shrugged a little helplessly. "He just never got better."

"I got better, Aadon. I'm getting better every day."

"Every time I go visit him at the center, I feel this agony of fear rolling off him. Like it did you, when…." He pointed at the head of the bed behind them. "With him, there's nothing I can do. I can feed him and dress him and talk to him, but so what? He's never going to recover. He's a grown man, in a grown man's body, with the mind of a child."

"I'm sorry."

"Nothing for you to be sorry about."

"Then why tell me all this?"

"What if the way I feel isn't about you at all? What if it's just about Ricky and what I can't do for him? Dad goes on and on about how he tried everything, he took him to shrinks, put him in rehab, kept him locked in his room, everything he could think of, and this happened anyway, because he refused to get help. He refused to acknowledge anything was wrong."

"I have never claimed there was nothing wrong. Just that I didn't want it to become my life, to consume me."

"But it does. Every time I get close, you start to shake. You were afraid to touch me when I had you in my mouth, for god's sake."

"I'm sorry." Jesse got up and stalked across the room. "I just—I haven't—I—" He slumped against the far wall but made himself stay upright this time. He would not collapse on the floor in a weeping mess like he had the last time they had talked about this. "Anthony." He had to take a deep breath. Some things about what Anthony had done even the lawyers didn't know. But Aadon wasn't a lawyer. Surely if Jesse could tell anyone, he could tell Aadon. "He used to take me out dancing, but he didn't want to dance. Not really. He wanted to hunt, for someone even more pathetic than me."

"You are not pathetic." Aadon got up and went to him, but Jesse wrapped his own arms around himself and hung his head. He couldn't tell this story with Aadon touching him.

Taking the hint, Aadon backed off.

"When he found what he wanted, he'd bring him home and—he liked to watch. I hated that, being with someone else, him watching. It was awful. Touching." He shook his head. "Not allowed. If I did touch the other guy, if I even looked like I enjoyed it, he'd—"

"He made you submit to strangers?" The idea clearly revolted Aadon.

"Not exactly. He just found people more submissive than me who didn't know any better and would do what he told them. He never did more than tie me down while they... and then only if I did something wrong. I learned what not to do, and touching was one of the things not to do."

"So he watched while other men raped you."

"You make it sound a lot worse than it was. They never did anything more than touch me, or maybe...." Jesse waved a vague hand. "What you did." He didn't know why he found it so hard to say the words, but he couldn't.

"Jesus, Jesse, you should have told me!"

"I don't actually make a habit of telling lovers the most humiliating aspects of my sexual history while I'm naked under them. Not that I've had anyone to tell before this, but still."

"Jesse, if I'd known, I wouldn't have—"

"Touched me, I know." Angry, Jesse pushed past Aadon and headed for the bathroom.

"No." Aadon followed him. "I would have been more careful. I would have—"

Jesse closed the door in his face, cutting off the rest of his speech. He didn't want to hear how sorry Aadon was for what he'd had nothing to do with, or how careful he had to be now, and he especially didn't want to hear how wrong Jesse was to think he was over Anthony. He knew he wasn't, that he never would be, and he hated the bastard for ruining his life. In the shower, with the hot water beating down on him, he allowed his misery to take over. It wouldn't hurt anything, just for a few minutes, safe from sharp objects and well-meaning boyfriends, to let it wash through him. He could blame his wet face on the water and his shaking limbs on cold air sneaking in over the door. He stayed there a long time.

When he finally came out he found Aadon fully dressed and sitting on the bed. He had expected it, but the blow still hurt. "You don't have to stay," he said, rooting through his dresser for underwear and pajama pants.

"I will if you want me to. I can sleep on the couch."

Jesse padded past him, needing not to be in the same room with him. "I have to sleep," he said over his shoulder. "I'm opening up tomorrow."

Stay.

How badly he wanted to say it, to plead. He wanted Aadon's strong body in bed next to him, curled around him to hold off the nightmares that would come. He wanted to feel safe, even from everything going on in his own head. He couldn't stand there and wait for Aadon to say the words, so he said them for him. "You might as well go home."

"Jesse." Aadon had followed him from the bedroom and stood on the other side of the kitchen counter as Jesse stared blindly into the fridge. The soft light of the under-cabinet bulbs illuminated his hands where they lay on the counter, but they left his face in shadow. "Please. Talk to me."

"What? I haven't told you enough of my humiliating past? You need more?"

"No! I mean, you're upset."

"Of course I am. You satisfied your curiosity. You know why I didn't have a boyfriend, how fucked up I am, so you can leave now. You have no obligation to fix me. I won't be a surrogate for your brother, and I sure as hell will not let you tell me I'm too damaged to possibly make another man happy. I made my decision about Anthony. It's past and over, and I won't go back there."

"Fine." Aadon gathered his coat and shoes and went to the door. "You've obviously made up your mind about me too. I tried to be honest with you, telling you about Ricky, and if this is how you want to look at it, go ahead. Filter everything that happens, everything anyone tells you, through what Anthony did to you and assume every man is as cruel and selfish as he was. See how long it takes you to put him in your past that way, but don't expect me to pay for what he did, or wait around until you get it right."

He slammed out of the apartment, his shoes still in his hands, and Jesse finally allowed himself to collapse on the kitchen floor. Burying his head in his arms, he couldn't hold back the shaking, and he didn't try. Only this time, he'd driven away the one person who might have held him and told him it would get better.

Chapter
Ten

AADON stopped just outside the door, dropped his shoes, but the fury evaporated. He'd been the one to bring Ricky into this in the first place. He couldn't fault Jesse for latching onto that and using it as a shield to protect himself from Aadon's own stupid bumbling.

He turned around, ready to go back in, to work out whatever they had to, because now that he'd dropped the "L" word, he couldn't just walk away.

Then his cell rang. The theme song for *The Greatest American Hero* trilled up and down the hallway. He couldn't ignore it.

"Dr. Carol?" His heart sank. She never called him unless Ricky had taken a turn for the worse.

"Hi, Aadon. I'm sorry to bother you."

"Is he okay?"

"Honestly? I don't know. He keeps asking to see you. I don't know why. He won't talk to me, and he doesn't want the orderlies, not even Katherine, anywhere near. I'd rather not force the issue if we don't have to. That could set him back months."

"I'm getting in the car now. Be there in about an hour."

"Thank you. I know it must be inconvenient. I hope you weren't in the middle of something."

"Just finishing up." He glanced at Jesse's door. *Finishing.* That sucked.

THE drive was a long one, with too much time to think. He'd screwed up. He shouldn't have let Jesse push him. He knew his lover wasn't ready. He *knew* it. He just wanted it, as badly as Jesse did, and he was the one supposed to be in control. He should have said no, should have waited.

But waiting was so hard, and the distance he had to keep from Jesse to keep from taking was also painful for his lover. He could see it in Jesse's frowns, in his sullenness, in the way he pouted, and it broke Aadon's heart to watch. It was worse, now he'd seen the real terror behind Jesse's desperate attempts to put Anthony in his past.

"Shit." He'd fucked up. He wasn't ready for this. He didn't know what to do. And the one person he really wanted to talk to about it probably wouldn't even answer his phone now.

He tried anyway, punching the speed dial to get to Jesse. Lights flashed by on the highway going in the other direction as he waited, listening to Jesse's phone ring. He didn't get an answer. Not a huge surprise. But then, hadn't Jesse unplugged his phone? He'd try again later. That was the only reason Jesse wasn't picking up. If he said it to himself enough times, he might begin to believe it. Tossing his cell onto the seat beside him, he concentrated on the drive, on not letting the gritty feel lack of sleep was depositing under his eyelids distract him from the road.

It took him less than the promised hour to get to Ricky's clinic, and Dr. Carol was waiting for him at the doors. It had to be bad if she was there waiting and not in her office on the fifth floor. It meant she wanted to go directly to Ricky with the least amount of delay possible. Aadon put thoughts of Jesse out of his head and sprinted for the front entrance of the building.

"I'm so sorry for dragging you out here in the middle of the night," she said as they hurried along the quiet corridors toward Ricky's room.

"No, don't be. It's fine. What happened?"

"I don't think anyone really knows. He was just in the common room, watching TV. He does that a lot at night. It's his pattern, and he sleeps better during the day anyway."

"Yeah. I know. It's one thing the last place tried to change, forcing him to sleep at night when that didn't work for him. They were idiots. He backslid fast there."

"Every hospital is different," Dr. Carol demurred, but her eyes flashed, and she frowned. "I hoped maybe he might tell you what happened."

"I'll see." Ricky didn't always talk to Aadon. Sometimes, he just wanted Aadon's presence and never opened his mouth.

They arrived to find two orderlies sitting on chairs to either side of Ricky's door. One of them Aadon recognized, and a moment of searching his memory brought her name, Katherine, to mind. He nodded at her, noticing that they both looked concerned and tense. The door to Ricky's room stood halfway open, and every light was on.

"Tried turning the bathroom light off," Katherine told Aadon from her chair. She looked tired and stressed and kept shooting worried glances at the half-closed door. "He freaked out. He's in the corner behind the bed now." She shook her head. "Good luck. Hope you can sort him out. He hasn't been this bad since he got here."

Aadon just nodded and slowly pushed the door open. "Ricky?"

"A?" Ricky's voice came from the corner on the far side of the bed, just as Katherine had predicted. He was crunched into a tight ball, knees up close to his chest and arms wrapped around his shins. It struck Aadon that that was exactly the pose Jesse had adopted the night he confessed his frightening past to Aadon.

"Hey, bro," Aadon said softly. "What's going on?"

"Martin…." Ricky gazed up at him, just peering over the sharp bones of his knees. "Don't let him… don't want it."

"I know." Aadon settled on the floor, back against the bed and hands in his lap. "I know you don't. It's okay. I'm not going to let Martin anywhere near you. I promise."

"Pathetic." Ricky drew in a deep, shuddering breath, and his eyes went a little vacant.

"No." Aadon bit his lip. He wanted to reach over, touch Ricky, offer some sort of comfort, but he didn't know if his brother would accept that for what it was, or if it would only frighten him more.

"Not twelve anymore," Ricky muttered.

Aadon smiled. "We all feel twelve sometimes, Ricky. That's okay."

"He can't." His throat worked, and Aadon waited, glad he'd lifted his head a little more. "Am I gay?"

"What?" That hadn't been even remotely close to what Aadon expected Ricky to say.

"You are." Ricky's feet shifted slightly, sliding out and clearing space in front of his face so Aadon could see him better.

"I am." Aadon glanced toward the door, but if Doc Carol was there, he couldn't see her. This was more lucid than he'd seen Ricky literally in years. His heart stuttered, his palms broke into a sweat. Did she know he was this aware of things? Was he supposed to get her? What? He didn't know what to do.

"Guys turn you on." Ricky was watching him, thoughtful, as though he were a complicated Chinese box, and Ricky was trying to work out where the secret latch was.

"Some do, yeah."

Ricky opened his mouth, shut it again, licked his lips. "Me too. Some. I think."

"Okay."

"Is it?"

Aadon turned that question over in his head, realized Ricky was asking him if it was okay that he thought he was gay. "Sure it's okay. That's natural."

"Martin said I was a freak. 'Cause...." His voice trailed off, his gaze went far away.

Aadon saw him retreating, and this time, he did reach out and let his fingers rest lightly on Ricky's knee. "Because why, Ricky? Why did he say that?"

"Don't want to." Ricky shook his head. "He...." A scowl twisted his delicate features. "Hurt and scared and... and...." He hauled in a ragged breath, and then tears were spilling down his face.

Aadon moved closer, slowly invading his brother's space until he could wrap an arm over his shoulders and pull him close. Ricky let him, collapsing against his chest into a heaving ball of snot and tears and what amounted to a twelve-year-old's terror.

"It's okay, Ricky. He's gone now. He can't hurt you."

The man who had done this to Ricky *was* gone. Jailed sixteen years ago when his molestation of Ricky had come to light, he'd lasted six months in prison before he took his own life. Aadon couldn't find it in him to care about the bastard's fate as he sat on the floor of a hospital room nearly two decades later and held his sobbing brother.

The crying jag lasted until the pink glow of morning drifted across the white bedspread, and Ricky was half-asleep in his arms. When Dr. Carol knocked softly, Aadon nodded her into the room, and together with Katherine, they managed to get Ricky onto his bed, curled on his side and staring into space.

"Okay?" Dr. Carol asked Aadon, who nodded as he settled on the edge of the bed and rested a hand on Ricky's shoulder.

"Yeah, Doc."

"I'll be upstairs in my office. Come up when he's asleep."

"Sure."

She and Katherine left, closing the door gently behind them.

Ricky's gaze slowly came into focus on Aadon's face. "You think… you going to tell her what I said?"

"I'd like to talk to her about it. Do you not want me to?"

Ricky shrugged. "She'll ask me anyway."

"Ricky, you don't have to tell her you think you're gay if you don't want to. That's private, and she'll respect that."

"She's always so nice," Ricky whispered.

Aadon smiled. "Yeah, she is."

"Just a doctor, though. Like the rest."

"No, I don't think so." If anyone knew about doctors and their indifference, it was Ricky. He was a tough case. He'd been through any number of doctors, psychiatrists, psychologists, and everything else in the past sixteen years. "I don't think she's anything like the rest," Aadon assured him. "I really think she cares."

Ricky's gaze slid away again. "You know what's the worst, A?"

"What?"

"I can be fuzzy and drugged up all the time, or I can remember everything. Can't have both." Another tear leaked out and dripped sideways off the bridge of his nose. "How come some people can get better and I can't?"

Aadon moved so he was kneeling beside the bed, so he could see into his brother's face on Ricky's level. He stroked his fingers through the stiff, coarse hair at Ricky's temple and found a small smile. "However you are, Ricky, whatever choice you make, you're my brother. I'll always be here. I love you."

"You're here when I don't even know you're here, A?"

"Yeah, of course."

"Not Dad. Or Mom."

Aadon wanted to lie and tell him that wasn't true, but Ricky was staring straight at him, silently demanding truth in exchange for this painful return to reality. A crooked flash of a half smile twisted his lips. "Doesn't matter, bro. You got me, and I got you. We're golden."

For a few minutes, Ricky just watched him, and Aadon waited, relearning the contours of his brother's aging face. He was still handsome, if too thin, and Aadon didn't ever think that haunted look would leave his eyes, but for the first time in ten years, he had hope there maybe was a person in there who wanted to come out and be part of the world again. Slowly, Ricky's eyelids drooped, closed, and flickered open a few times before he yawned.

"Tired, A."

"I bet. Bedtime for you, bro."

Ricky muttered something that sounded like, "Love ya, A." And then he was asleep.

Aadon closed his eyes, rested his forehead on his arm as he listened to Ricky's steady breathing, and felt the warmth of his being through his palm still resting on Ricky's head. "Love you too, bro," he whispered, finally.

He'd been crouched there long enough, getting to his feet was hell on his knees, but he didn't care. He'd just had a coherent conversation with his brother; something that hadn't happened in years. It didn't matter that Ricky had spent hours crying his heart out. It was progress that he actually felt something, and Aadon was confident in Dr. Carol's ability to care for Ricky in the aftermath of that great avalanche of hurt and anger. Maybe, just maybe, she'd be able to sift a few more pieces of Ricky out of the rubble.

The first thing she did when he made it upstairs to knock on her office door was wrap him in a warm, firm hug. He accepted the embrace and returned it, grateful for the unconditional support. She held him a good few minutes before stepping back to peer up into his face.

"You did good, Aadon." She smiled and pushed the long hair out of his eyes so she could see him better. "I'm so proud of you."

"He cried for hours," Aadon said, surprised how his voice cracked and his own throat closed. "Just… blubbered." His eyes stung, and he sank onto the couch opposite her desk.

"I know." She perched beside him and took his hand. "I know."

"It was… so much. There's so much in him. God." He drew in a shaking breath. "I didn't know what to do."

"Just what you did do, Aadon. That was the exact right thing. Just what he needed."

Aadon nodded, unable to get anything else out past the heaviness in his own throat. So who held him when he broke, he wondered. Then Dr. Carol was pulling him forward, patting his head onto her shoulder, and that was all it took. His own tears spilled out and soaked into the wool of her sweater. God, it felt so good, just to let it out, and he didn't even know what *it* was.

He didn't take as long to pull himself together as he thought he might, though Dr. Carol was patient with him until he did.

"You can't drive back in this state," she told him firmly. "Let me see if I can't find you an empty bed."

"Can I just sleep here?" He felt a little bit like a lost kid. He wanted the familiarity of this space, rather than the shock and confusion of waking up in a strange hospital room, even one made palatable for residents needing something that looked like a home.

"Sure." She smiled kindly and pulled an afghan off the back of the couch. "Rest. I have rounds to make, and I'll wake you when I'm done. We'll go for some breakfast." She touched his cheek, exactly like a mother, like his mother used to, before their family had disintegrated. "We'll talk."

And there it was. She wasn't going to let him take this home with him. They were going to hash it out and figure out what it meant. Only he wasn't sure he wanted to. Maybe he just wanted this tiny piece of his brother for himself.

"Aadon, in case he can't tell me himself, and you know how he gets lost inside himself so much of the time, I need to know. I'm working blind, here. I know it's been difficult for you. For all of you—"

"Not hard for mom and dad, now is it. Just write us both off and move on."

"Your father is fragile, Aadon. Your mother just wants to protect him."

Aadon stared at her. His *father* was fragile? His father was a cold bastard who turned his back when Ricky needed him. Who didn't want to hear that his second son was gay, who just excised from his life that which didn't fit his ideal.

Carol sighed. "We'll talk later. When you're rested. Now get some sleep, and I have work to do, okay?"

Aadon pulled in a labored breath and nodded, kicked off his shoes, and lay down on the yielding leather of the overstuffed couch. "Thanks, Doc."

"You're welcome."

Chapter
Eleven

EVENTUALLY, Jesse had to rouse himself from the cold tiles. He made it as far as the sofa but didn't bother with lights or the TV. Rolling himself into a ball with a blanket, he managed to fade off to sleep. He slept poorly on the lumpy couch and woke to a still dark apartment. Shifting under the blanket, he felt for the scars on his arm. Still there. All the scars were still there. Sitting up, he eyed the bathroom door.

He used disposable razors now and tossed them in the kitchen garbage after every use. Buying a new one every two days was a pain in the ass but better than keeping them around, even the safety ones. He just didn't want to tempt himself. He had bought one today so he could shave for tonight, and he knew it still sat on the edge of the sink. Rising, he wrapped his blanket tight around his shoulders, took the apartment keys from the hook by the door, and went down the hallway to Sarah's.

It took two tries to wake her, but finally, she appeared, bleary and frazzled, in the crack between the partially open door and the frame. "Jesse?"

"Hey, babe. Can I sleep here tonight?"

She didn't hesitate but closed the door enough to release the chain and let him in. In the light from a lamp on the table, he could see her concern and regretted using the pet name. "What happened?"

"I'm tired."

"Jesse?"

"I just want to sleep."

"Okay." She sat on the sofa and pulled the comforter from the back, lifting her feet and resting her head on the arm. The whole time, she didn't take her eyes off him. "Take the bed."

"You don't have to."

"I'm shorter. Go to bed."

He loved her for not pressing, not demanding answers. "Thanks." He smiled faintly and kissed her hair. "You're the best."

"I know." Her tone said, more than her words, that she knew why he'd come to her. Jesse just turned toward the hallway.

"I'm here for you, babe." She emphasized the name, and he turned back around. "You know that, right?"

"I know. Thanks." He went to the bedroom, closing the door behind him, pretending he didn't hear a few minutes later when she went into the bathroom and clattered around in the cabinet.

Chapter
Twelve

JESSE stumbled through the rest of the week, going to classes, handing in papers, and showing up at work when expected. He avoided Sarah, though, and locked himself in his apartment every night, curled on the couch with the TV on. Nothing really interested him there; he just couldn't stand the silence. He couldn't sleep in the bed, either, fancying it still smelled of Aadon and sex, even though he'd changed the sheets and washed the comforter, and he knew that was ridiculous.

A few days after his blowup, a heavy envelope arrived in his mailbox from his lawyer. He brought it up to his apartment and set it on the table without opening it, opting instead for a thick anthropology text, a highlighter, and the muted television. He read until none of it made sense and he couldn't keep his eyes open, then curled into a ball to sleep. His alarm, moved to the coffee table, woke him, and he barely had enough time to race out the door and make it to work on time.

"Well, hello there." He looked up to see Miss Stathopoulos watching him drag his ass in the big glass doors.

"Hi, Miss Stathopoulos." He tried to shift past her, lifting the section of counter that would let him into the checkout area, but she laid a hand on the surface and shook her head. "I have you in the back today, Jesse. A shipment of textbooks came in, and I need you to enter them into the system. You can use the computer in the back."

Knowing how her varicose veins and thick ankles made standing behind the checkout desk painful for her, he braved a smile and handed her the cup of tea he'd brought. "That's okay, ma'am. I'll work the desk for you."

"Not today, Jesse." She almost sounded kind, and he frowned. "You've looked tired lately. Don't you have exams coming up?"

"Well, yeah, but—"

"Go." She took the paper mug from him but pointed one long finger to the door leading to the back office. "If you finish early, you can use the peace and quiet to catch up."

"I'm not behind."

She raised both eyebrows and jabbed her finger once more at the door.

Jesse sighed and took his own coffee and book bag to the back room. No point arguing with her. Maybe after lunch, after standing for hours getting sore and cranky, she'd listen to reason.

He did relieve her for a break that extended ten minutes into his, but he said nothing. After all, even if she wasn't the boss, making it not his place to say anything about it, he knew she was no longer capable of enduring a full day on her feet. That she came back to the desk at all made him suspicious, but he said nothing, and refrained from arguing when she told him to take a longer lunch.

He went to the back and spent the precious extra minutes rooting in the bottom of his bag for spare change. Grocery shopping hadn't made it as high on his list of things to do this week as moping had, and now he had to pay for it. He'd have to brave the cafeteria and hope for the best. At least it was marginally better than the pub, even if he would have to pay through the nose for a fresh banana.

Scrounging a few dollars in loose change, he stashed the bag under the desk and went out to the main library. And stopped in his tracks. The door swung shut behind him with a muffled thump, making Aadon look up from a nearby cubicle where he sat poring over his books. Their eyes met for the briefest of instants before Aadon's head turned back to his work, and Jesse practically ran from the room, his heart in his throat.

He didn't slow until he'd almost made it to the cafeteria, and even then, he kept his head down and his steps purposefully quick. He could handle things if he just went about his business, didn't think about it. Didn't remember the less than thoughtful things he'd said when Aadon had tried to help. He made it to the cafeteria, but his appetite hadn't. For a few minutes, he gazed at the offerings behind the glass without finding anything that tempted him. He could sit, miserably, in a corner of the room until his lunch break ended, or he could go back and at least do something useful and distracting with the time. He'd just have to run the risk that Aadon hadn't left yet. He couldn't bear to contemplate sitting alone in the crowded room in his current mood.

Shuffling his feet down the hall, he made his way back, pausing to let a group of chattering first-years exit before he entered the quiet space himself. He made his feet move across the carpeted floor and forced a smile onto his face as he passed his boss. She merely frowned at him. He passed the checkout desk and made directly for the office. He couldn't resist checking the cubicle. An untidy stack of books and a few crumpled sheets of paper sat on the table, evidence of a hasty exit, but he saw no sign of Aadon.

Jesse sighed and went into the office, slumping in the chair behind the desk, ignoring the computer. The thought of spending the rest of the afternoon at the mind-numbing task of typing textbook titles into the system depressed him mightily. He'd barely settled into his brood before Miss Stathopoulos appeared at the door. Jesse leaned forward and attempted to look like he wanted to sit there doing his job, which normally, he did.

Stathopoulos heaved a sigh and came into the room, carefully closing the door behind her. "Perhaps you should go home," she suggested.

"No, I'm fine." He unlocked the computer and proceeded to type in his password, but she crossed the room and flicked the screen off. He glared up at her, but the expression softening her face kept his mouth shut.

"I might very well be an old battle-axe, Jesse, but I'm no fool."

Jesse flushed, but she didn't give him the opportunity to say anything.

"I don't like to meddle, but I like you. You're a good boy." She patted his hand, and he looked up to find her smiling down at him a little sadly. "I know I may have led you to believe Aadon frivolous in his affections."

"I didn't—"

"Pay any attention to what I said. Somehow, I'm not surprised, and I'm glad you didn't, because I shouldn't have said it. He isn't."

"How would you know?"

"His aunt and I were…." She hesitated, glancing over her shoulder and then sighing. "Close. We were very close." Something tightened around her eyes and drew the corners of her lips down into the habitual, severe frown he knew. He recognized it now, having seen it in his mother's face too many times after his father had died.

"I see." Then he did see and knew his eyes widened slightly as he caught what she hadn't come out and said. She smiled at his sudden comprehension.

"Surprise you to know I'm not just a dried-up old crone?"

"I never thought of you that way at all, miss."

She actually laughed, and Jesse flushed. "Never mind. I didn't want to talk to you about me."

"If you're here to warn me off your nephew, you're too late. We stopped seeing each other." Jesse's chair creaked as he slumped back in it. "Should have known he was too good to be true." This last he muttered, more to himself than her, but her eyes narrowed just the same.

"I had no intention of warning you off. I simply hoped to implore you to be gentle with him. He's had a hard time of things. He has a lot on his shoulders."

"I know. He told me. But it doesn't matter anymore."

"That's unfortunate, Jesse. I thought you a good match for him. He needs someone to take care of. Someone to love, and I thought you needed that too."

Jesse actually stood, his anger propelling him to his feet and pushing the chair back against the wall. "I don't need taking care of. I need leaving alone." His fists clenched at his sides, and he gritted his teeth over a tirade he didn't want to let loose on his boss. Her face had gone hard again, and he trembled with the effort of keeping his next words calm. "I am perfectly capable of looking after myself, thank you. I don't need you, him, or anyone else trying to fix me. I'm not broken."

Her eyebrows went up again, but she said nothing, letting Jesse know exactly how childish he sounded.

"I can see that."

His face went hot, and he tried to relax his fingers. "I'm not feeling very well."

"I can see that too. Why don't you take the rest of the day off?"

"Thank you." He dug his backpack out from under the desk and stomped out of the room, his feet making barely any noise on the carpet as he left.

Once back in his own apartment, he found himself slightly nauseated by his own behavior. Yet another person trying to help, and he managed to piss her off. His eyes fell on the still sealed envelope from his lawyer.

"Son of a bitch." Tossing his book bag under the table, he picked up the yellow envelope and tore open the seal. Inside, a thick document waited to remind him of all the nastiest details of the worst year of his life. And people wanted him to relive it yet again. He pulled it out and set it on the table, running his fingers over the smooth surface of black on white. If only any of it were that simple.

The walk home had at least restored his appetite somewhat, so he made himself a sandwich and poured a glass of milk before sitting down at the table with the papers. Much of it rehashed what he already knew; the details of how Anthony had ended up in jail in the first place. With a little more distance now, the ins and outs of how the laws worked actually began to make some sense to him, and Mr. Nivens had thoughtfully excised most of the more grisly details from the documents. He didn't need to read any of it in print. He'd lived it. Not having it set out there in Times New Roman twelve point didn't keep the memories from swamping him, though.

He'd also lived through the bits that hadn't made it to print; the bits he'd only ever confessed to Aadon. Those things he didn't want his mother to learn from Anthony or through lawyers and courts. He had no idea how he'd tell her he'd let it happen, not just once when Anthony got violent, but over and over again because he'd been too frightened to stop it. The appeal of curling back up on the couch and hiding until it all went away almost won, but in the end, he made himself get up, clean his dirty dishes, and make a few phone calls.

He even held out another hour before the barrage of memories and the twisting snake of anger and fear in his gut got too much. He couldn't go to Sarah again, couldn't bring himself to dial Aadon's number, though he sat with his phone in his hand and ghosted over the numbers a dozen times, wishing he knew how to make things right with the other man. But the hurtful things he'd said, that they both said, the fact that Aadon had run from the library instead of risk seeing him—it was a pile too huge to crawl out from under.

There was one thing he knew worked to clear his mind every time, and he didn't really think about what he was doing until he found himself standing at the bathroom sink. Then he blanked his mind because so much of him knew this was not the way to deal.

He always wondered why it felt cold before it hurt. Why his hands might shake, constantly, all day long, but for this moment, they were completely steady. He watched the blood bead before it dripped into the sink, a single crimson tear, maybe to take the place of the ones he didn't have. It left a thin trail along the porcelain before it rolled over stainless steel and down the drain.

"Fuck." This wasn't who he was any more. He wanted to throw the blade across the room. He rinsed it carefully and set it in the empty soap dish, washed the cut, and carefully pulled his sleeve down over the bandage. Who was he kidding? He curled under the blanket on the couch. He didn't deserve the solace of kicking Sarah out of her bed now.

Sometime in the dead of night, he called his mother.

"Mr. Nivens still need me?"

"Jesse—"

"Yes or no, Mom?"

"Yes, honey."

"'Kay."

He hung up. Didn't matter if his mother sounded happy to hear he would come home for a few days. He didn't want to talk about why. He'd have a gutful of it when he got there, and he loved her for letting him come round to it his own way. He rubbed a thumb over the fresh bandage, knowing he couldn't wait for it to heal before he went home, and that he couldn't let her see it. He couldn't face her disappointment.

THREE days later, he decided to take the train home. Not because it cost less, but because it took longer, and fewer people crowded train stations than airports. He liked the long, rhythmic ride, the trees flashing past, the view into the backyards of people who only thought they had to put up a good front and never thought someone might watch them from behind. At the station, finding Sarah standing on the platform waiting for him gave him mixed feelings.

"My mother called you," he said.

"Of course she did." She stood up on tiptoe and pecked his cheek.

"She asked you to see me off?" He wouldn't put it past either woman to connive behind his back like this, but he smiled anyway. At least he knew they cared.

"Better than that. I'm coming with you."

His smile faded. "I don't need—"

"Yes you do," she said easily, picking up the heavy backpack he hadn't noticed sitting at her feet. "But I don't require you to admit it, tough guy." With a light mock punch on his bicep, she sauntered to the train and swung up the stairs. At the top, she turned and looked back at him. "You coming?"

He almost said no, almost turned around and stormed off. Almost. Sighing, he mounted the steep steps and took a seat in front of her, ignoring her wide grin and staring out the window. She respected his annoyance just until the train started moving, and the ticket man came by to rip off a portion of their tickets and hand them a menu from the dining car.

"Don't be mad at your mom," Sarah said as she slid into the seat beside him. "It was my idea."

"I don't want you here."

"I know." She looked past him as the fire escapes and fences slid by outside. "But you shouldn't do this alone."

He glanced at her, and the fierce scowl on her face surprised him. "My mom will be there."

"Of course she will." The scowl fell away, but her tone crystallized around the words. "And so will I. You'll have us, at least. You'll see. It will be okay." She patted his arm, and he flinched before he thought.

"Jesse?"

"Please don't—"

But she was already peeling his coat and shirtsleeve back to reveal the evidence of his complete breakdown.

"Damn it, Jesse."

"I said don't." He yanked his arm free, hauled his sleeve down to hide the new cuts.

Sarah leaned her head against his shoulder, gently wrapped her arms through his so as not to knock the tender area again. "We'll get you through this, babe."

He refrained from pointing out that no one could do anything. Once the truth came out, he couldn't go back, couldn't pretend it hadn't happened. He'd have no way to make a life for himself that didn't include the fact he'd been a victim and a fool. And everyone who had loved him would know.

Sarah fell asleep leaning on him after only a very short time. He gazed down at the top of her head, still resting on his upper arm.

"Thanks, babe," he whispered, kissing her hair. Maybe she was mad about his lapse, but she wasn't turning her back on him for it. There wasn't really any way to thank her for that properly.

He settled in to watch the scenery flash past until darkness hid it all from view. Then he just watched the reflections of the other travelers in the window and tried to imagine his life had things not happened the way they had. He tried to form words that would tell his mother and his best friend what he'd told Aadon and couldn't imagine how they would react. By the time the train pulled into the first stop, an hour and a half into the fifteen-hour trip, he'd twisted himself into such knots, he could no longer think straight. Sarah had shifted her slumber to the arm of her seat and curled so her feet lay across his lap. She seemed peaceful, and he didn't want to disturb that. The doors at the end of the car opened, and a few passengers trundled off, a few more came on, and Jesse still had Anthony on the brain. The closer he got to home, the more likely it was he could run into someone he knew. Someone who knew him from when he'd been with Anthony. He hoped that wouldn't happen. When he looked up, he found that one of the new passengers had stopped in the aisle beside his seat to stare at him.

With memories still roaming through his head, for a minute, he thought the man standing there a figment of those memories come to life. Then the woman behind him made a noise of disgust at his blocking the aisle, and he started.

"S-sorry." He glanced over his shoulder, shifted his big bag, and moved past, as though wading through honey, his gaze still riveted to Jesse's face. Finally, he passed, though the woman continued to curse quietly for the delay.

The man's face left an afterimage on Jesse's mind. He didn't know why he remembered that face in particular. The others, whose names he never learned and whose faces he had willed himself to forget, had faded to vagueness and shadows. This one man, with his soft ways and his soft voice, he hadn't managed to banish. Maybe because he'd been the last one, the one that tipped Jesse over the edge into finally wanting to leave. Maybe because he'd told Anthony he wouldn't do anything Jesse didn't want him to do. At the time, Jesse had thought it all part of the act, his cue to beg until the guy sucked him off and satisfied Anthony. Except something different, something hard and angry in the guy's eyes, made him stand out. Too frightening at the time for any other reaction, Jesse had closed his eyes and waited for it to end. He'd never seen the guy again. Anthony never invited any of them back, but Jesse hadn't forgotten that time and couldn't live with himself, or Anthony, after that.

The train started moving again, jolting Jesse from his thoughts and Sarah from her sleep. She sat up, mumbled something about the bathroom and a snack, and wobbled off down the aisle. Jesse sank into his seat and stared out the window. He knew he'd made a mistake. The odds of seeing the one familiar man out of so many he couldn't remember were astronomical. He'd seen someone who looked a little like someone he thought he knew from a different life. Leaning his forehead on the cool glass, he watched the shadows fly by outside and tried to put it all out of his head. He'd have plenty of time to wallow in the misery of it all later.

The train made good time, and they arrived at the station only a few minutes past schedule. His mother smiled warmly at them and gave him a hug.

"Welcome home, Jesse."

"Thanks, Mom." He gripped the handle of his duffle bag and waited, but she only moved on to Sarah and gave her a hug too, whispering something in her ear he couldn't hear. After that, she led them across the bustling lot to her little red Toyota, and they climbed in. She asked him politely about the trip, about school, asked Sarah how her exams had gone and suggested they go to the little vegan place he liked so much. It was near her house and on the way from the station, so he agreed, even though he wasn't very hungry.

Jesse stared out the window at the familiar sights and answered her questions, wondering when she would get around to the reason he'd come and gearing himself up to answer questions about Aadon.

Neither came.

She just pulled into the tiny lot outside the restaurant and turned off the ignition, twisting around in the seat to look at Sarah. "Why don't you go inside and find us a table, dear."

Sarah smiled and climbed out.

"Real subtle, Mom."

"I wasn't going for subtle, dear." She settled back into her seat and studied him for a few minutes.

He endured.

"You haven't been sleeping."

He didn't answer.

"Or eating. I almost want to make you eat a steak just to put some meat on your bones."

He made a face at her, but she only smiled gently. "Come inside and eat your rabbit food, then."

He followed her in, amazed at her restraint, which continued through the meal and into coffee. Finally, he had to break the ice himself. The moment he did, Sarah bolted for the ladies room.

Good he'd allowed her to come for moral support, though. He frowned after her only briefly before turning back to his mother for an answer. "So? You haven't said a word about any of it, or asked about Aadon."

"Do you want to talk about Aadon?"

"No."

"Then why would I ask?"

He scowled, recognizing his own turn around the corner toward unreasonable, but his mother reached across the table and touched the knuckles of his clenched fist.

"I'm going to ask you one thing, and then I don't want to discuss it any more tonight. I want to just enjoy having you back for at least one evening first."

He nodded, studying her delicate fingers with their tiny pink fingernails and too fragile looking skin.

"When was the last time you cut yourself?

He started. Of all the things he expected her to ask, this topic she normally avoided like the plague had not even made the list. For a minute, he just stared at her. "I—" He pulled his hand away from under hers and sat back. "Did Sarah say something?"

He watched his mother, small, contained, fierce, as she blinked once, twice, swallowed hard, and then gave her head a little shake, as though settling the pile of coifed curls into place, though they hadn't budged from their perfect set. "She didn't have to." She met his eye, leaned forward until she could reach his hand again, and closed her fingers about his, her grip too tight for him to escape again. "You're my son. I know."

"I'm sorry… I—"

Her look of shock closed his mouth. "You have nothing to be sorry for, Jesse."

"You're not mad?" Confusion made his head spin wildly out of control, and he gripped the edge of the table with his free hand. He must have been crushing her delicate fingers, but she didn't even flinch.

"I'm desperately worried about you, Jesse. You're my boy, and you're in pain. I am not mad." She drew in a deep fortifying breath and managed to smile. "We can do this. We'll get through this."

Jesse offered a weak smile. He loved her for those words, more than he could express, but they both knew the only one who could get him through this was him, and he'd adequately proved how weak he really was.

The bright smile she offered next surprised him more than the question had. "Okay then." She picked up her water and took a sip, and he didn't mention the slight tremor in her hand or her rapid blinking.

"Why did you ask me that?"

She straightened the napkin on her lap into neat folds and pressed it with her hands. "Because you're my son. I love you, and I worry."

"But you never asked before." He leaned toward her, wishing she would look at him. "You never said the words before."

"There are a lot of things we've never said to one another, Jesse. A lot of things we've never talked about. That doesn't make them less real. It just makes them harder to deal with." Now she did look at him. "Do you understand?"

He nodded, tried to convince himself to tell her everything, that he had no secrets, nothing he couldn't tell her. He was her son. She loved him. She'd never stop loving him. But tonight, she didn't want to talk. She wanted just to spend time with him and share a meal and an easy conversation. Lord knew they would have few enough of those in the near future.

They took dessert to go and made the drive home in silence as comfortable as he could make it. As they made the trip through his old neighborhood, he really began to understand what his mother had meant. The weight of not having to hide, or pretending he hadn't had this latest lapse was gone. They both knew. And instead of turning their backs, they'd closed ranks, a couple of she-dragons and him the whelp they were determined to protect.

It made him smile. Even though he knew they couldn't really do anything to protect him from what was to come, the idea they wanted to, that they would, no matter what, made the world a little less dark.

Sarah sat in the back seat humming to the radio, and Jesse looked out the window, watching his neighborhood pass in all its mundane glory. The car pulled into the drive, the garage door opened at the touch of the button, and he was home. For the first time since he'd run away to school, away from the memories, he was home. No one rushed him to get out of the car, but he couldn't very well sit there all night, so he made himself get out and go inside.

His mother already had the kettle on, and Sarah unpacked the desserts onto plates and set them around the table. The two of them worked in easy unison that didn't surprise him, but that made him a little bit sad. His mom had only ever met Anthony across the courtroom, and there hadn't really been anyone worth bothering to introduce before that. He wondered how she would get on with Aadon and had to remind himself it didn't matter. He'd lost the chance to find out.

"Up there, dear," his mother said to Sarah, pointing to the cupboard holding the mugs before Sarah had even had a chance to voice what she needed.

Sarah pulled down three mugs and popped tea bags his mother handed her into them. He watched from the tall stool on the other side of the counter and let himself relax into the safe domesticity of it all. Once the kettle boiled, they sat around the table discussing exams, the coming term, and Sarah's ongoing debate about switching to an honors program. She had the brains, but it would require a level of commitment she hadn't decided she could maintain.

"In my experience," Jesse's mother offered, "if you can't decide, you aren't ready." She glanced up at Sarah and smiled. "You'll know when it's time."

"Would you tell my father that, please?" Sarah grinned and licked the last of the chocolate icing off her fork. "He seems to think I'm way overdue for a little bit of commitment of one kind or another." She shot a sidelong look at Jesse.

"Um. No." He flicked her hair into her face. "I like you, but not that much. You're entirely the wrong shape. Don't tell me he's still pushing that."

"Oh, he knows you like boys. In his eyes, that makes you perfect for me."

"Just keep pointing out how much he wants grandchildren," Jesse's mother said. "That will straighten him out."

Jesse watched his mother for a minute as the silence settled over the table.

"Mom, you know if I could—"

"Oh, nonsense, Jesse. My wanting grandchildren is not going to straighten you out. I knew that before you turned ten. I've had a long time to get used to the idea." She stood, gathered up the dirty plates, and headed for the sink.

Jesse and Sarah exchanged a look, and Sarah made a motion with her hand.

Getting up to follow his mother, Jesse took the dishes from her hands and put them on the counter beside the sink. He turned her around and hugged her close. "I really wish I could, Mom. I want kids, too, sometimes. I'm just not made that way."

"Stop it." She straightened and pushed him gently away. "We are over this. We dealt with it a long time go. Now collect those mugs and pick up a towel. It's late, and we have a long day tomorrow."

She said it all with infinite gentleness. Hard as he searched, Jesse could find no sadness or regret in her eyes. How had he gotten so lucky to have a mother with so much understanding and patience? Jesse would have hugged her again, but she'd already dismissed the entire topic by turning to the sink and filling it with sudsy, steaming water.

Shooing Sarah to her seat, he brought the mugs to the sink and picked up the towel as he'd been told. He was lucky to have them both. Now if only he didn't have to break both their hearts tomorrow and tell them how foolish and careless he'd been.

Chapter
Thirteen

AADON snarled at the television and all but threw the game controller onto the floor at the foot of the console.

"Seriously, dude?" Leo scowled at him. "It's just a game. I cannot afford to replace another controller because you're a sore loser."

"Sorry," Aadon mumbled.

"Addy, why don't you just call him?" Leanne asked from where she was curled on the couch watching.

"Yeah, Addy," Leo agreed with his girlfriend as he retrieved Aadon's discarded controller and examined it for dings and scratches. "Call the man."

"I tried."

"Try again because you, like this? Seriously getting on my nerves."

"Thanks, asshat." Aadon rose and wandered to the kitchen to pull a beer out of the cooler sitting beside the fridge. "You want?"

"Nah, man." He glanced over at Leanne and grinned. "I'm good."

"Spare me," Aadon muttered and wandered to the back door of their house instead of back to the living room. They maybe needed space for a little nookie, and he needed space from the togetherness. He could hear the smack of lip lock, even from there, and it set his teeth on edge. Not that he had anything against them, in particular. Leo and Leanne had been going strong since middle school, and he was happy for them. He gritted his teeth. Really, fucking happy for them. Maybe he should call Perry. But he dismissed that idea in the same moment it occurred. The idea of getting his rocks off with a guy he could barely tolerate on any other level turned his stomach. He wasn't sure when or why, exactly, that had changed, but it had.

"Hey." Leo entered the room, and Aadon realized he didn't even know how long he'd been standing there gazing out into the backyard. Leo clapped a hand on his shoulder, rested his chin on that hand, and nudged Aadon's hip with his own. "Talk to me, man."

"What's to talk about? I screwed up."

"You really dig this guy."

"Dig?" Aadon snorted. "Yeah." He took a swig of his beer. "Sure."

"Hel-looo!" From the front of the house, a loud crashing and happy whoop drew their attention, and Aadon sighed with relief that he didn't have to explain just exactly how much he "dug" Jesse and how hard it was not to be able to talk to him.

"Hey, Sweet Thing," Leanne crooned. "How are you, baby?"

"Ah." A loud smack of lips on cheek followed by Leanne's squeal of laughter preceded both parties into the kitchen. "I am fabulous, as always. Boys."

Aadon and Leo turned to greet him.

"Don't tell me I've finally witnessed the apocalypse and you two have at last settled unsolvable sexual tension."

"Never happen, cousin mine," Aadon said, forcing the gloomy thoughts away and smiling at his cousin. "Leo will never submit, alas."

Behind him, Leo sputtered loudly.

"You just don't have the right set of cuffs, darling," Leanne put in, winking at Aadon.

"The pink, fluffy ones, you mean?" Aadon grinned at her and opened the cooler. "Who's getting drunk with me tonight?"

"Oh hell yes," Sweet Thing hooted. "You know it!"

"You are *such* a flamer," Aadon muttered, handing him a beer. But he smiled and received an answering grin in return.

"You wouldn't love me any other way, Addy," he replied. "I gotta be me."

"Of course you do, *Mike*."

"Oh! You did *not* just call me that!"

"If you think I'm ever calling you Sweet Thing, you really are delusional. I've seen your junk, and it ain't all that sweet."

"Oh!" Feigning complete horror, Mike snatched the offered beer and grabbed up the cooler he'd carried in with him. "You can eat hot dogs, my man. The rest get steak."

Aadon stuck his tongue out at his cousin's retreating back.

Leo shook his head, but looked over at Leanne. "Lee?"

"Up to you, babe. You know the rules."

"Rules?" That stopped Mike at the door, already halfway out. "There are rules in this house?"

"Ah...." Leo ducked his head. "Kind of."

"Never you mind, sweets. Just go light the BBQ," Leanne ordered.

"And the noose grows ever tighter," Mike said in a soft, sinister voice as he left, letting the screen door bang behind him.

Aadon watched as a flush crept up Leo's neck and stained his cheeks. "What's going on?"

Leanne shifted where she sat on the kitchen table, glanced at Leo, who shrugged. "'S'okay, Lee. He gets it."

"Gets what?" Aadon glanced between them, completely confused.

"You remember when I asked you why you were still banging Perry when you clearly had no other use for him?"

Aadon narrowed his eyes. "Yeah." He wondered suddenly if he should regret telling his best friend he'd kept Perry around for the kink.

"Well, I thought...." Leo took a swig of Leanne's beer. "I kind of tossed the idea past Lee. Just to see, you know, what she thought. I mean, I didn't say anything about you and Perry... uh." He stopped, his eyes went wide, and he glanced between them. "Well. Until now."

Aadon shook his head. "Okay." He already had a glimmer of an idea where this was going and realized he wasn't going to get grief for that particular activity from either of his friends.

"So. Turns out, there's something in it for us."

"Oh." This was probably a little more information about his friends' sex lives than he really wanted, but they were both looking at him now, waiting. "That's... good. I guess." He frowned, wondering what they were waiting for. Some kind of sanction? A medal? It wasn't really any of his business, and he didn't want it to become so. Really didn't.

Leo gulped down more of the beer, draining half of it, then draining the rest.

Leanne grabbed the empty bottle back from him. "The rule is, if he wants me to tie him up and spank his ass"—she gave him a fierce look and held out her empty bottle—"no booze."

Aadon nodded. "Sensible rule."

"I was nervous," Leo protested. He slung an arm over Aadon's shoulders. "And Addy needs me tonight. You understand?"

"I might spank you anyway, for drinking my last Corona."

"It was warm, anyway," Leo mumbled.

She hopped off the table and rooted through the fridge for another of her favored imports. With a small crow of triumph, she came out again with something German and grinned at them as she popped the top. "But yes, I understand completely. Addy needs us."

"DUDE, you are not a happy drunk." Leo flopped down in the lounge chair next to Aadon's.

"Not a happy anything right now."

"It isn't Ricky, is it?" Leo asked, genuine worry coloring his tone.

Aadon peered at him through one half-closed eye. He was still blurry. "Nah." He waved a hand. "'S doin' great." He picked at the label on his beer bottle. "Really great."

"I just noticed, you've been going up there a lot more, recently. Since...."

"Since?" Aadon straightened.

"Since The Split," Mike said, joining them by swinging a leg over the end of Aadon's chair and planting his ass where Aadon had just had his feet.

"What the fuck are you talking about?"

"Oh please." Mike rolled his eyes. "Do *not* pretend like we're that oblivious. You and Jesse."

"What gives?" Leo asked.

"Nothing *gives.*"

"But you have split?"

"We weren't... we haven't...." Aadon dropped his head back against the chair with a grunt. "It wasn't working out."

"Do you need me to kick his ass for you?" Leo asked.

"No! No! God, no."

"Then what?" Mike pressured. "Talk to us, because the way you've been dragging your ass the past month, you would think someone died. This is not like you. You bounce back. You find another guy. You don't mope and get depressed."

"I am not depressed."

They both gave him raised eyebrow looks.

"I'm not. I'm... worried."

"It's Ricky, then. I knew it was Ricky. Why didn't you tell us? We could help—"

"It's not Ricky! Ricky is fine. In fact, he's better than he's been in ages. It is Jesse, and I can't tell you because it isn't any of your business!" He got up, irritated by their crowding concern and lurched away toward the swing at the far end of the yard. The chair tipped, and Mike flew off onto his back.

"Hey!" Leo hurriedly helped the other man up, and they both pursued Aadon across the yard.

"Fuck off!" He didn't want to do this. It was enough he was visiting Dr. Carol once a week and bemoaning the turn of his love life on her shoulder. He was damned if he was going to do it here too. It was none of their business.

"Addy, stop acting like a complete jerkoff and talk to us!" Mike's hand descended on his shoulder, yanking him around. Aadon whirled, giving his cousin an almighty shove.

"I said leave me alone!"

Mike stumbled and tripped, landing hard on his ass, bleached hair flopping in front of shocked eyes as he landed. Aadon advanced a step, fists clenched, anger riding high. "Just butt out! I don't need you, of all people, horning into my personal life! You wouldn't know a real relationship if it smacked you down and spat on you!"

"Aadon!"

Aadon turned only just in time to catch Leo, who flew at him and took him to the ground. They landed with a grunt, and Aadon finally let go of the savage fury he'd locked away. He had no idea how many punches he landed, but it took them both to pin him down. The minute he was immobilized, everything snapped back into focus.

"Oh shit." His throat tightened. Tears welled and spilled, and they let him up. When he would have made a break for the darkness further from the house, they both moved in and sat, Mike facing him, his legs draped over Aadon's, ass planted on the grass between his knees, and Leo behind him, legs wrapped around them both.

Firmly secured between the two people in the world who'd known him longest and knew him best, every pent-up emotion Aadon had so desperately tried to hold in came out. He made a mess, and they held on tighter.

Long minutes passed as they sat like that, three heads close together, arms and legs entangled in an impenetrable knot, like they had innumerable times, like they were kids again, the three of them against the world. Nothing could get in unless they let it, and for now, they let nothing in at Aadon and absorbed everything he needed to let out. When he finally began to wind down, they loosened their hold.

Mike sat back enough to focus on him, took his chin in a tight grip. "You going to tell me this isn't real?" he asked, jaw tight, eyes blazing.

Aadon shook his head the slight amount that grip would allow.

"Good." Mike shook him a bit. "Because I love you, you dumb jackass."

Aadon laughed, a soggy, heartfelt sound, and patted Leo's hand, still flat against his chest. "You bleeding all over me back there, straight boy?"

Leo grunted. "You couldn't hit the broad side of a barn sober, fucktard."

They all laughed, and it was as much, if not more of a release than the fighting and crying.

"Ice packs all round, boys?" Leanne called from the back door.

They hobbled to their feet and stumbled inside, past Krissy, who had arrived home sometime while they were brawling and now huddled in the kitchen doorway, eyes wide and mouth tight. She followed them inside and helped Leanne hand out the ice. "You see why I date girls?" she asked. "Bunch of Neanderthals, the lot of them."

"Pass me a beer, will you, Krissy?" Aadon asked, holding an ice pack to his jaw and one hand out toward her.

Leanne slapped the hand down. "Not bloody likely. You're going to sober up, and in the morning, we figure out how to fix this because, Addy, I love you, but you have to get a handle on this. It's killing you."

"And me," Leo complained.

"Oh, suck it up." Mike punched him on the arm, and Leo yelped and cradled his shoulder.

"Easy! I bruise!"

They all laughed, and for the first time since he'd admitted to Jesse how he really felt, Aadon thought maybe there was a chance the world wasn't going to collapse on top of him. Whatever happened with Jesse, he had these people, this little family held together with spit and knuckle cracking and a lot of love that had grown up between the cracks of his life without his noticing.

Chapter
Fourteen

DISHES done and house quiet, it was a long time before Jesse found sleep. Instead, he found himself lying in bed remembering. How many times had he let it happen? Had Aadon really got it right, calling it rape? Could Jesse really say he'd been against it all? He didn't have to pick the guys to bring home from the bar. He didn't have to lie passively and let Anthony tie him to the bed. A lot of things he didn't have to do. A lot of things he did do, and the end result had been what it was. How could it not be at least partly his own fault?

Finally, he rolled to face the wall. Whatever it could or couldn't be called, he knew if he had it to do all over again, he would wish things had been different. Sex, after all, wasn't supposed to be about fear. He thought about his encounter with Aadon and wondered if it could ever be anything else now.

Morning brought weak sunshine, a fitful breeze in the open window, and a ball of uncertainty, malformed and sticky, in Jesse's belly. He lay in bed as long as he reasonably thought he could get away with, then he stayed a little longer. He knew he couldn't avoid doing what he came here for. Not practically, but he hardly wanted to jump into a detailed confession at the crack of dawn, either. When the smell of coffee and frying bacon wafted up to his room, though, and the volume of the radio became conspicuously loud, he knew he couldn't procrastinate any longer.

He went down and received good morning hugs from both women and a huge steaming mug of coffee from Sarah. Perched on a stool once again, he watched as they did their kitchen dance to the tune of sizzling bacon and more coffee dripping through the machine. If he had even a remote interest in girls, he would have given serious thought to making his mother happy and marrying Sarah. He didn't, though, and however well the two of them got on, neither of them would thank him for even bringing it up. They had put the subject of grandkids firmly to rest last night.

His late start meant breakfast, and the tidying away of its aftermath, took up most of the morning. Through it all, still his mother pretended not to notice his nervous fidgeting or clipped responses to her questions. She didn't say a word about the case or Anthony, and the glaring omission did more to stress him out than if she'd insisted on discussing it over the toast and eggs. He hadn't decided if he should tell them about the other men now, before the lawyer arrived, and give them a chance to assimilate it, or if the necessity of then telling it twice was too much to take.

He selfishly only wanted to do it once, but it would affect them both, and to make them go through that in front of a virtual stranger was cruel. He knew exactly how cruel. When, at close to one, his mother announced that the lawyer had unexpected meetings all day and would probably be unavailable until after supper, Jesse couldn't quite contain his sigh of relief.

"Right, then." She patted his arm. "I guess I call him back and tell him not to bother until morning."

Jesse flopped onto the couch and stared up at her. "I thought we had a plan…." He trailed off, not even sure what he was getting at or what the plan might have been. He couldn't tell if he was relieved or disappointed. It took his mother's gaze, fixating on his movement, to realize he was rubbing a hand up and down his lacerated forearm. He stopped, moving both hands to pin under his thighs against the couch.

"He says he can come tomorrow, honey. If we give him the word, he'll clear his schedule now. Do you want him to? Whatever it is you're debating telling us can wait that long, can't it?"

Jesse nodded, a little numbly. "Yeah. Sure. I guess." So she wasn't oblivious. On one hand, he was glad. Maybe she was mentally preparing herself. On the other, what was going through her head, and should he just tell her and keep her from any more worry?

Before he could make up his mind, she disappeared back into her office, presumably to call the lawyer back, and Jesse slumped further.

"You okay, Jess?" Sarah sat beside him. "You look a little…."

"I'm just…. I…." He shrugged. "I was ready." He looked at her and smiled a bit crookedly. "Now I'm going to have to psych myself up all over again."

"You can tell me." She didn't look at him, but her fingers tightened on the throw pillow she had clutched against her chest.

"Tell you."

"A test run." She shifted to face him. "Jesse, you can talk to me. Tell me anything."

"I—" Jesse studied her face.

She put the pillow down and laid a hand on his thigh. "Don't worry. It's just one more retelling. There's nothing going to happen you haven't already endured once. You can do it again. And you aren't alone. It will be fine, you'll see." She patted his leg, capitulated, and he knew she knew her placating words were not going to work.

"It isn't just one more." He didn't have the heart to tell her there were things she didn't know. He hoped he still had the heart to even go through with it. Maybe he could just stick to what they already knew, and that would make enough of a difference. How much easier to just keep it simple and forget about the rest. But the rest had crept into his bed, insinuated itself between him and Aadon, and now it visited him in his dreams at night. Every night. These same dreams had woken him hour after hour at first, had led to him trying to distract himself in the worst way possible, not once, but now a second time, and he was ashamed of that weakness.

He found himself rubbing a hand over his forearm again and stopped the motion with a soft snarl. Maybe this trial was the only way to banish it once and for all.

"We'll go out," she declared, rising and pulling him up with her.

To distract him, and he knew he needed the distraction, Sarah insisted he take her shopping. What she expected to find in his dinky corner of town she couldn't find more of and better in the city they'd just traveled from, he had no idea. He braced himself for the reminders. He'd left so soon after Anthony, he suspected everywhere he went there would be a reminder. Maybe even people who remembered him. He prayed they wouldn't run into anyone who knew what kind of relationship they'd had. Plenty of people had known what kind of man Anthony was. What that made Jesse, they'd never had much doubt.

To try and combat the restless memories roaming through his head, he brought Sarah to some of his favorite used bookstores, places Anthony never went. They stopped for a late lunch at a café he'd spent a lot of time at when

Anthony still let him go out to lunch alone or with his friends. It was one more place he had avoided after. Just the fact he'd let Anthony take this away from him too had made it less a place of familiar comfort and more an ugly reminder of how foolish he'd been. Going back now, he hoped, would let him defy the memories.

They chose a table on the street side, Sarah wanting to enjoy the still mild weather, and Jesse wanting to just have the fresh air to filter the stale feelings of inadequacy and humiliation that were continually growing in him.

He told himself it was because fall would have set in for real once they got back to school. Here, further south, the fair weather held on a little longer. He didn't want to sit outside because it felt too claustrophobic to eat in one of the booths he used to share with friends before he'd deserted them all for Anthony. He wasn't avoiding thinking about the last time he'd sat in there and listened to them all warning him Anthony was bad news, trying to talk sense into him. He certainly didn't want to think about how he'd fallen for Anthony's manipulations. Or how he'd repeated them to himself and convinced himself his lover was right, that people just didn't understand the lifestyle and would try to talk him out of it because of that.

In retrospect, he knew the arguments had been against the man and not the kink. He just hadn't listened then. By the time he figured it out, those friends had all disappeared. Given up on him, and he didn't blame them. He'd been an idiot. He'd pushed them all away with anger and hurt over the perceived misunderstanding, the idea he was being judged. An idea Anthony had put in his head. In reality, the only people judging him were Anthony and himself, with Anthony deeming him weak enough to manipulate, and himself agreeing with that assessment by letting it happen.

They'd almost finished their meal, and he was feeling more uncertain than ever when a familiar voice hailed him, and a shadow fell over his plate. He had a hard time hiding his start.

"Jesse, right?"

He glanced up at the tall blond standing over him and nodded, hating the way his palms sweat, and he felt like hunching his shoulders.

"Yeah, I remember you. You used come into the bar with Anthony Bruno. Heard he got jail time. Eventually. Thank God someone had enough balls to speak up." His voice held a scowl, and Jesse sank a little bit into himself. "'Course, you know all about that, right?"

Jesse shrugged and glared at his plate.

"Always thought he was a prick."

"A bit, yeah." *Understatement of the decade.*

"You're better off, I say."

Jesse glanced up at him again, finally recognizing where he'd seen this guy before. He'd been a bartender at Anthony's favorite dance bar. Jesse remembered the free drinks, the sly smiles, and shivered.

"Haven't seen you around in a long time."

"No." Jesse didn't bother to explain why. It wasn't any of this guy's business.

"You don't remember me, do you?"

"Yeah." Jesse glanced at him. "Sure. You bartended."

"Still do. Name's Justin."

Jesse scowled. "Right."

Justin pointed down the street. "You used to come dancing at Stripes. With him."

Jesse grunted. Justin used that pronoun as though he was referring to something particularly vile.

"Guess."

"The two of you would pick guys up. Bring them home."

"Yeah." *I remember. God, please don't bring this up here.*

"You ever have contact with any of those guys? You know, after you were done with them?"

Jesse kept his head down. "No." Barely above a whisper. *Just stop.*

"You ever do, can you let me know? Still work at Stripes. It's Moondance, now."

"Uh." *Why?* What did this guy want with one of Anthony's conquests? Jesse remembered the way the guy always gave him speculative looks. Did he want to find someone as vulnerable as the guys Anthony tormented? Jesse shivered under the warm sun. Maybe he was just seeing all the ugly he'd been too innocent before to notice. Maybe he was seeing more than was really there.

"Really appreciate it," Justin was saying.

"Sure."

Justin wandered off, hailing someone else he knew further down the patio.

"Jess? You okay? What was that all about?" Sarah asked, taking Jesse's hand from the table where his fingers flipped his fork over and over. "What's he talking about?"

He pulled free and managed a weak smile. "Nothing. I need to use the john, babe."

She nodded. Her fist clenched, though, and she searched his eyes. "Jess?"

"I'll be okay." His chair scraped across the pavement, jarring to a stop before he could stand. "Sarah, I'm fine. I just need to piss."

She took a deep breath, nodded, and let him go.

How would he get through this? Just seeing someone who associated him with Anthony made him want to vomit. What would happen when he sat across the room from the man and had to look him in eyes, call him out on what he'd done? The last time, he'd backed down, not called it what it was. The last time, he'd let Anthony get away with it. Aadon would expect him to be braver this time. But Aadon wasn't here.

Jesse sighed. Aadon didn't have to do this. The only one making him do it was him. And he had told Aadon he was a different person than he had been the first time. He just didn't know if he really was any stronger. As he had the night his mother had first called, he wanted someone who could hold him and tell him it would be okay, that it would work out. He wanted Aadon.

He was still standing in front of the sink when the bathroom door opened.

"Ummm…."

He looked up. The face in the mirror over his shoulder swam a little. He was still dizzy, and his eyes stung, so he couldn't make out anything but that the guy was dressed in black with a red apron circling his waist.

"Your girlfriend asked me to check you're okay."

"I'm fine."

The man frowned at him. "You don't look okay. You look…."

Jesse glanced back up when his voice trailed off. "I know you." There was a pause, and to Jesse's surprise, the man fumbled behind himself for the wall. "You're him."

"What?" Jesse whirled. "Him who?"

"Anthony's—"

"I am not Anthony's anything!" Jesse would have stormed out, but turning had given him a good look at the guy. In an instant, he plunged into a nightmare. Instead of rushing for the door, he ran for a toilet, the contents of his stomach coming up in a rush. His throat burned. Sweat broke out across his back. The splashing water and sounds of his retching filled his head. He continued to heave emptily long after there was nothing left to come up. By the time it stopped, he had no strength to even stand and sank onto the floor.

The guy was still there by the door, watching him.

Jesse could only sit and shake. After a minute, the waiter moved, carefully tiptoeing to the sink. He ripped a few paper towels from the dispenser and wagged them under the tap. When they were wet, he handed them to Jesse. He left a lot of space between them.

"So you remember me." His voice was quite, gentle, but tense, just like Jesse remembered.

"Hard to forget," Jesse muttered. He accepted the towels but held them in limp fingers. The guy crouched on the far side of the room. Not having him standing over him made it easier for Jesse to pull his gaze from the cracked grout to look at him. "I mostly remember you sucking me off and then fucking my boyfriend."

The guy's face paled, but he didn't look away. "Yeah. Well. If you remember that, then you remember how much I enjoyed it."

Jesse swallowed. "I'm sorry." He did remember. He remembered the struggle and the tears and Anthony not caring about any of it. Worse than not caring, liking it, and Jesse helpless to do anything but watch. He hadn't been that animal's only victim.

"Why are you sorry? It wasn't your fault."

"I should have warned you."

"And what would he have done to you if you did and he found out?"

Jesse shrugged. Anthony was unpredictable to some extent, but it didn't take much imagination to know he'd have been pissed. Jesse had carried a lot of bruises as reminders how Anthony dealt with things that pissed him off.

"I don't blame you," the guy said. "In fact, I heard what happened to you when you tried to leave him. I was glad you put him away."

"Yeah." Jesse tossed the paper towels into the toilet and reached to flush it. The roar filled the room for a second, and when it died away, Jesse looked up to meet the other man's gaze. "I have to tell them about you."

"What?"

"Well, not about you personally, but about what happened. He's got this new lawyer. New story. I have to tell everything, or they'll let him out. I have to tell them everything, or he'll be out in a week."

With a squeak of sneakers and a soft, strangled moan, the waiter slumped to the floor. For a long minute, he stared off into space.

Jesse wondered if he was remembering the night he'd stepped into his own nightmare and said nothing, just waited.

"What will you tell them?" he asked at last. Big brown eyes shifted, his gaze drifting over Jesse's face, and Jesse was shocked to realize he recognized that vague, dazed expression from so long ago.

"I'll tell them it wasn't your fault. That you only did it to protect me."

"How do you know that's why I did it?" He looked at Jesse, and his eyes came back into focus.

"Because. You told me, after, when you were leaving, that someone who actually cared would save me from that crap, not get off on watching it." Jesse fell silent.

Aadon's face, his dejected posture as he sat on the edge of Jesse's bed came back to him. He could only imagine what Aadon must have felt like, realizing after the fact how terrified Jesse had been while he was getting off. And then Jesse had thrown it in his face. Worse, he'd accused him of actually liking it, of feeling good about the fact he had a second chance to try and fix what he hadn't been able to fix for Ricky. He'd been the worst kind of idiot. Pushing to his feet, he looked down at the waiter still miserably squeezed into a ball.

"I have to go." He didn't, though. He waited until the man looked up at him. "I don't have to tell them who you are, but I have to tell them what Anthony did. You weren't the only one he did it to."

The man nodded.

"It might not make any difference. They might not believe me, since I didn't say anything about it before, but I have to try."

There was a long, tense silence as the other man crouched, staring off into space. "They'll believe you if you aren't the only one saying it."

Jesse frowned.

"If I come forward, they'll have to believe you. If I do, someone else might too."

"I'm not asking you to. I only told you so you'd know he wasn't going to get away with it. In case you found out. I didn't want you to find out on the news or something, when you weren't ready to hear it. He's not going to get away with it this time. This is what I always wished I'd done the first time."

"Did it help you?" Huge brown eyes suddenly fixed on him. In the center of that soft, pale face, they were every bit as impossibly deep and hurting as Jesse remembered. "Knowing he was in jail and that you put him there, did it help?"

"Knowing he was laughing at me for not being able to tell the truth? Finding out now he plans on using everything he did to me against me? No. I wanted it to help. I tried to make myself believe it did, but no. Because I never really let myself believe what he did was rape."

Jesse watched his companion's entire body tense, pull in. His breath sucked in through his teeth, and he dropped his head.

"It is what it is," Jesse said quietly, wishing he was brave enough to reach over and touch this guy, to reassure him, as he'd done for Jesse back then. "You were right about what you said to me that night. Those words, that's what made me decide to finally leave."

The man snorted. "That worked out well for you."

Jesse lowered himself to the floor beside him. "Yes, it did. In the long run. I couldn't stay with him. I had some weird idea at the time you were trying to tell me something. I thought I would just walk out, find you, and everything would be fine."

"Find me?"

"I told you, it was a weird idea. I thought…." Jesse sighed. "I guess it doesn't really matter what I thought. It was just a desperate grab at something that wasn't him. It was enough to make me get out."

"You know, it's funny. I went home with you that night because I thought maybe…." He paused, ran a hand over the back of his neck. "But I guess you're right. It doesn't matter now. I did find someone, eventually. He gets my issues." He smiled faintly and twisted a ring on his finger. "And he'll understand why I need to do this. He won't like it, but he'll understand." Big brown eyes fixed on Jesse again. "You shouldn't have to do it on your own."

Jesse stared at him for a minute. He hadn't changed all that much, really, this guy, this stranger who knew way too much about him. His hair was a different style, his eyes were less open, more guarded, and the easy smile that had drawn Jesse to him in the first place was less easy. None of that was very surprising. Jesse only felt a kind of loss, some strange sadness that the boyfriend this guy had now hadn't known him before he lost that easy charm.

"You don't have to," Jesse said at last.

"Yes, I do." The waiter got up and held out a hand to pull Jesse to his feet. "I'm doing it for myself. For all the people he'll hurt if he gets out." He glanced at Jesse's arm, where his shirtsleeve had ridden up to reveal the old scars and the new cuts. "For everyone he already hurt who might never get this chance." Very gently, he lifted the edge of the sleeve, ran his thumb over the cuts, and Jesse had no idea why he let him take the liberty. Except maybe, because on a night a long, long time ago, he'd done the same thing to the bruises riddling Jesse's ribs, and then he'd done everything in his power to keep Jesse from earning any new ones that night. They both had paid too high a price for that protection.

Jesse understood him.

"And for you. So you can put it behind you; find that person who will protect you like you deserve."

Jesse smiled. "I found him."

"Good." He carefully pulled Jesse's sleeve back down and laid a hand lightly over the thin covering. "I hope he knows what he's got."

"Actually, I was a jerk to him, and that's why I have to go. I have to find a way to make it up to him. Here." Jesse pulled out his wallet and rifled through it until he found what he was looking for. "My lawyer's card. Call him if you really want to do this."

The waiter took the card and studied it for a minute, then nodded. "I will."

"Okay." Jesse pulled in a breath and let it out. "Then I guess I'll be seeing you."

"I guess." He held out his hand. "David, by the way. David Younge."

Jesse took his hand and shook. It was the first time he could remember not flinching, not feeling like he needed to pull away from contact with another man besides Aadon. It brought a smile to his lips, and David responded, his face lighting up.

"Jesse Turbul."

"We can do this, you know."

Jesse nodded. "Sarah will be worried if I don't get back." He hesitated. "Thank you."

David smiled again and held open the door. "You're welcome, Jesse."

Chapter
Fifteen

AADON did his very, very best to ignore the hangover he woke with. He was sprawled half on Leo's couch, one leg dangling over the side of the too short piece of furniture. He could hear movement in the kitchen, but didn't really want to get up to see who else was awake. He ran a hand through his hair and couldn't ignore his skinned knuckles, which just reminded him of his flare of temper the night before.

Groaning, he shifted his weight, feeling the strain in his back from yet another night on someone's couch. Why he even had an apartment, he was beginning to wonder. He'd spent most of the last month either crashed out here or on the even more uncomfortable futon in Mike's living room. He'd had a gutful of long lonely nights in the huge, mostly empty house he'd grown up in with his confused brother and distracted parents. He wasn't one to wallow, but the thought of his empty apartment always drove him to seek company.

Last night had been no exception, and the reminder of how he'd abused his friends made his gut twist. A soft huff from the floor beside him made him lock over, and the first thing he noticed was the livid bruise across Mike's cheek when he looked down at his cousin, lying on the floor, snoring softly.

"Not like that was your first drunken brawl, Addy." Leanne smiled at him from the living room doorway, where she lounged against the frame in her flannels, two cups of coffee in her hand. Aadon sat up to give her room on the couch, and she came over to sit beside him. She handed him one of the cups with a smile. "Probably won't be your last, either." Sitting back, she curled a foot under her. "Though you don't usually start them." She paused to sip and watch him. "Want to talk about it?"

"I miss him."

She chuckled. "Really? We hadn't noticed."

Aadon made a face. "I don't know what to do. He won't take my calls. I tried going to his place a couple times, and his bulldog neighbor ran me off both times. Wouldn't even let him know I'd stopped by."

"Sarah?" Leanne smiled. "I have to say, I understand how she feels. I'm not very inclined to feel welcoming toward Jesse right now, either. Whatever happened between you two, you're hurting because of it, and you know? I'm not really required to like him for hurting you."

"I hurt him, Lee."

"Not saying you didn't, but this"—she waved her hand up and down in front of him—"is a portrait of a man who had something pretty nasty thrown at him."

Aadon nodded assent. "But deserved." He sighed and turned his attention to the hot, delicious coffee for a little while. "And not all that far from the truth."

"So. Is this truth something the two of you can't work out?"

"I don't know. He's avoiding me."

"Did you talk to Mom, Addy?" Mike's voice drifted up from the floor, and Aadon stared down at him.

"Why would I talk to your mother?"

Mike rolled his eyes. "Because she's his boss, bonehead. He spends every other day with her. Maybe she could talk him into at least listening to what you have to say." Mike sat up with a groan and touched tentative fingers to his discolored cheekbone. "Not sure which hurts more. My head or my face."

Leanne leaned over the back of the couch and came back with a bottle of aspirin, which she tossed into his lap. "I think this calls for a little bit of Boys Breakfast, don't you?" she asked them. "The three of you should go out, eat some of that disgusting greasy food you swear by, and then stop by the library and talk to sweetie's mom." She fixed a look on Aadon. "While I might be reserving a bit of an opinion on the guy, if Jesse's in as bad shape as you are, honey, the very least you both need is to hash it out once and for all. Make it work, or move on."

"Always so practical is my lady," Leo said from the kitchen doorway. He was already dressed and looking chipper despite his black eye. "Let's go, ladies. Chop, chop. I'm starving."

"Don't you ever get hung over?" Aadon grumbled as he hunted around for his jeans and T-shirt. He frowned when he found it, complete with dried blood dripped down the front.

"Here." Leo tossed him a fresh one from a laundry basket in the hall, and the three of them trooped out the door.

Breakfast went a long way toward helping Aadon feel human enough to face his aunt. A feeling that fled about the moment he walked into the library, and she beckoned him, alone, into the back room.

"Who started it this time?" she asked him, turning his face this way and that to examine the bruising. Aadon blushed and fixed his gaze on the floor. "No doubt my idiot son managed to say just the right thing."

Aadon couldn't help but grin. "He did, Thea. He said exactly the right thing, and once I got over being mad, I realized he was right. That's why I'm here. He might piss me off, but that's only because he has this really annoying habit of being right so much of the time."

A small grunt was her only reply for a few minutes. "You three can't just settle your differences like everyone else, can you? You have to shout and hit and blubber all over each other."

Aadon's grin only widened at the realization of how well she knew them, and he nodded. But the grin faded when she finally let him go. "I'm glad I take after Thea Mira more than I do Mom, even if it means losing my temper once in a while. At least I *feel* something."

"So am I, Sobrino." She settled in a chair, brusquely tugging at the sleeves of her blouse as if they needed straightening. "Not that your mother doesn't feel. She just learned too well how to hide it. A lesson she never un-learned, unfortunately. So I'm glad you're more like her sister too."

Knowing talking about his aunt, even now, years after her death, perturbed her lover, Aadon pressed on as gently as he could. "Thea Ada, you once told me when you met her, she terrified you."

"And so she did. Marpessa was a wild creature." She eyed him. "Much like you've been up until very recently. In our day, what she and I found when we met was far more dangerous than it is for you, Aadon. You're lucky. The world has changed a great deal."

"Yes. I know. But you found a way."

"Because we were in love."

"Was it her wild ways that frightened you, or the situation?"

"Both. Why?"

"I just… you've always said she was the brave one. That she was terrifying and wonderful and all these things. I'm just trying to understand."

"And why do you need to understand the ins and outs of a love affair between two old women?"

Another small grin flashed across Aadon's face as Adara crossed her arms over her chest and peered at him over the rims of her glasses. "Because. You weren't always old. You weren't when you met, and you always tell me my 'wild ways' are going to drive all the other boys away, but they didn't drive you away from Thea Mara. I want to know why."

"Probably because I was more stubborn than anyone else she met." That made Aadon laugh out loud and finally brought a smile to Adara's lips too. She leaned forward slightly to catch his eye. "What is this really about, Sobrino? And why aren't you speaking to your parents about it?"

Aadon just scowled at that. "You know what they're like. They wouldn't understand. They wouldn't want to." He glanced at her nervously, but plowed on when she simply sat there, waiting for him to get to the point. "I know some pretty bad things happened to you. When you were young. When everything first started with Ricky, and you and Thea Mara tried to help, I heard you talking to Mom. I heard how she just didn't listen, didn't want to know."

Adara drew in a deep breath. "Is this about Ricky, then?"

"Not really." He bit his lip, but eventually her patience drew it out of him more than her questions. "Jesse."

She was already shaking her head. "You have to ask Jesse about anything, Aadon. Even if he had said anything to me, which he hasn't, it would not be my place to tell you."

"I know what happened to him already. He told me. It was bad. I just… I want to know what Thea Mara did. How she helped you trust again. I mean, you fell in love with her, but that couldn't have been easy, after everything that happened to you."

"What happened to me, unfortunately, was more common than you might think, and yes, it was unpleasant, but I wasn't as alone in the feeling it left behind as I might have been." She leaned even further forward. "As, perhaps, a young man might feel under the same circumstances. I got help, Aadon. Mara simply loved me. The rest, I talked through with a therapist. I did a lot of hard work to get over that experience. I focused on Marpessa, on

Michael, because he certainly was the best thing that could have happened to me, all things considered, and I got through."

Aadon remained quiet for a long time. None of this was exactly a revelation. Mike had actually been the one to tell Aadon and Leo how he'd been conceived, so even that wasn't news. He supposed he'd hoped for some kind of magic solution. Some *thing* he could do to help Jesse. He wasn't really surprised at her reply. Hadn't he watched Ricky slowly self-destruct because he *wouldn't* face the truth? He didn't want the same thing for Jesse. He didn't know how to prevent it.

"All you can do, Aadon," Adara said gently, "is love him. Tell him every day you love him. Remind him in little ways. Ways he can accept, that don't frighten him. You have a powerful, loving little family in Leo and Leanne and Michael. Let them help you so you can help Jesse. Lord knows, that boy needs support."

Aadon nodded at the floor. "I would, Thea. He won't talk to me."

"Why?"

Aadon cringed at giving her any details. "I pushed too hard, I guess. I knew it was too soon."

"Oh, Aadon."

"I know." He felt the tears starting again, miserable, not because he missed Jesse, which he did, but because for all he wanted to make everything better for the other man, he was the one who'd made it all infinitely worse. "And now he won't answer my phone calls, and I don't... I don't know what to do."

"Well, for the time being, you'll just have to pull yourself together and wait. He's gone home."

"Home?" Aadon lifted his head to look at her. "What do you mean home? Where's home? Is he coming back?"

"Of course he's coming back. He went home, he told me, to take care of some legal matters. I don't know what, so don't ask. He didn't elaborate."

"I know."

"Then you already know more than I do."

"Did he give you a number?"

"I'm sorry. He didn't. Just told me if I needed to reach him, I could call his cell."

"Which I've been doing, and he never picks up."

"Well, Aadon." She rose and patted him on the head. "I don't know what to tell you. Maybe you just have to let this go."

"I can't. I love him. And I hurt him." He scrubbed his hands over his face. "I love him. He doesn't have to love me back, but I have to at least talk to him one more time. Tell him I'm sorry. That I know what I did, and I'm sorry."

"The very most I can do is tell him you want to talk to him, Aadon. Other than that, he has to want that too."

"I understand, Thea. Thank you." He got up, and she immediately pulled him into a hug, making him wince from the bruises left over from Leo's tackle.

She pushed him away and held him at arm's length. "None of you have broken bones?"

She could always get a laugh out of him. "No, Thea. No broken bones."

"Good." Opening the door and ushering him out, all she had to do was give her son a look, and Mike trotted over to kiss her cheek. "You be good to your cousin, Michael. No more brawls."

"He swung first!" Mike pointed in Aadon's direction, complete innocence on his face.

"Mmmm. And without provocation, I'm sure."

"Well...."

"Why am I not surprised, Hmmm?" She hugged him tight, though, and kissed his cheek before moving on to inspect Leo's black eye and click her tongue at him. His wide grin still earned him a hug, and she tucked a wild strand of his red hair behind his ear.

"Auntie," he complained, batting it free and shaking his head.

"Now get out of here, all of you. I have work to do."

Aadon gave her one last hug before he left. "Yes, ma'am. Love you, too, Thea."

"You're suddenly very chipper," Leo pointed out as they piled back into his car. "What did she say?"

"Jesse's gone home."

"And this is a good thing?"

"It is, because he told her he's gone home to take care of some legal matters, which means he's doing something positive."

"About what?"

"It just means… it's good, okay? Trust me."

"Please tell me," Mike put in, "it means you two will get back together, because I cannot stand much more of Gloomy you on my couch."

"I think I'm pretty much over couch living too. Leo, can you drop me off at mine?"

"Finally," they both chorused, and Aadon smacked them both across the backs of their heads from where he sat in the back seat. But he couldn't really be angry. He had been relying heavily on them, and they had been great. But it was time to get a grip and get back to his own life. If Jesse could sort through his shit, Aadon could surely deal with one shattered relationship, even if he couldn't fix it.

Chapter
S i x t e e n

BY THE time Jesse arrived back at their table, Sarah had chewed the straw from her drink to a tiny plastic ball. She watched Jesse make his way back through the dining room and jumped up as he neared the table. "Are you all right? Jesse, what happened?"

"It's fine." He hugged her, trying to reassure her, and led her toward the door. "Something big happened. Come on." They paid quickly, and he hustled her down the street to where fewer people lined the walks and he could talk in more privacy. He told her everything. From how he met Anthony to the night he left, and everything in between.

Walking along the streets where he'd grown up, passing the places he'd known when he was a kid made the details less real, somehow, like they couldn't be a part of the innocent playgrounds and the wooded lot or the ball field.

She didn't interrupt. After the first few minutes, she took his hand and held it but didn't speak.

He couldn't look at her, but in the end, telling it wasn't as hard as he'd feared. They sat in the swings in the playground nearest his home, and he waited while she stared at the sandy depression under her feet. "Aadon knows all this?" she asked at last.

"Yes. Well. Most of it. The most important parts." He dropped his voice. "The worst parts."

"You told him, and he walked out on you? After all this time?"

"No." Jesse sighed and pushed his feet into the sand, driving the swing into motion. "I told him, and he understood completely. He walked out because I treated him like shit. I accused him of using me." For a few minutes, he pumped the swing hard, rocking the entire piece of equipment, focusing all his anger on the effort of making the swing go higher, but eventually, he stopped. "We made love, and he was terrified, Sarah. He thought he hurt me."

"Did he?"

"He didn't mean to. I pretended he didn't and told him he didn't have the power to hurt me."

"But did he?"

Jesse nodded. "I was as scared as I had been with Anthony near the end. As much as I knew I was safe, I was still terrified. I should have stopped him. I should have told him. He would have understood. He wanted me to say it, and I wouldn't, so he pushed. I made him push, didn't give him any other choice. He felt like shit after, and I let him feel that way."

"Jess—"

Jesse threw himself out of the swing and started walking. He didn't want to listen to her well-meaning, understanding concern. He wanted to talk to Aadon. He had to speak to him.

Sarah jumped up and hurried after him.

Terse and quick, he told her about David and his willingness to help, handed off the napkin David had given him when he paid that had the other man's phone number on it, but he had only his own guilt on his mind. He didn't even hear her responses.

At the house, she stopped in the garden to talk to his mother as she clipped her roses in the dying evening light.

Jesse didn't stop but went straight to the office and closed the door. He dialed Aadon's number and listened to it ring a few times. The answering machine came on, and he cursed. "Shit. I forgot," he said after the beep. "You're still driving from visiting Ricky, probably. Guess the time zone thing is genetic." Suddenly all his conviction fled, and he didn't know what else to say. "Sorry" seemed beyond inadequate and trying to explain over the machine crass. "Listen. I'll call back later. In the morning. I hope you'll answer. There is something I have to tell you."

Aadon picked up. "Jesse?"

"Hi." It was all he could manage before his throat closed. He wondered how he was ever going to get anything out at all, let alone find the right way to say it.

"Jesse."

Silence. Long, thick, clumsy silence.

"How?" A deep breath. "Is it over?"

"Hasn't even started." Jesse sank to the floor in front of the couch and tucked his feet up close to his body. "Doesn't matter."

"Oh." Resignation rang through the short syllable, and Jesse knew he was off to a bad start. "It doesn't matter. If he goes to jail or he doesn't, nothing changes." He picked up a toast crumb from the short pile carpet and crushed it between his thumb and fingernail, absently wondering how it got there, under his mother's fastidious nose. "I'll still be here, where he left me. I can't move forward." His voice broke, and he had to stop. He wasn't going to cry over the phone. He wasn't going to do that to Aadon. After a minute of catching his breath, he tried again. "I needed to confront him and tell him—"

"Tell him what?"

"It doesn't matter."

"Tell me."

"You're not him."

"Just say it. It doesn't matter to who. Say it out loud." There was a pause before he spoke again. "My therapist says say it out loud. Put it out there where you don't have to carry it alone, and won't be so big."

"Your therapist?"

"Well, Ricky's actually. But I've been seeing her too. Recently. Trying to sort shit out. Look. It doesn't matter. Just tell me what you want to tell him. It doesn't matter who you say it to, as long as you say it."

"It does."

"What difference does it make? I'll listen."

"He wouldn't. That's the difference. Whatever I said, he wouldn't care. He never listened."

More silence, like molasses, thick and dark and sticky. Jesse tried. In a tentative voice, hearing it shake, forcing the words out through his teeth, he spoke, "Okay. Fine. You want me to say it? You hurt me. You shouldn't have done it. I didn't want it. I was scared…." He paused, swallowed hard. "Not ready."

"I know." Such a neutral tone. Jesse could tell nothing from it.

"I couldn't stop you. I wanted to. I wanted—" He closed his eyes, remembering, but it all blurred together. He didn't want the memory of Aadon to blend with the others, but it did. It was the same. "I wasn't ready," he said again, barely a whisper, and knew he wasn't pretending to talk to Anthony any more. From the broken sound on the other end of the line, he knew Aadon knew it too.

He took a deep breath and clung to the phone. "I wasn't," he whispered. "I'm sorry. I just wanted not to hurt any more. Please—"

"Shhh." Aadon cut him off. "Don't say anything."

"But—"

"Don't. We made a mistake. We can't unmake it."

Over the line, Jesse heard him take a deep breath and let it out. There was more silence, but it wasn't as heavy. It didn't smother him.

"Aadon?"

Aadon cleared his throat and spoke in a voice gruff and full of edges. "I can't hurt you like that again. I'm sorry."

"Don't hang up!" Desperate, Jesse bolted to his feet, as though he would run out the door and back to Aadon if it was the only way not to lose him.

"I don't know what to do, Jesse." He sounded so bleak.

Jesse almost thought he sounded frightened.

"Someone told me once," Jesse began, "that a person who cared would save me from what Anthony did, not watch it happen and g-get off on it." He heard a tiny intake of breath, but he went on. "That's why you were so upset, isn't it? You thought you were like him, knowing I was terrified and not stopping. The thing is, he liked seeing me like that. Aadon?" There was no reply. "Aadon, you're not like him."

"I should have stopped. I knew it wasn't okay with you. I knew it was wrong."

"I'm always going to be scared, Aadon. Always. He ruined me. He took that from me, and I'll never get it back. Not like it should be. But you make it better. I can be afraid with you and still know I'm safe. That's the difference. That's why I love you."

He hadn't meant to say it.

Aadon would throw up a fuss about him not understanding what love was, not knowing, but he knew he was right. He'd thought he was in love with Anthony, but love should never look that much like fear. He'd thought, in some vague, unformed way, he could run away and have something with David, but he knew he'd only latched onto that thought because it looked like escape.... He loved Aadon. He had no doubts about that, hadn't from the first date.

"What if—"

Jesse waited. This was a different voice, one small and uncertain. One he had to be very careful not to tread on.

"What if you're wrong?" Aadon asked.

"What if I am? I can't take the chance I'm right and still just walk away." He swallowed. "That didn't make much sense."

"Yeah. It did, actually." Aadon let go of a wet laugh. Suddenly, everything made sense. Despite all the complications, it was really very simple. "It made perfect sense."

Jesse heard a lot of rustling and the sound of a door closing.

"When do you meet with the lawyer?"

"Tuesday afternoon, I hope."

"I'll be there." He wasn't completely sure how he was going to manage it, but he knew he had to try, to show Jesse he wasn't just talking about this. That he meant it. "I'll be there," he said again.

Jesse's heart leapt. He sank onto the couch, shock folding him like a house of cards. "You'll what?"

"I'll be there. To hold your hand, or make coffee, or sit out on the porch and wait, whatever you need."

"You should know Sarah is here."

This time Aadon's chuckle was closer to the one Jesse knew. The one that sent a shiver of joy through him.

"I'll bring a treat. Do you think a big slab of steak will distract her?" Aadon was not going to be put off by her guard-dog act again. She wasn't Jesse's keeper, and if she really loved him, she'd let him go, let him make this decision for himself.

"I think she'll behave, or I'll have to pen her in the backyard." More seriously, he said, "She knows everything. She won't give you a hard time. How are you going to get here by tomorrow?"

"I'm getting in the car now. I can be there in less than twenty-four hours."

"You'll be exhausted."

"Probably."

"You can't drive that long. It isn't safe."

"What would you have me do?" Aadon held his breath, willing Jesse not to tell him to stay home.

"Call someone. Leo, or… what's-his-name at the restaurant. Maybe someone can come with you."

Aadon breathed a sigh of relief. "You're right. I'll pick Leo up on the way. Now hang up so I can call him. I'll call you back later for directions, when we get closer. And get some sleep."

"It's five in the afternoon here."

Aadon paused as the echo of Jesse's emotional stress rebounded through his own chest. "I know your tired voice. I'll be there by Tuesday morning. First cup's on you."

"It'll be ready." Jesse settled into the soft cushions of the couch, warmed by that tiny reminder that he wasn't alone. "Aadon? When this is over, we'll be able to talk, right? Figure things out?"

"I can't promise any answers, Jesse. I don't know how this works."

"Me either, but we know a bit of what doesn't at least." He smiled into the phone, hoping Aadon could hear it in his words and know he wasn't laying any blame. "All we have to do is keep talking."

"I hope you're right, Jesse."

Aadon hung up the phone after he heard the soft click of Jesse doing the same and let out a long sigh. He let himself flop back onto the mattress and just process. Jesse had called him. And told him exactly what he had hoped never to hear; that he'd hurt him in the worst way possible. But he had called. He had said they could work it out, that there was something worth talking about.

One thing at a time. He sat up and dialed Leo's number, quickly explaining what had happened, and before he could even ask if his friend would help, Leo was waking his girl up and telling her he had to take a road trip.

"Thanks, man. You have no idea how much I appreciate this."

"Oh, yes I do. Wait until I call in this favor. We'll see how appreciative you are."

Aadon chuckled. "I'll pick you up in an hour. I want to stop by the clinic on the way. I have to tell Doc Carol I'll be out of town and make sure she has Ada's number if anything happens."

"Sure thing."

The ride to the clinic was a quiet one. Leo might be a loudmouth brat, but he was not much of a night owl. He dozed as Aadon drove and offered to stay in the car when Aadon went into the building. He'd called the doctor to tell her what was going on, and she'd agreed to meet him at the clinic. Since they both knew Ricky would be up this time of night anyway, it seemed appropriate to go and see him and tell him in person what was going on.

With his recent bouts of lucidity, Aadon wanted to spend as much time with him, talking to him, keeping him up to date with the world, as it seemed his brother could stand. He was sitting in the lounge when Aadon arrived with Dr. Carol. She waited at the door so the brothers could have a few private words.

"Hey, Ricky."

After a heartbeat, Ricky's blond head lifted, he gazed at Aadon, and then a happy smile lit his face. "Hi, A. What're you doin' back here?"

"Came to see you a minute." Aadon sat on the couch next to him, but not touching. Ricky had to invite touch most of the time. "Something's going on, and I have to go out of town a few days."

"You comin' back?" Ricky' eyes got a little bit wide; his mouth went a little bit slack.

"Yeah, Ricky. 'Course I am. I just have a friend. He needs my help. I'm going to go help him."

"Like you help me?"

"Something like that."

"That why you've been so worried?" Ricky sat up a bit. "You worried about this friend?"

"Um…." Aadon glanced at Dr. Carol who only shrugged and indicated he should go ahead and answer. "I am, yeah. He had this thing happen. Someone hurt him." Aadon bit his lip, trying to decide how much to tell his fragile brother.

Ricky stared at him, eyes bright and wide. "Martin hurt me."

Aadon nodded. "Yeah. Martin hurt you," Aadon said softly, amazed to hear Ricky say it out loud.

Ricky shuffled a few inches closer, then a few more, until their knees touched. He focused his gaze on that contact point as his hands twisted in his lap, twined together in a tight tangle of fingers and whitened knuckles. "Was your friend hurt… like *that*?"

Aadon took in a deep breath, but he didn't look to Dr. Carol for guidance this time. He had to go with his gut, and his gut told him Ricky had a reason for asking, and if he was brave enough to risk the fallout of recalling those memories, he deserved a straight answer. He nodded. "Yeah, Ricky. Something like that. He was older when it happened to him, though, and he wanted to pretend it didn't happen. But it did. Now he needs me to help him."

"Then you should help him," Ricky whispered. He lifted his face, and there were more tears on his cheeks. Not like last time, when he had sobbed like a broken child, but still tears and sadness in his eyes that cracked Aadon's heart. "Can't pretend it didn't happen. Doesn't work, A."

"No. It doesn't."

"You worry about everyone."

Aadon smiled. "Didn't know you'd noticed."

"I notice." For a split second, Ricky' eyes clouded, his brows knotted a bit. "I notice when I don't take the fuzzy meds." He looked shyly up at Aadon. "Tryin' not to take so many fuzzy meds."

"I know. That's good. If you're happy."

"Not always. But… sometimes. I forgot what happy felt like."

"Geez, Ricky." Aadon wanted to hug him, but Ricky hadn't made any indication touching would be okay, so he just smiled. "Happy's good, yeah?"

Ricky nodded. "Where you goin'?"

"Well, across the country, actually. Long drive. But I promise, I'll be back for your eval, and in the meantime, if you need anything, you ask Doc Carol, or ask her to call Thea Ada, okay? She's got Thea's number."

"Okay."

They sat for a few stiff seconds, then Ricky leaned over, arms held out, and Aadon practically threw himself into the rare hug his brother offered. "Thanks, Ricky. Thanks."

"You get happy too, A, okay?"

"I'll try, Ricky."

"So?" Dr, Carol asked as he made his way back across the darkened room to her.

"He seems okay with it." He considered a moment, thinking about Ricky's acceptance, calm despite the tears, of what he'd told him. "He's okay with a lot of things that used to send him into screaming fits of rage. What changed?"

"It's so hard to know, Aadon. He was stunted, and it was easy for him to regress. Something made him suddenly want to try. He spends a lot of time with Katherine. She even visits off duty."

Aadon nodded. He knew that, and he'd talked to the young orderly about it on one of his visits. She'd told him Ricky reminded her of her younger, autistic brother, Mark. She'd talked to Dr. Carol about trying a few techniques that seemed to work with Mark, and when Ricky responded, they had both decided to keep going. Besides, she'd told him, Ricky was the nicest, gentlest person she'd ever met. Aadon couldn't argue with her on that point, and if he had a friend in her, that could only be a good thing.

"She's good for him," Aadon admitted.

"And for you. You need the break."

Aadon just shrugged. "He's my brother. I don't need a break from that."

"I think it will do both you and Ricky some good if you have a chance to focus on something other than trying to make him better. He's doing just fine. Space to feel his way through this is what he needs. He'll fall, I'm sure, but he knows you'll be there to help if he needs it. Now it's time to let him do some of this on his own."

"You're telling me to back off. Now that he's finally alive, and real, you want me to leave him alone?"

"I want you to stand back and give him room. Not leave. The best thing you can do right now is show him how life works by living yours. You have a chance now to show him the difference between what happened to him and what love really means. Don't think for a minute that he doesn't understand who this 'friend' really is to you. He knows. Show him how it's supposed to work. And at the same time, show Jesse. Ricky needs you to let him go. Sounds to me like Jesse needs you there to hang onto while he does this thing he has to do."

Aadon gazed back into the room where Ricky sat, the light from the TV flickering across his profile. "You have Ada's number, right?"

"Of course I do."

Aadon continued to watch his brother, absorbed, now, in his program, seemingly oblivious to the world. "I want to be just happy and proud. I'm scared for him."

"It's all out of your hands. That is scary."

A small laugh escaped Aadon. "I don't suppose I ever really had any control over any of it."

"None of us really do. Not over anyone but ourselves. And Aadon." She laid a hand on his arm, drawing his attention back to her. "If Jesse ever decides to give you control again, it's your responsibility to make sure he knows why he's doing it. If it's because he's too scared to be in control himself, that's not a good reason."

Dumbfounded, Aadon nodded. "How did you know…?"

Her smile was slightly on the sly side of kind. "It's my job, Aadon. To listen to what you tell me. And what you don't. Almost always, the key is in what you don't say, and not once did you say you initiated things with Jesse, however much you might have wanted to." Her expression softened. "If he wanted that badly to thrust responsibility on you and not own what he was feeling, the outcome was almost inevitable. Neither one of you are in control of anything, at that point. Taking back ownership of his body was only the first step, and it was a good one, however painful it ended up being for him. Now he's ready to move forward, and while you can't do this for him, you can hold his hand, like you've been doing for Ricky all these years."

"He called me." Aadon brought his attention back to the doctor. "He told me… he wasn't ready. He pushed, and I let him. I wanted. I didn't want to hurt him. God. I didn't know what to do. I'm as bad as Anthony."

"Aadon, you know that isn't true."

"I'm going to have to tell him that I talked to you about all this."

"Yes, you should, but one step at a time. Go do what he needs you to do right now. Help him get through whatever it is he's doing, and go from there. You don't have to fix anything, Aadon. You just have to be there."

"It's hard. Not doing anything. Not being able to do anything."

"But you are doing something. You're showing Ricky he's strong enough to do this on his own, and you're showing Jesse he doesn't have to do it alone. What they both need right now." She cupped his face in a very motherly gesture. "And you need to believe in your own ability to be strong for them. You have good instincts. Don't think so much. Don't be so afraid of what you feel."

"Since when do you give so much advice?" he asked. "You usually make me work a lot harder for this."

"Since I'm fairly certain you already know everything I'm telling you anyway. Otherwise, you would not have dragged me out of my pajamas this time of night, decided to leave Ricky, and arranged to trek across the country to Jesse if you didn't think it was what needed to be done."

"I suppose." Aadon snorted. "Yeah. Guess you're right. You have Thea—"

"Yes! You already asked."

"Oh." He gave her a sheepish grin. "Sorry. But you'll call her before you call my folks, right? If something goes wrong. Just… she'll get in touch with me. I'll come back." He shot a nervous glance back to where Ricky sat, seemingly oblivious to everything but the TV.

"Don't worry so much. For right now, you need to concentrate on you and Jesse."

Aadon nodded. "I told him I was seeing you. Just not that I talked so much about him."

"And?"

"He didn't say much."

"Well, the offer stands. If he wants to talk, I'm here to listen. We'll work out the billing with student assistance or something. Don't let that be a barrier."

"I know."

"Good. Now go. The sooner you get this over with, the sooner you two can move on, whatever that means for you."

"Thanks, Doc."

"You're more than welcome."

When he got back to the car, Leo was already sitting in the driver's seat.

"All clear?" he asked as Aadon shuffled around in his seat and pulled out the seatbelt.

"Yup."

Leo still sat, both hands on the wheel, staring forward. "You're sure about this? Because you know I will follow you anywhere, but if this guy hurts you again, I will kick his ass—"

"I'm sure," Aadon interrupted.

Leo nodded. "Okay, then."

"Okay, then."

He started the car, and they drove into the night. It was some time before Aadon managed anything resembling sleep.

Chapter
Seventeen

Awake long before anyone else, Jesse carefully tiptoed around the kitchen, making coffee as quietly as possible. He hadn't mentioned Aadon's arrival to the others. His day Monday had been spent locked in his mother's office with the lawyer telling him everything and figuring out how David's willingness to come forward affected things. Like he'd predicted and told Aadon, the meeting between lawyer and family and himself had been pushed back another day.

Steven Nivens had been completely supportive and understanding through the whole thing. In a way, Jesse, was glad to have had the chance to tell him before he told his mother. The man was sympathetic and gave every sign that he actually cared what Jesse was going through and how this new information would affect his mother. He was almost as glad to have the other man's support as he was for Sarah's and Aadon's. When he sat down with his mom and told her the truth, he knew she would be devastated. It was one thing to know her son had been raped and beaten, to know he had tastes she didn't understand, but to know how far he'd let the abuse go, how much he'd kept from her over the year he'd been with Anthony, would make her doubt everything she wanted to believe about herself as a parent.

The last thing he wanted to do was make her think she had not done a good enough job raising him, or regret that she'd never found a man to help. He doubted seriously whether any man who wasn't the father he remembered from when he was twelve would have been able to make any difference in the choices he'd made in college. And, it didn't matter. It was all over and done. He couldn't go back, and he didn't want to be stuck any more.

Now he sat at the kitchen table, his own mug in hand, and watched out the window as the day slowly snuck in and stole away the power darkness held over the house and the yard. He recognized Aadon's car when it stopped at the corner and had two cups of coffee poured and waiting. He stepped out onto the porch, mugs in hand to wait.

"You found it okay," he called, once Aadon had parked and stepped out of his car.

"Yeah. Your directions were good."

"Good." Jesse held out a cup. "Just like you like it. Hot, black, and strong. Where's Leo?"

"Sleeping in the back seat. Don't want to wake him. He did most of the driving."

"What happened to your face?" Jesse stared in shock at the fading color under Aadon's left eye.

"Oh." Aadon touched it gently. "Leo and Mike had to knock a bit of sense into me." Aadon took the offered coffee, set it on the railing, and took Jesse's hand instead. "Don't worry about it. No permanent damage, and I needed the wake up."

"I don't get how beating you up is helpful."

Jesse's face crumpled into a frown, and Aadon reached for Jesse's other hand too. "They didn't beat me up. It's...." Aadon thought about it a minute, trying to figure out how to explain. "Hard to explain," he said finally. "Just how we work. I promise, no one got hurt, and it seriously reminded me how worried they were."

"Okay, well. I still don't get it, but, if you say so." It took only a gentle, abbreviated tug to get Jesse to move, and then Aadon's arms were around him, and he was sinking into a warm embrace.

"I say so." He tightened his arms around Jesse. "God, I missed you so much." He closed his eyes, pressed his cheek against the soft fall of hair at Jesse's temple.

"Thanks for coming."

"Knowing you were here, doing this on your own...."

Aadon's hand rose up his back and cupped the back of his head, pulling Jesse closer, cradling his head against his shoulder, and Jesse at last surrendered to the exhaustion of holding up to the strain. He needed this so much. Letting his own arms rise up to circle loosely around Aadon's waist, he leaned and marveled at how Aadon just took his weight and felt like shelter and safe and home.

"It was killing me, being so far away, Jesse. Even Ricky noticed I was distracted."

"He did?"

"Yeah." Aadon pulled away slightly to look into Jesse's face. "Shocked the shit out of me when he pointed it out. I didn't think he noticed much of anything. So I told him. Told him you were doing this thing, that something happened to you, like happened to him, and you were trying to fix it."

Aadon stopped talking. His eyes had gone glassy, and the corners of his mouth pinched tight, and Jesse reached up to touch his fingers to the hard line drawing those perfect lips down.

"He started to cry."

"I'm sorry—"

"No." Aadon's hand on the back of his head shifted, his fingers sifting lightly through Jesse's hair. "No. It was good. It was something. Don't know if he really understood himself why he was upset, but...." His lips twitched in a slight smile, but still, the tell-tale pinch of worry remained. "It was something, Jesse. More than I've ever seen in him in years. His doctor says he's been hiding, not really trying to get better. That the drugs have given him the perfect excuse not to deal with anything. He can just pretend he's too messed up to really try. And he's been doing it so long he really convinced himself he was that far gone. But maybe he's coming around now."

"You think so?"

"I don't know." Aadon tugged Jesse close again, rested his chin on Jesse's head and sighed. "I don't know. Sometimes, I think he might be able to process stuff. Sometimes...."

"And you came here to be with me instead of staying there with him, when he could be on the verge of a breakthrough. You could get him back."

"You listen to me." Aadon tilted Jesse's head back to better look him in the eye. "I made up my mind to come the second I heard your voice on that phone. To come get you, to come hold your hand, whatever it took. Whatever you wanted." He bit his lower lip and struggled to keep his emotions in check when all he really wanted was to haul Jesse close and never let him go. "Whatever I could talk you into accepting. What you said, about me and Ricky that night, it wasn't that far off. It pissed me off because you were right, and I hated that. But it was wrong of me to walk out because I didn't like hearing the truth. Just as wrong as it was for me to force you—"

"That isn't what happened."

"I knew you were scared. I knew I should stop. I thought if I was gentle, didn't push too hard...." He blinked down at Jesse, his eyes once more going glassy. "I wanted to be the one to make it all go away."

"Don't." Jesse pulled free of Aadon's grip and crossed to lean on the deck railing, arms crossed over his chest and staring out at the quiet end of the cul-de-sac. "I wanted you to be that too. Like none of it ever happened. But it did. And I haven't dealt with it. That isn't your fault, or your problem. But it's like you said. It was a mistake we can't unmake."

"I never wanted to hurt you, Jesse." Aadon's hand rested briefly on Jesse's shoulder, but fell away before Jesse could react to the touch by pulling away again. He didn't think he could take him pulling away again.

"I should have told you. Everything." Jesse turned around, propped his ass on the railing, and stared at Aadon, searching for the only strength he could muster: defiance. "And I will. I've started. I told you, the lawyer, Sarah. Now I just have to face Mom. Hell, soon, it'll be a matter of public record. But you'll know everything. Then you can decide if I'm the kind of project you really want to take on."

Aadon pursed his lips. "Don't talk about yourself like that."

"I'm not easy."

Aadon laughed, and the sound was infectious, leaving Jesse chuckling, as well. He had his head down, his gaze directed at his bare toes when he realized Aadon had moved close again. His hand under Jesse's chin was warm, eliciting that now familiar tingling tension in his gut. He let Aadon lift his face and met the taller man's eyes.

"One thing at a time, okay? Let's just get through today."

Jesse nodded.

"Good." Aadon kissed him then, a soft, undemanding touch of lips against his.

The sensation of falling was immediate and surreal, and Jesse found himself gripping Aadon's arms, clinging, even as his lips parted, and he leaned closer. The dual sensations of anxiety and need turned him inside out, and he moaned. "Aadon...."

Aadon's lips left his, and his voice soothed the ruffles of emotion. "It's okay." Aadon hugged him close. "It's going to be okay."

For once, Jesse didn't fight the need to be held and reassured. It couldn't hurt to accept the comfort some of the time, could it?

They stayed that way for a long time, it seemed. The sun warmed Jesse's back, and Aadon's strong body against his grounded him. All the tension and pent-up fear of the last few weeks began to melt away until he could finally step back and remember what it was like to not be living under the shadow of Anthony Bruno.

"We should go inside. Mom will be up soon."

Aadon nodded and turned toward the front door, but his arm remained draped across Jesse's shoulders.

"What about Leo?"

"The man sleeps like the dead and growls like an old bear if you wake him up. Let him sleep. He'll come in when he wakes."

"Wouldn't he be more comfortable in a bed?"

"Probably."

"Aadon."

"Trust me on this." Aadon tightened his arm when Jesse made a move as though he would go back to wake Leo. "I've known the guy since we were five. You wake him from a sleep like that, he comes up swinging. Let him be."

"If you say so."

Aadon kissed the top of Jesse's head. "I do."

"Okay, then." Jesse smiled to himself, leaned a little into Aadon's body and the security of his presence. He'd managed so much on his own in the past few days. But having Aadon close made everything less scary. Now he knew he could do what he needed to do, he didn't mind sharing his fear with the other man and letting him ease some of it away.

IN THE kitchen, they found Jesse's mother sitting at the small breakfast table near the window that looked out over the front porch, and Sarah, with her back to the door, pouring coffee.

"So." Jesse's mom smiled. "You must be Aadon."

"Yes, ma'am." Aadon held out a hand to her, and she stood, sizing his six-foot frame up from her five-foot-one perspective.

Aadon bit his lip and offered a tentative smile.

"Miriam," she said at last, taking his offered hand in both of hers. "Call me Miriam. Sarah?"

"We've met." Sarah's terse comment, with the underlying anger, didn't surprise Jesse one bit.

"Set four places at the table, please, dear. Aadon's had a long drive."

Aadon nodded, but his attention was mostly on Sarah.

"You'll be tired," Miriam went on. "A bit of food, and then some sleep, I think, before Steve gets here."

"Mr. Nivens," Jesse said, tossing a tight-lipped look at his mother, "will be here after lunch."

Sarah slammed her mug down on the counter. "Oh, Jesse, for God's sake—"

"Sarah." Miriam turned, cut off whatever she was about to say, and pointed to the table. "Please, dear." Her voice softened immediately. "Let's just get some food on the table, and we can clear the air, yes?"

Sarah nodded. "Yes, ma'am."

"Good. Jesse, if you could make some juice, and Aadon, the toaster and bread." She pointed to the spotless counter and the gleaming appliance sitting next to the breadbox. "A nice scramble, I think. Mushrooms all right, Aadon?"

"Yes, ma'am. Mushrooms would be fine."

They worked in silence, except for Miriam's soft hum as she cracked eggs into a bowl and whisked in milk. Jesse chopped some mushrooms, and the whole breakfast was on the table in fifteen minutes, his mother's perfect, light and fluffy eggs mounded on everyone's plates next to slightly burnt toast.

"I'm... not much in the kitchen," Aadon mumbled, fingering his too crispy slice.

Jesse smiled at him. "It's perfect."

"You are so full of shit," Sarah snapped.

Miriam pursed her lips. "Sarah, please."

"Well...."

"Well what?" Jesse asked, glaring at her.

"He walked out on you, Jesse. He was a shit."

"You weren't there, Sarah," Jesse reminder her. "You don't know what happened."

"I know you came knocking on my door in the middle of the night. I know you were upset enough to need someone else around to stop you cutting yourself." She jabbed her fork into her eggs, spearing a mushroom and dropping the utensil with a clatter. "I know enough."

"You don't—"

"Did you?" Aadon's head snapped round from where he'd been staring at Sarah, and his gaze pinned Jesse.

"Did I what?" Jesse frowned at him, dread growing in his gut. This was not how he would have wanted to have this conversation.

Aadon just tilted his head, his gaze dancing down to Jesse's arms and back to his face.

Jesse flushed and looked away, but not before he saw Aadon's eyes close in defeat.

"It wasn't your fault," he said, mostly to his eggs. "Everything... got so big."

"I'm sorry," Aadon whispered.

Jesse looked over to find him pushed away from the table, face pale, gaze riveted on Jesse. His eyes were too big, his hands too tense on the arms of his chair.

"What? No! Aadon, don't be sorry because I did something stupid. It wasn't you're fault." He pushed his own chair back from the table and glared at Sarah. "Thank you for your fucking support, because this is *exactly* how I wanted to tell him," he shot at her. "Next time, I'll just keep it to myself."

He stood, whirled on his heel, and fled.

Caught up in his own rage, he realized too late he had nowhere to run to. The living room was wide open to the kitchen and his mother's office locked.

"Well." Miriam's voice clipped off her words. "We handled that well."

"He had to know," Sarah mumbled.

"Not like that." A chair scraped across the kitchen tile as Aadon's voice rose. "You keep trying to protect him, but you just make him doubt himself. Every time he tries, you pull him back, like you think he can't do it on his own."

"And you push. Make him do stuff he's not ready for."

"At least I listen to him!"

"Stop it. Both of you!" Jesse's mother never raised her voice, but now he heard her clearly, even a room away. "You sound like children fighting over a favorite toy. Jesse needs our support."

Jesse glared out the living room window, not seeing much of anything. To have them fighting over him, talking about him like he was some broken prize trophy that needed gluing back together made him sick. Bile burned his throat, and sweat oozed out over his whole body. Careful footsteps approached from behind, and he wrapped his arms around himself, knowing even that was not enough to stop or hide his trembling.

"Jesse?"

"I'm fine, Aadon."

"I'm sorry."

"I *am* stronger than that."

"Then why?"

Jesse shrugged. "I don't want to talk about it."

"You said you were ready to tell me everything," he said softly but firmly. "Are you, or aren't you?" Aadon dropped his hands onto Jesse's shoulders and let them travel lightly down his arms. Dr. Carol had told him to follow his instincts. His instincts told him Jesse needed grounding. Needed safety and support, so he did his best to give him that, gently holding the shorter man against his chest.

Jesse turned, buried his face against Aadon's chest, and sighed. "At least it's out there now, you know?" He settled a little more as Aadon's hands continued to rub lightly up and down his arms. "All this time I've been wishing Mom wouldn't ignore it, or talk around it. I guess part of me wanted attention. Wanted everyone to see how much I was hurting and fix it. And she couldn't even say it out loud. Couldn't ask me why I was doing it, or even *if* I was doing it." He stepped back and scrubbed a hand over his face. "And when you all finally do acknowledge it, I rip you all a new one. I'm sorry."

"You don't have to be sorry."

"Yeah, actually, I do." Jesse managed a smile. "It was a fair question. And the answer is yes, I did think about it. I did go over to Sarah's so I wouldn't be alone in my own head until I got to that point. She means well. I know she does, but it's hard for her to watch me make a mistake that she sees is going to hurt me. She can't just let it happen." He sighed. "Probably because she knows she's the one who has to pick up the pieces, because up to now, I haven't been willing to see I was falling apart." He looked up at Aadon. "Don't be mad at her for trying to hold me back. She's been trying to protect herself, too, and she has every right to do that. I stopped going to her to hold me together. I couldn't hold myself together. And before you go off on a guilt trip, it wasn't your fault. It's the way my brain works, and it's part of what I have to fix. She was there for some, and I'm grateful she was. But this is a thing in me no one can fix but me, and I—" Jesse hauled in a deep breath. "I had to know."

"Know what?"

"Hard to explain. I couldn't understand why I was doing it unless…. God it sounds stupid to say it out loud. Before, I cut myself because everything hurt so much. I couldn't get out of my head, and it gave me something to focus on, something to chase the rest away for a little while. When I started feeling like that again this time, I had to know if it really helped. Or if it just hurt and made me bleed."

"And?" Aadon couldn't quite wrap his head around what Jesse was getting at, but he sensed this was important to him to try and get it out.

"I don't want to be that person. I don't want to bleed everything I am, everything I feel out down the drain. I want to be able to feel it and know I'm still me, even when it hurts."

"When it hurts?"

"Especially when it hurts."

"Do we have the hug fest now, or later?" Sarah asked from the doorway, her voice small and not at all like her usual biting self.

"First." Aadon turned from Jesse to face her. "You obviously have something to say to me."

Sarah's lips went tight, her eyes narrowed, and Jesse cringed. "You hurt him," Sarah accused. "Walked out on him when he needed you."

"Sarah, I'm a big boy," Jesse said.

"Of course you are," she snapped. "And I'm your friend, and he's an ass."

"You're not required to like him," Jesse said stiffly, inserting himself between his best friend and his boyfriend. "But you are required to be polite and keep your shit to yourself."

"We've been friends a long time, Jesse."

"Yes. But that doesn't give you the right to run off my boyfriend or pass judgment."

"Don't worry." Aadon dropped an arm around Jesse, wrapping his forearm across his chest. His glare was all for Sarah. "I'm not running anywhere. Not anymore, and certainly not because of her."

"This is fucking brilliant," Jesse muttered, slithering out from under his arm and leaving them both there glaring at one another. "Just what I need. You two figure out how to get along, because I don't need this, and neither does my mother."

He reentered the kitchen to find his mom still sitting at the table, fork in one hand and charred toast in the other.

She pointed at Jesse's plate. "Sit. Eat your eggs, dear."

"Yes, Mom." He sat, picked up his fork, and glanced up at her. "So. You and Mr. Nivens...?"

When she didn't say anything, he prodded further. "You want to tell me about that?"

"Steven said it might be better if you got a different lawyer, under the circumstances. He's more than willing to talk to one of his colleagues."

Jesse speared some eggs, ate a few bites, and looked back at her. "Is he nice to you?"

"He's a very good man, Jesse, and he wants to see you get the justice you deserve."

"Is he nice to you?" he asked again, frustrated that she was talking around his questions.

At last, she set her fork down and looked at him. "I suspect if I needed him to drive across the country to support me in doing something very frightening and very brave, he wouldn't hesitate for a minute getting into his car and making the trip. Does that answer your question?"

Jesse nodded. "Unless there's some legal reason he can't represent me, I don't want another lawyer."

"I'll let him know."

A few minutes later, both Sarah and Aadon came slinking back to the table to sit and eat their cold eggs.

So much for clearing the air, Jesse thought.

They were almost done with the meal when the there was a knock on the front door. "Hello?"

"Oh!" Aadon sprang up from his chair. "Sorry, Mrs. Turbul. I forgot to tell you. My friend Leo came with, to help with the drive." He rushed to open the door, then turned to look apologetically at Jesse's mother. "Sorry."

"No, no, of course not. Invite him in." She got up and bustled about the kitchen, rounding up fixings for more eggs. Sarah got up and helped her, this time manning the toaster while Jesse made yet more coffee in his mother's tiny machine, and Aadon made introductions.

Leo leaned on the counter near Jesse, and in a lull, he leaned over and winked. "Didn't I say we'd see more of each other?"

Jesse flashed him a nervous smile. "Yeah. Thanks. You didn't have to—"

"Aadon would have made the trip anyway. I thought it would be best if he had a wingman."

"I appreciate that. Thank you." Jesse met his eye. "Really. Thank you for looking out for him."

"I always look out for him. He's my best friend."

Chapter
Eighteen

TELLING the tale for the third time was hard. Talking about sex in front of his mother was bad enough. Talking about kinky sex and how fast and how horribly it could go wrong in front of her was an infinity of discomfort for both of them. When Nivens suggested she might not need to know all the details, she resolutely shook her head.

"I'll leave if Jesse asks me to." She looked over at him, her eyes glassy behind the determined façade.

Jesse could see the tears she wasn't shedding, and the fragile, all-over shivering she couldn't stop. He could also see her resolve to help him through. "This is too hard on you," he said softly.

"It was harder on you when it was happening, and I couldn't be there for you then. I always wanted to be the kind of parent you could talk to, Jesse."

Nivens reached out and took her hand, closing her frailty in his blunt, strong-looking fingers.

"You are, Mom." Jesse managed a small smile as he ripped his gaze up from that connection between his mother and Nivens. "A guy doesn't talk to his mother about sex. Not ever. None of this happened because you weren't there for me. It just happened."

"Well." Nivens let out a huge sigh, placed Miriam's hand on her knee, patted her gently, then rose from his seat beside her. They had been sitting next to one another on the small couch in her office, while Jesse sat in the office chair, pulled around in front of the desk, and Aadon leaned on the desk behind him. Sarah had found a spot with her feet curled under her, her back against the desk within easy reach of Jesse's hand. He had no idea where Leo was. Probably sleeping somewhere, he guessed.

"As I see things," Nivens said, tugging the tails of his shirt straight and sauntering around the desk to where he'd left his briefcase. "If this David person really does want to come forward, there is every chance Bruno is not getting out of prison for a very long time, Jesse. This is an entirely different case, if we have another victim."

Jesse's mother made a small sound in the back of her throat.

"Mom, it's okay." Jesse leaned forward, reaching for her. "I'm not a victim anymore."

She nodded vigorously. "I know." But she was clearly at the very end of her rope, and Jesse didn't know what to do to help her.

"I think we've talked enough for one day," Nivens said brusquely, ushering Jesse, Aadon, and Sarah from the room.

Jesse turned back at the door to peer past him at his mother. "She's—"

"I know, son." Nivens patted his shoulder. "I know."

Jesse wasn't sure how he felt about this guy calling him son or herding him off. "Just—"

"I'll take care of her."

Jesse pursed his lips, and suddenly, he had a good idea how Sarah must have felt, seeing Aadon walk into the kitchen this morning. "Okay," he said at last, casting one last look at his mother. He was leaving her to this man's care. He had not one single reason to doubt Nivens would be gentle with her. He'd been nothing but gentle throughout the entire case, beginning to end. Obviously, his mother liked this guy an awful lot. She stood now, leaning on the desk, one arm across her middle and the other hand playing with the ring she still wore on a chain around her neck. Jesse's father's ring.

She smiled a watery smile at him. "Get some rest, honey," she advised. "This is just going to get harder, from here."

Jesse nodded and turned back to Nivens. "You care about her?"

"I do."

Jesse bit his lip, squared his shoulders. "Do you love her?"

At last, Nivens smiled. "Very much."

Jesse nodded. "Okay." He brought his gaze back from his fidgeting mother to look Nivens in the eye. "Okay, then." He turned and left Nivens to calm her down.

It wasn't all that late in the day. Aadon had slept for a few hours after breakfast, until Nivens had appeared, and he had not left Jesse's side since. Now the three of them stood in the hallway, shuffling feet and looking everywhere but at one another.

"Fifth wheel, again," Sarah commented at last, shoving her hands into the back pockets of her jeans.

"Not fifth wheel," Jesse assured her, dragging her over for a hug. "Not to me."

She sighed heavily and leaned on him. "I wish none of that happened to you," she said at last, her words soaking into his shirt, into his skin, bleeding into his heart.

"It did," he said simply. There was nothing else to say about that. Wish all they might, there was no going back to undo any of it. "You can't take it away. No one can." He rubbed her back and, just for a few minutes, basked in the fact she was there, with him, doing the only thing she could. "I used to think I could just forget about it. That if I didn't think about it, it would go away." He glanced over her head to where Aadon was watching them. "As long as I didn't have any reminders, that was fine, I guess."

She pulled herself upright and gazed up into his face. "But that's no way to live, never having any of the things that remind you what happened."

"Not really." Tucking a bit of stray hair behind her ear, Jesse found he had forgotten just how very real and honest she was, how much she cared about him. "You tried to tell me that. I know. I didn't listen. But I'm doing it now, yeah?" He smiled at her. "And I'm glad you're here."

"I'm glad you're doing this, Jess. However hard it is. You deserve to be happy, finally."

He tossed that remark off with a shrug. He figured the humiliation now was about what it should cost to deal with the mess he'd made of things. Anthony was not going to stop doing what he did, and maybe Jesse could make up for what he'd done to David, and the other guys like him, by making sure Anthony couldn't do those things to anyone else. At the very least, it might help him purge the memories once and for all.

"I could use some food," Aadon announced. "Who's up for a lunch out?"

Sarah pulled herself upright and smiled at them both. "You guys go ahead. I didn't sleep much last night. Think I'm going to find a good book and curl up. Maybe take a nap."

"I could eat," Jesse admitted.

Aadon grinned at him "There must be a good place to buy a veggie burger around here."

"There is a little bistro. Nice walk."

"Sure."

They walked mostly in silence, but Jesse was glad his mother lived in a neighborhood where they could hold hands and not feel conspicuous. He needed the connection right now, still shaky as he was from the afternoon of revelation.

"Your mother is strong, Jesse," Aadon said as they took the same table Jesse and Sarah had sat at two days before. "It's all a shock, maybe, but she'll be okay." He smiled and touched the back of Jesse's hand. "Besides, your lawyer is solidly in her corner."

"I know." Jesse found the more he thought about it, the easier it was to accept. After all, his mother had been alone for over a decade now. Why shouldn't she have someone in her life to care for her the way she deserved? "He loves her."

"They are pretty perfect for each other, if you ask me."

"Okay. It's my mom. I like the guy she's dating." Jesse gave a mock shiver. "That's enough of that."

Aadon laughed, and the sound seemed to brush away a month's worth of shadows and doubts. It felt like the sun had just come out, and Jesse grinned.

"You again." Jesse almost jumped at the sound of an angry voice slamming into the atmosphere. A ripping cold jolt of fear straightened his spine, and he whirled.

"Justin."

The newcomer stood on the other side of the fence, arms crossed rigidly over his chest, face stony.

"Problem?" Aadon set his water glass down and all but got up. He didn't know who this guy was, but he'd be damned if he'd let anyone intimidate Jesse or intrude on their much-needed alone time.

"No." Jesse reached a hand across the table and held Aadon in place with a soft touch. "Aadon, this is Justin. Justin, Aadon."

"I suppose you heard about Anthony," Justin said, barely acknowledging Aadon's presence.

"Yeah."

"You knew all along. That's why you're back in town."

Jesse fought his impulse to lower his gaze. "Yes. I knew. That's why I'm back."

"You came here to find David, didn't you? To talk him into this insanity."

"I swear, I didn't even know his name, or anything about him. I came back to find a way to keep Anthony in jail. That's all. Sarah and I just came here for lunch. I had no idea I'd run into him. Or you."

"That's a lot of coincidences."

"Is it?" Jesse felt the tension pulling his shoulders taut. "This is our neighborhood. Why wouldn't we run into each other? You work at the same place you did two years ago. My mom hasn't moved. This is still a gay-friendly restaurant. So why is it so surprising?"

Justin stared at him for a long moment. "You just leave David out of this. He's been through enough."

"I didn't—"

"Bring him into it? You took him home that night. You let that happen to him."

"I was tied to the fucking bed," Jesse hissed. "I couldn't stop it." Uncontrollable shaking made Jesse's voice quiver, and he balled up his fingers, as though the tight fists would help him hold on to the here and now while his thoughts swirled down the drain into memory.

"You didn't have to bring him there in the first place!" Justin shouted.

"I didn't—I couldn't—" How did he tell this guy, all six foot two of him towering and threatening and angry, that he couldn't have said no to Anthony. He hadn't been strong enough. He'd been too scared.

"That's enough!" Aadon was up now, towering and glaring right back at Justin.

"I'm glad he did come home with us that night," Jesse said quietly. Both men stared at him in shock. Under the thick silence, Jesse found the strength now to look up, meet both of their disbelieving glares in turn. He settled his focus on Justin. "Not at all happy about what happened to him.

That was horrible. No one should have to go through that, and I wish it could have been me instead of him but...." He blinked back the sting in his eyes. "Even after, even when he was... hurt, he said something to me. He stopped, and he untied me, and he told me someone who cared wouldn't do that.... He could have hated me just as much as he hated Anthony, but he didn't. He helped me. He probably saved my life, even if he didn't know it."

"And it almost cost him his," Justin growled. "Do you have any idea how wrecked he was? How many times he didn't come in for a shift, didn't answer his phone? How often I went looking for him and found him passed out drunk just so he didn't have to think about it anymore?"

How many other men had Anthony done that to, who Jesse had never seen again; who weren't as lucky as he'd been to have his mother, or David had been to have this hulk of a man to watch over him?

Jesse pulled in a deep breath, uncurled his fingers, already sore from the tight grip on reality. He pushed his chair back and unbuttoned a shirt cuff. Keeping his focus tight on rolling up his sleeve, knowing Aadon was going to curse hard when he saw, Jesse gritted his teeth, made himself face the truth. He couldn't run from it, couldn't hide from it, with both men standing there watching him. Maybe Aadon would walk out, but even that didn't matter. His face flushed hot as the freshly healing cuts laid over old scars came into view. He kept his gaze on those red lines, remembering the cold nights in his bathroom, watching the blade and the blood, finally understanding the self-mutilation wasn't going to free him of the ugliness inside.

"I know how much it hurts," he whispered. "I know how hard it is to find the right way to deal with it."

"Jesse—"

"Don't, Aadon. Just don't." He looked up, into those deep, beautiful blue eyes. "This had nothing to do with you. You walking out that night... that hurt. This is way older than that. A last, little bit of the guy who didn't want to call a rape a rape." He pulled in a deep breath and found the space inside to appreciate that breath held the scent of his home, of the man across from him, of a whole lot of new things that this old, fading pain couldn't touch. "I'm not that guy any more. I know what happened. I can deal with it."

Aadon sank back into his chair, his gaze never breaking from Jesse's. "Okay." He placed his hand on Jesse's lying palm up on the table and was gratified when Jesse's fingers curled around his. "Okay."

Jesse looked to Justin as Aadon's fingers tightened around his. He could have cried when Aadon reached over to lay his other hand protectively over Jesse's arm. "I didn't ask David to get involved this time. But when I saw him here the other day, I knew I couldn't let him find out in the news or some other way. I had to tell him myself what was going on, so he'd know. So he'd be prepared. He offered to come forward, and all I did was say thank you and gave him my lawyer's card. I told him to really think about it. It doesn't… go away. Pretending it didn't happen, or that it was something else, none of that helped. So I'm not going to pretend any more. I'm going to do what I should have done the first time. I can't put Anthony on trial for raping me that final time. I gave up the right to accuse him of that when I didn't man up the first time. But I can tell them everything else he did. I can tell them I wasn't the only one he did it to.

"I thought it would be okay, because I could tell myself he was behind bars, and he couldn't hurt anyone else. But it wasn't okay, and now, he might get out if I don't do something, and someone else might get hurt. I didn't stop him before when I should have. I'm going to stop him now. I have to. It's the only way I can fix…." He stopped, gulped in a few soggy breaths, and gritted his teeth. "I can't fix what I did. I can't take my part back in what happened to David or the others. It happened, and I can't make it un-happen. But if I tell the authorities what kind of man Anthony really is, maybe it'll never happen again. Maybe that's what David is thinking too."

"He's hell bent on doing this thing. No matter what I say. I don't want him to. He's been sober for months. Good. Strong. If he has to live through it all again…."

"He will anyway," Jesse told him. "He'll live it because he saw me again, because we talked about it, because he probably remembers every time he closes his eyes, or walks into a bar or—" Jesse swallowed hard and lowered his gaze further. "—goes down on you."

"He doesn't—wait. How did you know we were even together?"

Jesse smiled and glanced over at Aadon. "Because I'm beginning to understand how a person reacts when someone they love is in pain and they feel like they can't do anything about it."

Aadon ground his teeth, gripping Jesse's hand almost too tight, but said nothing. He didn't trust himself to speak.

"You said you gave him your lawyer's number?"

Jesse nodded.

"He's a good lawyer?"

"The best."

Justin turned to Aadon. "How do you do it? How do you sit there and be so calm?" He waved a hand at Jesse. "Over all this?"

Aadon grunted. If this joker thought he was in any way calm about any of this, he had no idea. But Jesse didn't need Aadon freaking out. He needed to feel like he was in control, and Aadon hitting the roof over new cuts or having a meltdown of his own watching Jesse, practically in tears as he admitted to a load of guilt he shouldn't feel, would not be helpful. Besides, as much as he hated that Jesse had so much pain to deal with, Aadon was also incredibly proud of him for stepping up, for facing it, no matter how hard it was.

"You just do what you have to," he said at last. "What he needs you to."

"Right." Justin backed up a few steps. "Uh."

"Probably see you around," Jesse offered.

"Yeah." He ran a hand over the back of his neck and nodded. "I guess. Probably. I mean. If he does this, and all." He met Jesse's eye for a moment before his gaze flickered to Jesse's forearm. "You really think it will help?"

"Yeah." Jesse began to roll the sleeve down, once again hiding the marks he'd made on himself. "I think it will. He needed to stop and help me, even back then. I think he probably needs to do this. Why else would he have offered?"

"I guess."

"Just be there for him," Aadon put in. He reached and took Jesse's hand again. "Especially when he's mad and scared. Don't ever walk out on him. Don't let him push you out the door." He glared at Jesse. "Don't ever push me out the door again."

Jesse flashed a guilty smile at him. "'Kay."

"Right. I'll, uh, leave you to it, then." Justin backed away a bit further. "Thanks."

Jesse waved him off. "He'll be all right," he said to Aadon after he'd gone.

"Hope so. For this David person's sake."

Chapter
Nineteen

IN LIGHT of the new testimony Jesse was willing to give, and the fact that David was now going to come forward with his story, the trial date Jesse had come home for was moved, first to a week off, then a month and a half. When David claimed to know other men Anthony had abused, and those men also decided it was time to speak up, Jesse's testimony seemed incidental. In fact, when he was finally ushered in front of the judge, sat in his chambers, and told everything to a video camera, it seemed wholly anticlimactic.

Anthony's get out of jail free card was revoked almost instantaneously once all the evidence was heard. It should have put it all to rest. Should have been the end. Jesse wished it was over.

The thing about wishes and genies and bottles, was that nothing ever went back the way it had been. Aadon had been very careful with him before. Now the kid gloves came out. Dates happened in neutral territory, and kissing, if it happened at all, was next to chaste.

"I have a fucking boyfriend," Jesse whined, flinging books onto the wheeled rack shortly after the last browser had left the library, and he and Sarah were the only ones remaining to clean up the cubicles and replace the reference materials.

"No, you have a boyfriend who doesn't fuck," Sarah pointed out.

Jesse heaved a sigh and gave the cart an almighty shove. It wheeled silently over the carpet and came to rest with a soft clink against the nearest stack, denying him even the satisfaction of a good crash. "Thank you for that assessment. It helps. Really."

"Jess, you have to relax, babe. You know he's just being careful."

"Careful, my ass. He's scared."

"And can you blame him?" Picking one of the books from the cart, Sarah glanced at the spine and wandered off down the next row to shelve it. "Look what happened last time he blew you."

"I should not have told you about that." But he had told her, figuring the best way to get her off Aadon's back was to explain to her just exactly what had happened the night Aadon had left and Jesse had slid into the null space where cutting himself had seemed like a reasonable thing to do. He couldn't say his boyfriend and his best friend were really all that happy about sharing him, but at least they no longer went for one another's throats at every opportunity.

Jesse spent the next few moments fuming and glaring at the taped white stickers on the spines of the books without really seeing them, or the numbers carefully coded to tell him where they fit on the shelves. Not that he was mad at Sarah. Just angry in general and frustrated at the confusing mix of emotions roiling around inside.

Like so often now, a small sifting of memory came back to him. A different library in a different university, and he couldn't even remember why he'd been there. A research paper, maybe. The first one of his freshman year. Only he could clearly remember staring at the shelf beside him, at the yellow stickers with black skateboards. Young Adult fiction, it had been. A dusty, unused section of the library where he could hide and nurse the first bruises. Not the worst. No they'd gotten much worse before he'd managed to get out. But he remembered that corner.

"Jess?" A hand on his arm made him jump. "Babe, you okay?"

"Yeah."

"What were you thinking about?"

"Nothing." He said it too quick. Her expression said she knew he was lying, but for once, she didn't call him on it. She just squeezed his arm and picked up another book. "Let's get this done and get home, yeah? I'm starved. We can order pizza."

"Sure." But that was another thing. He never had a chance to be alone. If Aadon was carefully distant and neutral, Sarah was not. She clung. She hung out, ordered pizza, brought him coffee in the morning, walked him home from work, like she thought the moment she turned her back, he'd be cutting again, or worse.

He couldn't really assure her the thought hadn't crossed his mind, but he could say, without doubt, that he never wanted a reason to hide from

Aadon, and if he had any hope of their sex life picking up, he wanted to remain as scar free as could.

"Actually." He glanced over at her and offered a limp smile, which just made her frown, but he didn't let that change his mind. "I thought I might stop by Aadon's instead."

"Does he know you're coming?"

"No." Jesse shoved the book he was holding onto the nearest shelf. "And I don't have to give him advance warning. He's my boyfriend. He isn't going to mind if I stop by on impulse."

"Okay, okay. Keep your pants on."

"Why would you even ask that?"

"Jess, calm down. No reason. I just wondered. I thought it would be nice to have a night in, is all." She wasn't looking at him. In fact, she was staring at the book in her hands as though she didn't really see it.

"We've had a ton of 'nights in', Sarah."

"I know." Her shoulders twitched, and like that, the pensive mood was gone and she once again bustled about shelving the books while he stood and watched.

"What?" Jesse followed her to the next stack and down the aisle, but she just shook her head. "Sarah, what?"

"Nothing."

"Bullshit."

"Nothing, Jesse. Just drop it. Go. Visit loverboy."

"Sarah, babe, c'mon. What's going on?"

"Jesus, you're fucking like a dog with a bone." Her voice had dropped, though, and he caught a slight sniffle. "Let's just get this done so you can—"

"Are you jealous?"

She snorted. "Of Aadon?" The book in her hand joggled, and she shoved it on the shelf hard enough that the sound of it hitting the metal backstop rang through the empty library. "Hardly."

"Yes, you are."

"I worry about you, Jesse."

"Sure, okay. And I'm grateful, but this is more than that."

"No, it isn't." As she tried to push past him, back to the cart, he stepped in front of her, forcing her to look him in the eye. "What?"

He just tilted his head, waiting.

"Look, I get it, okay? You don't need pizza and movie reruns and the old fag-hag down the hall bringing you coffee every morning any more. Fine. I'll back off."

"Oh, Sarah, come on." He wrapped his arms around her, and the familiar smell of her cherry-scented shampoo wrapped him in a comforting, safe haven of absolute calm. "You are my best friend. Practically my only friend. You've always been there, even when I didn't want anyone, and you did all the work."

"And fucking Aadon Adonis gets all the glory. Bastard."

Jesse chuckled at her deliberate mispronunciation of Aadon's last name. "Please tell me you knew that someday, this was going to happen. Or did you expect me to remain single and doting on you forever?"

"I knew." She really did sniffle, now. There was no mistaking the sound for anything else. "I knew. I just...."

"Just what?" he asked when all she did was stand there, leaning on him and gulping back small, wet sobs.

After a minute, she straightened and rubbed a hand over her damp face, turning from him to pick at the covers of the books still on the cart. "There isn't a straight guy on the planet who will ever be as nice to me as you are."

A sharp guffaw burst from Jesse. "You can't be serious. I'm, like the most neurotic, messed up freak there is. I've given you nothing but angst and worry, and you think that's nice of me? Honey, I am a gay boy with a million issues you cannot fix." He took her hands in his and turned her to face him. "Babe, you deserve so much more than to hang everything on a guy who gives you nothing but grief. You know I can never be what you really need. I'm gay. I'm always going to be gay. Aadon is not stealing me away from you because my relationship with him and my relationship with you are not the same thing." Carefully, he thumbed away the tears streaking her face. "God, I'm an idiot. I was so not paying attention." He hugged her close, feeling, at the same time, like a complete heel.

All this time, he'd leaned on her, let her support him and look out for him, and never noticed how she felt. Of course she'd always known, from day one, that he was gay. But a person couldn't help who they fell in love with, and he'd treated her as poorly as any oblivious, selfish straight guy ever could have.

"Sarah, I am so sorry."

"I gotta...." She shoved herself away from him. "I'm going home." Quickly, she gathered her coat and purse. "I'll call you." Jesse was left standing there watching the door swing shut, a little shell-shocked at what he'd realized, but more so that she hadn't denied it. It took him a moment to realize Aadon was standing just outside watching Sarah hurry away, confusion written all over his face.

Dredging up a smile for his boyfriend, Jesse waved him inside.

"What's going on? Did she—"

"She didn't do anything. I just...." Running a hand through his hair, Jesse turned to the rack of books and began shelving them as quickly as possible.

"You finally noticed she's in love with you?" Aadon asked softly. He was close behind Jesse, and his body heat filled the space between them.

Jesse nodded.

"You know this isn't your fault, right?" Aadon placed a hand on each of Jesse's shoulders, tugging him back until Jesse's back rested against his chest. The poor guy looked so miserable and shocked. Aadon gave in to the desire to wrap his arms around his partner and hold him close.

"Doesn't make me feel like any less of an asswipe for not even noticing," Jesse pointed out. He relished the closeness, the support Aadon was offering, and let himself sink back into the comfort. Both his hands came up to rest on Aadon's bare forearms. "I don't even know what to do now."

"Nothing."

"What do you mean, nothing? I hurt her."

"No. She is hurting, but not because of anything you did. You just have to let her work through it. She does care about you. Give her time."

Jesse leaned his head back against Aadon's shoulder and closed his eyes. "I guess."

For a few minutes, Aadon stood still, holding him, enjoying the simple closeness. Just because he had carefully kept his physical distance from Jesse while the trial and testimony were going on didn't mean he didn't relish every opportunity he had to touch him. He closed his own eyes, concentrating on the feel of Jesse's chest, rising and falling under his arms, and the way his shoulder blades pressed against his chest a little more sharply with every intake of breath. He smelled so good. Felt good. Aadon couldn't remember when just holding another man had seemed like the best thing in the world, the way this did.

It wasn't even about protecting Jesse. Over the course of months since they'd returned from Jesse's hometown, and the trips back and forth to deal with Anthony, he'd come to realize that Jesse needed protection less and less. Not that every day had been good or easy, but Jesse didn't need or want anyone to protect him from what he had to do, once he'd made up his mind to do it.

"So," Jesse said at last, loath though he was to be the one to break the silent spell between them. "Why are you here? My shift doesn't end for another twenty minutes."

"Just came to let you know I was going up to see Ricky."

"I know." Jesse turned around, keeping close so Aadon didn't have to let him go. Thankfully, the bigger man's arms only dropped lower to circle his waist. "Oddly enough, I learned how to read a calendar at the shockingly young age of about six. It's that time of month. Besides,"—he gave Aadon a smile—"you go pretty much every weekend."

"I know." Aadon curled his lip in mock annoyance. "But I thought I would go up today. Stay overnight. Doc thinks maybe he's ready for a bit more. I thought I would take him out to lunch or something."

"That is really, really great news," Jesse said, quashing the stab of alarm. He'd spent so much time under either Aadon's wing or Sarah's, the thought of spending the night with neither of them at his beck and call made his breath catch in the beginnings of a panic attack. He nestled closer to Aadon and focused on the fact this was about Ricky, and not him. He'd just been lamenting the fact they were treating him like a fragile flower. Now was his chance to show them he was perfectly capable of looking after himself.

"It could be." Aadon kissed his hair. "The other option I thought about was bringing you with me." Aadon had entertained the idea enough his hotel reservations included the possibility for a second person in the room, but he'd hesitated to ask, unsure he could control himself alone with Jesse for that extended a period of time. He didn't want to set the other man's progress back even a little bit. He had seen the flash of fear in Jesse's eyes, though, at the mention of him being gone overnight. He knew Sarah was, at least for the moment, out of the picture, dealing with her own issues. He worried more about that anxiousness in Jesse's eyes than he did about his own struggle. If he had to keep his hands to himself, he could. Jesse being okay was more important than his own adolescent libido, or any discomfort he might encounter having to control it.

"Really?" Try as he might, Jesse could not keep the squeak of happiness from his voice.

Aadon hauled in a deep breath. That small sound of pleasure warmed him so much. But if Jesse was going accompany him, he had to know about the sessions Aadon had had with Dr. Carol, first. That could mean quashing that little bit of happiness for Jesse. At some point, Aadon was going to have to tell him. The longer he waited, the harder Jesse would take the deceit. Best to do now and get it over with.

"Jesse, there's something I have to tell you, and you might not be too pleased with me, once you hear it."

Jesse backed up a step so they were no longer pressed close. Only his hands remained on Aadon's chest, and his gaze, suspended somewhere around the level of Aadon's throat. "Okay." Another guy, Jesse wondered. Maybe Aadon was just tired of all the drama. He couldn't blame him, really.

"I've talked to Ricky's doctor a lot."

"Of course you have." A quick study of Aadon's face showed Jesse there was something pulling cords of tension tight within the other man, like bungee cords, and whatever they were holding down was suddenly too big for them to contain. "Maybe we should sit down," he suggested.

By now familiar with the waves of nausea and cold sweat that accompanied anything to do with Anthony or the vague but obviously similar past Ricky had endured, Jesse wanted the chair for himself. Aadon would probably pace. Jesse was familiar with that too. His partner tended to think better on his feet, and the lawyer in him was already striding past the mess of emotions Aadon was struggling to contain, and take over. Jesse could see it in the set of his shoulders and the no-nonsense look on his face.

In a way, it was a relief to see the transformation. It was a power Jesse felt comfortable around, giving him something to fall back on to keep his own nerves and fears under control. It was a power Aadon wore well, a well-fitted robe of confidence he shrugged into whenever his emotions rose close to the surface.

"It started because she was worried about me," he admitted. "Back before you went home that first time. I was a bit of a mess. I didn't know what to do, and I guess"—he shrugged—"I guess she saw that. She asked me what was wrong."

"And you told her?"

"Kind of. Mostly." As Jesse expected he would, Aadon began to pace, and that confidence he'd recently grown into smoothed the tight line of his shoulders. "I told her about you. Not all the details. She's worked very closely with Ricky. She probably knows more about exactly what happened to him with the guy who molested him than anyone but Ricky does. Certainly more than I do. So she figured out almost instantly what was going on with you."

Jesse nodded. So many people knew more than he wanted anyone to know about what had happened to him. He couldn't sort out how he felt about Aadon sharing his secret that wasn't really a secret with a stranger, and without talking to him about it first. He also knew, from watching Justin and David, as well as his own mother, how hard it could be on a person knowing someone they cared about had gone through it.

But Justin's family had rallied around both men, as had a coterie of close friends. And his mom had Steve Nivens in her corner, driving her home at night, holding her close and soothing her. Jesse had to admit the man had been far more than just his legal counsel and advisor through it all, as well. He'd been there, making coffee and sandwiches, fielding phone calls, and ushering everyone to bed when emotions ran so high no one could settle. Jesse had to wonder if his own soldier father, as kind and selfless as he'd been, would have handled it all as well.

Aadon had no one to talk to about any of it. Jesse could hardly begrudge the man accepting the help of a trained professional, when it was something Jesse still had reservations about doing himself, however much everyone around him seemed to think he should.

"So." Aadon glanced to where Jesse was sitting at the table, his hands clasped on it in front of him, beads of sweat forming on his brow. "So, I've been talking to her. Venting, mostly, about how stupid and helpless I feel that I can't *do* anything."

"You do plenty," Jesse said lamely, trying desperately to ignore how cold sweat coated his palms and began to trickle down the side of his face. His stomach roiled, and he tightened his fingers so Aadon wouldn't see them shake.

It tore at Aadon that Jesse fought so hard to contain the volatile sick he always seemed to feel when he was forced to face this, but Aadon managed a smile. "I watch. I stand here, and I watch, and you do all the work."

Miraculously, Jesse managed to shrug, as if he wasn't feeling like he might bring up his lunch any second, and he met Aadon's eye. "But you *do* stand there. Always. Right beside me, and I know you're there, and if that's all you can do, it's all you can do, but it's enough. You think I do it alone, but I don't. Because you're there, and Sarah and Mom and Steve. I'm not doing this by myself." Pushing onto shaky legs, Jesse crossed the floor space between them, needing to feel that cloak of confidence and strength wrap around him too.

"So maybe," he said, when he was securely safe in Aadon's embrace, and he could rest his cheek against the broad, strong chest. "I should also talk to this doctor of Ricky's. If she's worked such miracles with him, then possibly, she can do the same for me. Besides"—he looked up into Aadon's face—"look at you. All brave and confident. I used to wonder how you were going to be any kind of a lawyer if you couldn't talk, but here you are, telling me what had to be a hard thing to confess, and you didn't even flinch."

"Oh, I flinched." Aadon held Jesse tight. "I flinched plenty by not telling you months ago. And I'm sorry for telling your secrets out of turn."

"That's just it." Jesse leaned once again, trusting Aadon to take his weight. "They can't be secrets any more. They shouldn't have been then, and if I'd told back then, how many guys like David would have been spared what he went through? I'm not dumb enough I don't see that Anthony did a lot of damage to a lot of people, not just me. How many times when he left me alone in that shitty apartment was he out forcing some other kid into something he didn't want? We'll never know, but my secrets hurt a lot of people, and me most of all. I don't want to hurt any more. The more I say it out loud, the less power it has to hurt me. Some people might think less of me for letting it happen, but those people won't ever get it until they're in it, and I hope to hell they never, ever have to get it.

"The people who do understand can help me stop it. Knowing that I helped to make it so that he can't do it to anyone else makes me feel less like a victim, and more like I matter."

What could Aadon do in the face of Jesse's little speech but agree?

Chapter
Twenty

ONCE again, Aadon found himself driving down that long stretch of highway toward Ricky with company next to him, and he reflected how different it felt to not be doing this alone, like he had for so very long.

"I won't know until we get there how Ricky's feeling this weekend. If he seems up for it, I'll introduce you, but if not...."

"Don't worry. This is about him. If he's not ready, we'll wait and do it another time."

"I just don't want you to feel like I'm keeping you out."

Jesse smiled at the passing scenery. "I won't."

"Okay."

Silence settled, though Jesse felt it weighed down by something Aadon seemed unable to share or ask. "Are you protecting me again?" He asked quietly.

"I don't know what you mean."

"I mean, I can feel it. There's something on your mind, but you're not saying it. Is that because you're trying to protect me? Because you think I might get mad or be hurt? I'm not fragile, you know. I do get mad, and I do get hurt, but I don't appreciate being treated like I can't handle those things. I can. And I resent you making those kinds of decisions for me without even consulting me as to whether or not it's a subject that matters to me."

For a long time, the only sound was the low music of The Doors CD that was playing and the road sounds of the car whizzing down the highway. A few times, Jesse glanced over, but Aadon's expression was unreadable, his face stony and still as he watched the road ahead. Jesse let him keep his silence this time.

"Maybe," Aadon said at last. "It isn't you I'm protecting."

Jesse swallowed his surprise, which resulted in a strangled kind of grunt, and he felt Aadon glance at him. Did he think Jesse didn't get he had to be careful around Ricky? What did he think? That he'd go blundering in there and dredge up all the things Ricky had spent a decade avoiding? Jesse was in the throes of that kind of turmoil. How could Aadon think for a minute he would inflict it on anyone else?

"This is the first time anyone has come to see Ricky with me. Even Thea stays away. Leo and Mike have driven up with me once in a while, but they never come to the clinic, never mind coming in to say hi to Ricky, and they're my best friends. They knew him growing up, before he tuned the world out. Okay, maybe he wasn't the greatest guy back then, but he wasn't always bad, either. Our own parents can't stand to see what he is now, or admit he's their son."

"I'm not going to do anything to Ricky," Jesse mumbled, feeling at once angry Aadon didn't trust him and stupid for feeling angry. Of course Aadon would be careful. He was responsible for his brother's happiness and wellbeing, in whatever small doses Ricky was able to find either anymore. Jesse couldn't blame him for wanting to protect every scrap of joy they had left. "If you don't want to take me to see him, you don't have to. I understand." And he did. In his head. His heart would catch up.

"It isn't that at all."

"What, then?"

"I love you so much for doing this with me. For being the one to understand how much I need to not be doing this on my own any more, and being there for me. I can't even tell you what that's worth."

This time, Jesse's shock took even his breath, and no sound came out at all.

"I should be happy and grateful to you for that, and I am."

"But?"

"I spent three hours this morning before I came to the library to get you agonizing over how to make hotel reservations. I couldn't afford two rooms and didn't want to ask for two in case you didn't want to come. I can't even afford the cancellation fee. So one bed or two? I didn't know how to ask you to come with me. I worried seeing Ricky would just remind you of everything and you'd break down. I was so mad at you for making it so I had you to worry about, too, and furious with myself, because believe me, I know how stupid irrational all that is."

Jesse said nothing. For long minutes, he grappled with his own anger, even while he realized Aadon was trying to make him understand something important. He kept his mouth shut, fearful of saying something that would shut them both down.

"I didn't know what to do," Aadon said at last. "And I got all up in knots being mad that I had to come up here for his meeting for him, and that I had to worry about you, too, and what was I going to do with you while I went to my own therapy session, how was I going to tell you I was going to see a shrink to get my head around us, and I was mad and tired and—"

"And an idiot."

"What?" The car rocked slightly side to side as Aadon's head whipped around so he could stare wide-eyed at Jesse.

Jesse gripped the console. "Road!" He pointed.

"Sorry." Aadon turned, miserable, to glare at the yellow stripes swishing past the front hood. He should have kept his mouth shut. It was his own stupid inability to cope that was the problem, not Jesse or Ricky. He shouldn't have said anything.

"You got all up in knots over a hotel reservation? Did it occur to you to just ask me?"

"I know what you'd say," Aadon replied, resentment curling into tight curds in his gut.

"Oh, you do." Jesse crossed his arms over his chest. "So what would I have said?"

"You would have said one room. One bed, and I would have spent the entire night—"

"Fuck you, Aadon."

"Wha—" Air rushed out of Aadon as though Jesse had gut punched him.

"You've spent years looking after Ricky, making decisions for him because up to now he hasn't been able to make them himself. You think you can step into my life and start making those decisions for me too. Like I don't have a mind of my own, a right to want what I want and do what I want. Well, fuck you. I do have my own mind, and I do know what I want, and I am perfectly capable of making my own choices."

Aadon tightened his grip on the steering wheel, trying hard to suck enough breath into himself so he didn't pass out at the wheel.

Jesse turned until his leg was twisted up, and he could face Aadon. It was about time he said this, and for once, Aadon couldn't turn the tables on him, couldn't pat his head and walk away and avoid the conversation he'd been avoiding ever since their ill-fated first attempt at making love. If it was unfair to do this while he was a captive audience, too the fuck bad.

"I learned a few things under Anthony, Aadon." Jesse forced the nausea down. He was going to get this out, once and for all, and he was going to get over the feeling that screwed his gut into twisting agony. "Sure, I learned the hardest way possible, but I learned. If I didn't *like* being tied down and submitting, he never would have gotten as far into my head as he did. I confused what was happening between the sheets and what I wanted to happen in his heart that never did, and he knew that. He took advantage of it. But I came out of it all alive and smarter. I know what I like in bed, and I know wanting it doesn't make me weak. Being able to give me that doesn't make you stronger than me. That's what Anthony wanted me to believe because it's what he wanted to believe about himself. He was wrong.

"And I know how much you care about me to hold back. I know how hard that must be, because I've been holding back too. Believe it or not, I'm not the only frightened, fragile one in this relationship." He reached over and ran his fingertips over Aadon's knuckles, white on the wheel. "I'm not the only one who needs protection."

With a tiny sigh, Aadon tugged the visor down to keep the setting sun out of his eyes, and nodded. "I know." The words were so tiny. He barely moved his lips to get them out, but miraculously, he did get them out.

And like that, the nausea and the sick evaporated, and Jesse was left with a clear view of the man he loved now, the relationship he wanted now. "I might want to surrender to you in bed, Aadon, and I hope you still want that. But I am not ever going to surrender my life to anyone, ever again. Not the way I did with Anthony. He didn't deserve me, and I don't want that kind of helplessness ever again."

"And you don't think submission is a kind of helplessness?"

"No." Jesse settled around straight in his seat again. "I can give you control in bed. I can put my faith in you to look after me and not hurt me. That isn't helplessness. That's trust, and I think you're worthy of it.

"But I can't give over my life and everything I am and want and believe and feel, and it isn't because I don't trust you." Jesse fixed his gaze on the road ahead, on the tall trees guarding the pastures beyond with their wide old trunks and skeletal hands, now long devoid of leaves. "It's because I can't trust myself," he admitted quietly. "I can't trust myself to not lean on you too much. Outside of sex, I need to stay present in my own skin, keep track of the world and what I need, because I got lost once." He ran a hand up and down his forearm, still able to feel the tingling where the newer cuts had healed over the damaged nerves. "Got lost inside myself and tried to deny I was lost even while I was trying to slice my way out. I don't ever want to go back there, and it isn't fair to you to ask you to take on that burden of keeping me here. I can do it myself." He bit his lip hard, clenched his fists. "I *have* to do it myself. For both our sakes."

Silence rolled down the highway with them, cohabitating with the sound of the wheels on the tarmac and the stereo rocking through more Doors songs.

"I'll need help," Jesse said after a good chunk of time had passed. "I'll need to talk about stuff, and I might not want to talk to you about it. Again, not because I don't trust you. Just because I want my feelings about Anthony and what he did to be separate from us. From you. At least for now. And I want to be able to have something with you that isn't about you looking after me."

"And when something I do brings it all back? Like it did that night?"

"Then I'll tell you." Jesse reached over and rested his hand on the seat close to Aadon. "Like, for instance, one of the things Anthony used to do, at the beginning, that made me feel like he was taking care of me was to plan our dates. He wouldn't ask me what I wanted to do. He'd just assume he knew, I thought. Really, he just disregarded what I wanted altogether, but usually, he got close enough to what I liked doing, at first I just thought he was trying to be thoughtful, relying on his experience to show me a good time. Then, when it started to get too far from comfortable, if I said anything, he'd get sarcastic, condescending. I felt like a stupid kid. So I stopped complaining. Eventually, he had me so cowed, so bullied, I'd be the one to pick out the guys he'd make me do things with even though I hated it, and he knew I hated it."

"So what? You see me making hotel reservations without telling you was me treating you like Anthony did? How is that keeping me and him separate?" Aadon didn't want the resentment to come through, but he knew it did by the way Jesse's hand retreated across the car seat to rest in his own lap.

"I know it's different with you. You made the reservations before you even asked me to come, but that's because you had to make them before you got a chance to see me. And I don't for one second think you would have made me feel bad if I said I didn't want to come with you. But you assumed you knew what I would say about the beds without asking me, and I deserve more than that."

"Okay." Aadon pulled in a deep breath, trying desperately not to close up. This was hard, and he was so tired of everything being hard. "So what would you have said?"

"I would have suggested getting a double room. With a double bed, and a single one, because we can't know right now how the entire weekend is going to go, and that way, we'll have options."

Aadon huffed out a breath. "Why do you have to be so fucking reasonable?"

Jesse smiled a small, contented smile. "Because. Like I said, I'm not the only one who's vulnerable here. You think I don't see how strung out you are? You've been going nonstop since that drive to my mom's and what with Ricky turning around, and the trial, and exams. And on top of that, you worry about me all the time. How you keep your head above water, I don't even know."

"I'm not, Jess." Aadon swung his head back and forth, like he could shake off the cloud of emotion descending on him. "I am this close"—he held up a hand, thumb and forefinger scant millimeters apart—"to feeling like I'm gonna sink." He couldn't have stopped the stinging tears from escaping if he tried. There was no way to outpace the feelings, here, no way to turn his back long enough to draw that lawyer façade around himself for protection. Instead, he blinked rapidly, attempting to keep his vision clear so he didn't run off the road.

"Okay." Jesse put a hand on his shoulder. "Okay. Pull over. Stop, Aadon. Just stop for five minutes, and let me take care of things."

Jesse couldn't have said anything more right in that moment. Aadon pulled the car over to the soft shoulder, thankful they were close to the old parking lot of an abandoned building so they didn't have to leave the ass end of the car out in traffic. Dust billowed past them on the cold breeze as he lowered his forehead onto the steering wheel and tried to breathe without breaking down. Jesse just sat with him, an arm around his shoulders, his face close so Aadon could feel his warm breath on his neck and ear.

"Baby, if you're not ready to have sex with me, I'm okay with that," Jesse told him. "It's big, and it could go wrong. I'm not sure where my head's at yet. I'm not willing to pressure you into it any more than you want to pressure me."

"There." Aadon sniffled and released a wet laugh. "There you go being reasonable again."

"Well, so? I'm not a freaking diva drama queen all the time."

"I know." Aadon straightened and twisted around so he could pull Jesse into his arms, as awkward as it was with the steering wheel digging into his side. He wanted his boyfriend in his arms for a minute, to feel his breath and his warmth and be able to hide a little bit. "I saw you in court watching Anthony get his ass slammed back inside for the rest of his life. I saw you being calm for David and your mom. I'm not blind. I'm just...." He leaned back again, withdrawing his hands until he had them cupped around Jesse's face. "I'm not. I see you, what you're capable of. And I see the scars and the fear, and all I know is Ricky. Sometimes I get so afraid to hope."

"I am not Ricky." Jesse ran a thumb over Aadon's wet cheek. "I'm not. Don't be mad at me for saying this, but I'm stronger than that. He was so young. How could he possible process what happened to him when no one around him would see it? When everyone chalked it up to him being a high-strung kid trying to get attention when that horrible thing was going on, and the people who were supposed to protect him refused to see? He couldn't. It wasn't his fault. But I wasn't that young. People did see. My friends, David, and he made me recognize it for what it was. I got out. I'm still getting out, but I *am* getting out. Never doubt that."

Aadon nodded. "Sometimes I think you're actually the strong one here," Aadon said, sniffling through the confession.

Jesse smiled, warmed by that admission, not just that Aadon could see he *was* strong, but that he trusted him enough to admit he felt this weak, even if he was doing it obliquely. "You know, you can just let me be strong for you, sometimes. That's what this relationship shit is about anyway."

"Yeah." Aadon nodded. You're right. So, tough guy. Drive for a while?"

Jesse laughed softly, pulled Aadon close, and kissed him with conviction. "Gladly. You will sleep until we get to town and I need directions, yeah?"

"Sleep." Aadon nodded, surprised how good that idea sounded. "Yeah."

THE motel Aadon had chosen wasn't spectacular. It was what a student could afford for two nights on a limited budget, which made Jesse aware that sometime in the past few months when he was dealing with Anthony, Aadon had begun to behave more and more like any other destitute student, and Jesse had barely noticed. At some point, he was going to have to ask Aadon about that.

Now, he wasn't about to complain. The room was clean and sat at the far end of the motel, away from the highway. Sliding doors led to a small stone patio looking out over a duck pond and a line of trees that bordered a ball field on the other side. The two beds meant the desk clerk didn't raise an eyelash when they checked in, and though Jesse wouldn't have cared if he did kick up a stink, he could see Aadon was still very much balanced on the edge of his knife. Jesse didn't want anything to tip him over to where he wouldn't be able to get the rest he needed for the long meeting with Ricky and his doctor in the morning.

Inside their room, Aadon flung his backpack with his clothes onto the floor beside the small dresser and flopped across the nearest bed. "God. I'm more tired than I should be."

Jesse eased down beside him and ran a hand in circles over his back. "You've been under a lot of strain. Takes it out of a guy."

"I guess."

"I'm not guessing. I know." Jesse shifted his weight. "Get this shirt off. You need a good deep tissue massage and a nap. We'll go find some dinner after, and I'm buying."

"We can go ask the concierge for the nicest veggie plate in town," Aadon said sleepily.

"After you sleep, maybe." Jesse helped him pull the sweatshirt he was wearing off over his head and encouraged him to spread out on his stomach. He spent most of the next hour kneading softness back into Aadon's hard, tense shoulders and back. By the time he was done, Aadon was all but asleep, and Jesse nagged him until he'd slipped out of his jeans and crawled under the blankets.

Not tired himself, Jesse pulled out a textbook and settled on the mattress beside him to read. He was barely comfortable when Aadon shifted, wiggling until his back was pressed hard up against Jesse's hip. He subsided then and snored softly for more than two hours.

Jesse's stomach began complaining around the two-hour mark. He managed to ignore it for another twenty minutes before he had to leave Aadon snoring while he actually did go back to the front office and inquire after a place that would serve vegetarian food. The clerk recommended a nearby bistro and even handed over a menu for Jesse to take back to the room. He called the place, and the busboy who answered took his order and volunteered to deliver it on his way home after the end of his shift.

"I so live in the wrong city," Jesse murmured as he hung up the phone. He leaned over to get a glimpse of Aadon's sleeping features. "Sometimes I forget people can actually be nice just because." He stroked his fingers through the over-long hair falling across Aadon's eyes. Finally, he looked peaceful, and Jesse had to berate himself for not realizing how stressed the other man had become over the past few weeks. "That because of me?" he wondered out loud. "Well, no more. My turn to look out for you, for a change. I'm sorry it took so long for me to get my shit together."

He was just happy he had done so, before the stress split them apart.

Aadon noticed the moment Jesse's warmth left the bed, but he didn't stir. He heard the door open and close, but he didn't roll over or call out. He wasn't sure he was ready to face Jesse after his spectacular meltdown. A few minutes later, when the door opened again, and he felt Jesse's presence back in the room, it was all he could do not to breathe a deep sigh of relief. He listened to Jesse order their food, amazed that even through all his own hell, Jesse had been paying enough attention to know Aadon would prefer pork ribs and roasted potatoes over steak and fries. That made him smile and almost feel big enough to stop pretending to sleep.

Then Jesse was once more crawling carefully onto the bed beside him, and all that warmth and care wrapped around him from behind. He leaned a little into Jesse's body, stretched out at his back, felt where his own not-so-small ass curved in against Jesse's hips, and his broad back rested against Jesse's much thinner chest. And still, he didn't feel like the strong one.

With Jesse's last words, Aadon gave up the pretence and rolled a little more to blink up at him in the dim light from Jesse's bedside lamp. "Is what because of you?" he asked.

"The stress. You've been under so much strain, and I barely noticed. What's going on? Is it me?"

"No!" Aadon reluctantly sat up out of Jesse's embrace and drew his knees up so he could lean on the headboard and hide a bit behind them. It must be a natural thing. He'd seen Jesse do it, and Ricky, and now, it seemed, it was his turn. "It's…." He pulled in a breath and let it out in an exasperated sigh. "Everything at home's gone tits up. I called my mom a few weeks ago. Something Dr. Carol said to me got me thinking, and so I called Mom and asked if she would come visit Ricky with me. She might have said yes, too, eventually, but my dad got on the phone and—" He stopped, remembering the tirade, the cursing and vitriol his father had spewed across the country and the phone line at him, and closed his eyes against the memory.

"And what, Aadon? What happened?" Jesse laid a hand on Aadon's knee, moving closer so he could reach his other hand over and tuck it behind Aadon's bent head. Gently, he kneaded the neck muscles already cramping up again. "Talk to me."

"He's said it before, you know?" Aadon said finally, blinking hard, determined he wasn't going to cry over this again. "He's through with Ricky. He's said it, and he means it, even though up to now, he's paid the hospital bills, he's not set foot near the place in almost three years. Hasn't seen Ricky in over five. After all this time, he still wants to believe Ricky made it all up, that it was some excuse to explain the drugs and everything else. He's just decided Ricky's a fuck-up not worth his time. He's kept Mom away, too, because she won't do a thing to go against him. Some old-school crap loyalty to him. Against her own fucking son." He shook his head and realized he'd clenched his hands around the sheets. He let the creases go and spread his hands over his knees.

Jesse shifted slightly closer so he could twine his fingers through Aadon's "You said up to now he's paid the bills."

Aadon nodded. Now his anger far outweighed the need to cry. "He's cut us both off. Disowned me the minute I told them about you, and refused to pay another cent toward Ricky getting better. Now he refuses, just when he might actually *be* getting better." He let out a hard snort. "How's that for crap timing, huh?"

A long tingle of reality cascaded through Jesse, just under his skin, head to toe. "Yeah, well...." He moved, spread himself in a protective ring around Aadon and pulled him over until his shoulder thudded into Jesse's chest. "We'll figure something out."

Aadon said nothing, caught between deep gratitude to Jesse and a pit of worry over the fact his loving man had no idea what the stakes really were.

"I have a bit of savings. I can talk to my mom about getting my hands on it."

"No." Aadon sat up, pulled himself together as much as he could sitting on the bed, at the edge of tears and in his underwear. "No. You are not pulling your savings out to help me."

"Like hell." Jesse smiled and brushed hair out of Aadon's face again. "Even if just to get you a frickin' hair cut." That, at least, tugged a reluctant answering smile onto Aadon's face, and Jesse hurried on before he could interrupt again. "Ricky is your brother, and that makes him my family too. So you don't get to dictate what I do to help family. Also." He drew in a deep breath, knowing Aadon would probably turn down his next proposal, but determined to make it anyway. "I live in a rent-controlled building, and even now, the rent's a bit steep. If you move in, we can make it easily, and we'll have some left over for Ricky."

"Jesse—" A knock on the door interrupted him, and he yanked the slipping sheets over his pantless legs.

"Hold on." Jesse got up and hauled his wallet out of his pocket. "That's food. No more talking about this until you have something solid in your belly."

They sat at the small table in silence, each with his own thoughts. Jesse refused to talk about anything but the weather and the view until Aadon had eaten his fill. Then he insisted they watch *Breakfast at Tiffany's* on the hotel pay-per-view. There was a lot to discuss, but Jesse was determined to give Aadon one night of relief from all the stress and worries and just let him relax. He counted it a success when Aadon finally settled, peaceful against him where he sat with his back to the headboard. Aadon nestled between his legs, and Jess let his hands rove, slow and aimless over Aadon's Trent University T-shirt.

"God, you feel good," Aadon admitted.

Jesse smiled and kissed his hair. "You too."

"I didn't mean to fall apart like that, Jess, I'm sorry."

Jesse squeezed him and rested his cheek against the side of Aadon's head, breathing in the tranquility they'd managed to create between them. "Nothing to be sorry for. You might be used to carrying all this on your own, but you don't have to any more. I'm here. Let me help."

"By offering to share that itty bitty dinky little apartment?"

"It's got a perfectly good bed, and a decent kitchen. I think. Not that I ever use it, but it has a fridge and stove."

"You don't think we'd be cramped?"

"I think if it helps you take care of Ricky, I can stand the extra furniture." Jesse was amazed Aadon hadn't latched on to the one bed issue. He didn't dare mention it again. "Although, we can keep your couch and ditch mine. It sucks."

"Hard as a rock," Aadon agreed.

"Does this mean you're accepting my offer?"

"It's a huge step, Jess."

"The only other person I've ever lived with is Anthony. I know exactly how huge it is. What other choice do we have? You have bills to pay, tuition to pay, textbooks, exam fees, and you have to eat. If we share rent, that's one thing you don't have to worry about."

"And a whole host of others I do have to worry about. It's more than just sharing rent, and you know it."

Jesse stilled his hands on Aadon's warm body. "I'm far enough into this relationship, Aadon. I know I'm in for good. If it's going to work, I want to start. There's no more point in waiting. If you're not there, then maybe I shouldn't meet Ricky tomorrow." Jesse waited, his heart hammering staccato against his ribs. Surely it was pounding hard enough Aadon could feel it against his back. His skin prickled, another bout of reality skimming along just under the surface. "Say something."

Aadon didn't know what to say. From the beginning, he'd expected to be the one waiting for Jesse to catch up, and here he was, on the receiving end of what almost sounded like a proposal. And a well thought out one, besides. Every nerve ending in him tingled on high, waiting for his mouth to say yes. If he could just get his brain to shut the hell up and get out of the way.

"Okay." Jesse clamped his teeth hard on his lower lip to keep it from trembling. He was trapped under Aadon's silent weight as every muscle tensed for flight. He dragged his hands up Aadon's torso, ready to push him off, but Aadon grabbed both his wrists and held on. Tight.

"You are scary brave, Jesse, you know that?"

"I said already today, I want what I want. I don't see any point in dancing around this trying to guess what you want. Either it's me or it isn't. I have a lot of issues. You know what they are." He trembled in Aadon's tight grasp. "Either you want to take them on or you don't, and if you don't, that's okay. Just tell me now."

Instead of replying, Aadon pressed Jesse's right hand to his chest. "Leave that where it is," he instructed. He could feel Jesse's constant shivering, but the hand remained where it was. Slowly, Aadon turned Jesse's other hand over and pushed his sweater sleeve up. Jesse's shivering escalated to full on trembling, but he didn't otherwise move as his scars came into view.

Drawing Jesse's hand up toward his lips, Aadon let his thumb drift lightly over the fine white lines crisscrossing Jesse's inner forearm. "Do you know what I find the sexiest part of a man?" he asked.

Jesse shook his head, eyes riveted on his own marred skin. It took a moment to realize Aadon had stopped all movement, waiting for him to answer since he obviously couldn't see Jesse's head movement from where he lay facing away from him. Swallowing hard to get the fluttering nerves back down somewhere they didn't impede speech, Jesse dug for something coherent. "What?" Just a tiny, whispered word.

"Hands." Aadon ran his fingers over the back of Jesse's hand, gliding over the bones of his wrist. "Wrists, forearms." His fingers continued their path, sliding up over the many scars, some still pink, others almost completely faded away. "The way the muscles move, slide, and bunch when a person's hands move. That soft, pale skin here." He pressed his lips to Jesse's scars. "Even on a guy, this skin is so smooth and perfect over those muscles."

Jesse jerked his hand free, tried to yank his sleeve back down, humiliated at the mocking. His skin there was far from smooth or unblemished, but Aadon laid his hand flat over Jesse's right one, keeping it pinned to his chest. Everything inside Jesse began to unravel. After everything, there could not be a streak this cruel in the man he'd come to love.

Purposely, Aadon kept his restraining hand light. Jesse could choose to pull away if he wanted. Aadon gave him the choice. "Leave this hand here, I said."

"You're making fun—" Jesse curled his fingers, gripping folds of Aadon's worn T-shirt, fighting not to fold in on himself.

"No." Aadon released Jesse and rolled over, going up on his knees and placing a hand on the mattress on either side of Jesse's hips so he could look into Jesse's angry eyes. "No. I'm serious. I have a thing for arms."

"Yeah. Pure, perfect—"

"Strength. The way the muscles move. The way the delicate bones twist and reform every time a person moves their hands." Aadon sat back on his heels and took Jesse's bared arm in his hands once again and dropped his gaze to the trace work of lines. "The way all these scars put everything you are right there on your skin for everyone to see. They cover up that strength in you, disguise it so even I didn't see it. Not at first, but there it is." He kissed Jesse's palm, licked at the pulse point on his wrist, moved his lips and tongue along in slow, deliberate increments. Every once in a while he glanced up to see Jesse watching him, fascinated.

Jesse wasn't shaking any more. He wasn't sure if he'd gone beyond shaking right into shock, or what.

Aadon ended when he reached Jesse's elbow, planting a soft kiss in the fold and lifting his head. "I'll tell you what, Jesse Tyler Turbul. More than anything since the very first time I sat in a movie theatre beside you watching maybe the worst movie ever made, I've wanted to make love to you." He pushed his fingers into the hair at the back of Jesse's neck and plucked a quick, gentle kiss from him.

Jesse reciprocated, or tried to, as the other man's lips were there and gone so fast he barely had a chance to register the fact. Aadon's touches, his quiet strength fascinated him, made it impossible to control the wild beat of his heart shattering through his fear and drumming up desire from someplace in him he'd completely forgotten existed. Or maybe this was something new, something he'd never known. He didn't think, with the way Anthony had flayed him open and left him to bleed his life and his secrets out in a courtroom, that there was anything left in him not tainted by those experiences. But here was something he'd never felt before. He clung to it, eyes glued to Aadon's as the man spoke.

"I've wanted to spread you out under me, open you up, and get inside, figure out what it is about you that makes you this wonderful, amazing, intoxicating creature that I cannot...." Aadon clamped his mouth shut. Yes, he wanted all those things. Jesse was sitting there, staring at him, frozen, eyes wide while he ran on about taking him over. What kind of idiot was he? He couldn't think of a better way to completely freak Jesse out than to play this stupid Dom card now.

"Ca-can't what?" Jesse asked, aware his voice shook, and his gaze had gone a little glassy. That was probably because, as hard as his heart was pounding, it had just pumped every ounce of blood in his body into his dick and left his brain cells to die off one at a time. Another dose of reality skittered along under his skin and set it on fire. If Aadon said one more word in that soft, sexy, completely domineering voice, he was going to splooge in his pants, and wouldn't that just be the most perfectly humiliating thing he could do now.

"Jesse, say no."

"I don't want to say no."

"Because if you don't say it now...."

Jesse lifted both hands to cup Aadon's face and hold it still while he leaned forward to plant a silencing kiss on Aadon's parted lips. It took only a millisecond of tempting him with a flick of his tongue to get Aadon to kiss him back, and Jesse closed his eyes, sighed into the possession Aadon took of his mouth. He knew it was coming, and he welcomed it with everything in him.

It lasted forever and not even close to long enough before Aadon was moving his lips down along Jesse's jaw and throat. Jesse's hands trailed along his face, eventually sifting through his long hair as the kissing and licking continued toward his ear.

"Not ever going to say no to this," Jesse whispered.

Aadon said nothing, but continued to kiss and taste even while he forced himself to go slow and think things through. Jesse was strong. He believed that. He'd seen ample proof. He wanted the other man like a dying plant wanted sun and water. He'd pictured it often enough, Jesse arching up under his kisses, wanting more, always more, and he knew he wanted, needed to give until Jesse was so sated he couldn't move. But he had to do it right. It had to be everything Jesse had never known under Anthony and still fulfill the insatiable desire Jesse had to please and obey.

Aadon drew his focus back to Jesse's lips, kissed him thoroughly, and pulled back. "Your sweater's in my way," he said, fingering the material at Jesse's collar. "Take it off."

Jesse did, fingers shaking slightly. This was the true test. Aadon would see every scar. He'd seen the old ones. But now he would see the new, the ones too recent for Jesse to blame on Anthony. He tossed the sweater off the side of the bed and, for the life of him, could not raise his gaze to meet Aadon's. It was all he could do not to fold his arms around himself and hide.

"Hold them out," Aadon said, softening his voice to the gentlest of commands. He didn't have to elaborate. Jesse would choose to obey or choose to question, and that would give Aadon the clue he needed. If he could share this most soul-bearing intimacy with Aadon, then he really was healing, and Aadon knew he was ready to move forward.

Jesse did as he was asked, laying his arms and hands, palm up, along his jeans-clad thighs. For a minute, they both gazed at the tracery of pink and white lines like macabre lace covering his skin. "I'm not ashamed of anything I am, Aadon."

"What I can't do," Aadon said after a minute, as he traced his fingers down those pale, marked arms, "is ever let you go." He lifted Jesse's chin and looked into his soul-stealing brown eyes. "I am too far into you to ever get out. I'll have to move in with you, because I already need to breathe you like air."

Jesse touched just the tips of his fingers to Aadon's cheek, awed by the continued acceptance. "I cannot believe I ever thought you were too tongue-tied to be a lawyer."

"Very funny."

Jesse grinned, but it dropped away quickly. "You're going to make love to me, right?"

"Now?" Aadon lifted an eyebrow and tilted his head. "After that little remark? I should make you beg."

Jesse's grin came back, though shyness kept it softer than he might have liked. "I'm good at begging."

"You will be by the time I'm through with you." Aadon shifted backward, yanking Jesse by the legs so that he was splayed out on his back on the bed. "You sure you're ready for me?"

"Ungh." Jesse landed with a huff, but a shot of exhilaration flashed through him, and he nodded. "Positive. Do your worst."

"Oh, but Jesse, baby, you deserve the very best."

"You can be very cheesy, you know."

"And here I was going for silver-tongued. Now I'm going to have to kiss you stupid, since otherwise, you're far too mouthy."

Jesse grinned. "I'm hoping very soon you learn to appreciate my mouth."

"Hmm." Aadon ran a thumb over Jesse's lips and looked down on him from where he now straddled the smaller man's prone form. "I could fill it up. That would certainly cut down on the smart remarks." He leaned close to offer a fleeting kiss while one hand continued to flutter over Jesse's body, touching down lightly every few inches. "Do you like having a cock in your mouth?"

A delicate shiver ran through Jesse. "I might like anything we do when you touch me so gentle, like that."

"As long as you understand that's all it's going to be for now, gentle touching. We haven't talked properly about anything else, and we have to before we go into any sort of scene."

"Touching is good." Slowly, Jesse raised his hands and ran his fingers along Aadon's jaw. "Touching is very good." His gaze followed his fingers to Aadon's lips and fixated there. "Kissing too." He lifted his head, meeting Aadon's lips with his own, pushing at the kiss until Aadon took over, and his roving hand slid into Jesse's hair.

The grip was light, not enough to make Jesse feel constricted, but it was enough to guide him. It held him in place, and conversely, gave him the freedom to let go of some of the tight restraint he was holding onto.

As Jesse's light kiss turned into a parted-lip sigh, Aadon breathed in that tiny sound of surrender and took possession of the moment. Jesse was perfectly happy with the soft touches and firm, gentle control Aadon took of their lovemaking if his low moans and pleased gasps were anything to go by.

"Touch me however you want, Jess," Aadon whispered as he peppered kisses down his front. Tentative fingers played in his hair, and he pressed smiling lips against Jesse's belly so Jesse could feel his smile. "Yeah," he murmured, licking lightly into the neat divot of Jesse's bellybutton. "I like that. Keep going."

Jesse's fingers moved a tad more confidently, and his belly quivered with each tiny sigh he released. Aadon pushed aside the abiding anger that rose, thinking how Jesse had been denied this for so long he didn't even know what he liked, but only what he didn't. Resolute, he replaced the anger with a silent promise to teach his lover every joy his body had to offer.

Splaying his own palms flat over Jesse's body, Aadon explored with lips and tongue, alert for the slightest tension in Jesse's muscles. Taking his cue from his earlier misstep, he avoided Jesse's cock in favor of lavishing tender attention everywhere else.

"You're teasing," Jesse complained, his voice soft and breathy.

Aadon ran his tongue in a long sweep from Jesse's inner thigh to the soft crease at the top of his thigh, grinning through more feathery kisses. Jesse squirmed under him, fingers tightening in his hair.

"Oh! God, stop! That tickles!" Bright gasps and clear, tinkling edge to the words made Aadon look up to see Jesse's flushed face, lips parted and wet, eyes bright with laughter.

"Does it, now?" He lowered his chin, running his stubble across the sensitive area as he watched Jesse's head tilt back and his lips part wider, peals of laughter spilling out. He gave a little grind with his chin into the muscle, and Jesse convulsed.

"Aadon!" Shoving with both hands on the bigger man's shoulders, Jesse squirmed and folded up, a futile attempt to protect his most ticklish spot from Aadon's ruthless assault. Solid muscle strained against his palms through Aadon's shirt, and Jesse had the shocking realization he was nude, except for his pants around his ankles, and Aadon was still hovering over him, fully dressed and thoroughly enjoying his advantage.

"Hey." Jesse let his hand fall. "How did my jeans come off and yours are still on?"

"That's a problem?" Aadon finally drew his attention away from Jesse's intensely sensitive hips and gazed into his eyes.

"Yeah." Touching Aadon's cheek softly, Jesse let a smile curve his lips. "Huge problem. I can't see any way for you to have me with all those clothes in the way."

"Have you." Aadon sat back on his heels.

Not willing to let him get too far, or to think too hard, Jesse scooted after him and pushed his hands under Aadon's T-shirt. "You know what I mean." He leaned forward and managed to plant a kiss on Aadon's chest despite the awkward position of his knees crammed up and his feet trapped both in his jeans and under Aadon's ass.

"Spell it out for me."

Jesse shook his head in exasperation. "Kill the mood much?" But he grinned, dancing his fingers over Aadon's nipples and feeling a surge of intense satisfaction when Aadon's body arched into the touch. "There you go." He did it again, lingering, and Aadon's eyes dropped closed. A moan parted his lips. "And now I have my own ammunition." Jesse wiggled forward further, pushing the shirt out of his way so he could pinch a nipple up between his lips.

Aadon groaned. Jesse was like a heat-seeking missile, latching on to perhaps the one thing that could make him lose his mind in eight seconds flat. Then the little brat pressed a palm to his cock, rubbing his stiffy through his jeans, and he about came on the spot.

"Jess…." Aadon moved to grip Jesse's wrist but instead found himself pressing Jesse's hand more firmly against his aching cock. "If you're shooting to have me blow my load in my jeans, keep it up," he managed.

The touch of Jesse's lips and hands vanished, and Aadon's eyes popped open. "Hey—"

The protest died on his lips. Jesse had shuffled himself around so he had his back to Aadon. He was kneeling, trapped feet under his pert ass and hands on the bed in front of him. Muscles in his arms and shoulders rippled as he spread his fingers and lifted his ass slightly.

"Oh… my. Jesse—" All Aadon could see was the bottoms of Jesse's feet, his back, and the sweet curve of his ass. The gentle sway of his spine sweeping down to where his cheeks parted practically pointed the way to the most delectable hidden treasure Aadon had ever been offered.

"Yes." Jesse turned his head to peer over his shoulder. "Your Jesse. All yours."

"You're sure—"

The sight of Jesse lifting his ass another inch and swaying back toward him cut off his thought, his speech, his breath.

"I'm sure."

"I think I'm going to have a heart attack."

"Fuck me first, Aadon. Please."

"Please." Aadon at last found the power to move, and all he could manage was to reach over and trail the very tips of his fingers over the perfect curve of pale ass in front of him. "I mean, you asked nicely and everything."

Jesse chuckled. "Catch up, baby." He swayed back again.

"Condoms."

"Front pouch of my backpack."

"Lube."

"Hurry up!"

Aadon's palm itched, suddenly, to give Jesse's ass a slap for the demanding impertinence, but he hesitated. This was too precious a moment to ruin with the chance of a flashback. He opted for verbal control, instead.

"Don't move." Rising from the bed, he stood back to see if his command would be obeyed.

Jesse watched Aadon through the heat of lust, only his head moving to follow his lover's actions. The rest of him stayed perfectly still, ass raised just enough to make his thighs strain to keep it there. A trickle of sweat rolled down from under his hair to coast along his spine. Though it tickled, he managed not to squirm.

In profile, Jesse's submissive position only fuelled Aadon's desire. Coupled with the heated need in Jesse's eyes, he wasn't sure he would be able to put a condom on without even that slight touch making him come. "Very good," he praised, watching Jesse's face to see how he reacted.

An inner light flicked on. Everything in Jesse lit up like fireworks at Aadon's simple words. How hard he'd worked to earn them in the past. How easy it was to get them from someone who truly wanted to give them.

Everything suddenly made sense. He could see in himself all the broken bits left from the battering ram of Anthony's brutality. He could see how easy it would be for Aadon to be lacerated to death on the jagged edges, just trying to clean it all up. And he'd carried those sharp, dangerous pieces inside himself for so long. No wonder he had scars to show for it. They'd been rattling around, destroying him from the inside out, and he'd refused to acknowledge how much it hurt.

The trembling started in his legs but moved with lightning speed through his whole body. Sweat broke out for real, coating him in cold, clammy discomfort in seconds, and he dropped his gaze.

"Jesse." Aadon's arms surrounded him, Aadon's weight pulled him over to his side, and he curled into a ball, clinging to the strong forearms crossing his chest.

"Sorry," he muttered, fighting back the constricting, crushing mass of emotion.

"Shh, no." Aadon kissed Jesse's temple and shifted his weight to cradle the shaking man against his chest. "Not a thing to be sorry for. I'm so proud of you."

"What? For flaking out on you?"

"For finally understanding. For seeing it."

"I'm a mess." Jesse thought hard about freeing himself from Aadon's tight grasp but couldn't bring himself to let go of the lifeline that crushing embrace was offering.

"But you're my mess, and we are going to get you fixed up and working again."

Another kiss pressed to Jesse's temple, and slowly, he started to relax. "Why would you want to bother?"

Now Aadon did release him, and firm hands rolled him onto his back, still naked, jeans still rolled into a tight mass around his ankles, and his now flaccid cock sprawled across his thigh, just another broken bit of him. But Aadon didn't let him go. His body remained pressed against Jesse's side as Aadon leaned over him to look down into his face.

"Because I love you. And just because some of you is damaged and broken, so much more of you is whole, and shining and perfect. Because you're strong and generous and brave. You've had your share of dark, shitty things in your life, and I want to be the one to turn the lights back on, to show you yourself again."

Without thinking about it, Jesse glanced down at his forearms.

Aadon took his chin in hand and turned his face, gazing deep into Jesse's eyes. "You are more than what he did to you."

"And wanting to fix me, it isn't about Ricky?"

Aadon shook his head, far less disturbed by the question than he might have expected. It was a fair one. He knew that now. "Ricky doesn't need me to fix him, either. He needs to believe he can do it himself. All I can do for him is love him and take care of him the best I can. Make sure he has everything he needs."

"You know that's all you can do for me too, right?"

Aadon nodded. He knew he couldn't pick up Jesse's pieces for him, and he was well aware how easily he could be the one to get hurt in the rubble, but it didn't matter. The way Jesse lay there, calm in his arms, his expression as naked as the rest of him, fueled everything possessive and protective in Aadon. He'd take the bad with the good because the good was more perfect than he could ever have imagined on his own.

And right now, all that goodness was still sprawled out next to him watching him expectedly. "What?"

"You were going to make love to me."

"Was."

Jesse took Aadon's hand and laid it over his abdomen. "Did I tell you no?"

"Jess—"

Jesse stopped him talking by once again shoving his shirt up out of the way and attacking his nipple with his soft lips. When Aadon took too long to process the surprise, Jesse helped him out, pushing his hand downward toward his exposed groin.

"You're a brat," Aadon pointed out even as he closed his fingers around Jesse's growing cock.

"Can I help it if I'm so horny for you I can't keep my mind on anything else? Look at me." He directed Aadon's gaze down his body, shining with a sheen of sweat, a small pool of clear liquid gathering on his belly where his cock began to leak from Aadon's touch. "I'd tell you to whip it out and put it in me—"

"Jesse!"

"If I didn't think the refined lawyer in you would freak out." Jesse trailed a finger through the pool on his stomach and brought the finger to hover less than an inch from Aadon's lips. "Do it," he demanded, though his voice was merely a soft, husky whisper. His eyes glowed, and his cheeks flushed. "I know you want to."

Concentrating on getting air into his lungs, Aadon leaned forward to take the tempting offer into his mouth. He watched Jesse's eyelids flutter, his lips part and curl in a smile, heard the tiny sigh. Jesse wasn't consciously trying to seduce with those infinitesimal changes in expression toward happiness, but the effect on Aadon's body was instant, almost to the point of pain.

"Yesss." Jesse's cock jumped in his hand, very slight movements brought his body into more contact with Aadon, his hips rolled almost imperceptibly, and suddenly, his gaze was full and direct again, though his voice remained a breathy tease that Aadon had to lean closer to hear. "Don't be afraid of this. I'm not. I *want* you to enjoy me."

Aadon's cock stiffened. His chest went tight, and his head swam. Tying Perry's aggressive ass to the bed might have been fun and an exhilarating turn on, but watching Jesse voluntarily surrender to him hit deep. It was time to stop thinking about the potential for pain and accept the potential for joy.

Jesse wasn't giving him this because he thought it would stop the pain. He was doing it because it meant something to him. Because it was real, and it was who he was. Unlike Perry, he wasn't goading Aadon to let loose his aggressive side. He was offering his own submission as proof he already accepted Aadon's need for control, that he wanted it.

Pulling his lips off Jesse's finger, Aadon took his chin in hand, held it firmly, and bent for a kiss.

Jesse opened instantly, pushing his tongue into Aadon's mouth, sucking, greedy, full of desire for every taste and touch he could coax out. The kiss lasted and lasted as Aadon's hand roved over him, covering every exposed inch from collarbone to where his jeans stopped the touch at his ankles. He squirmed and writhed to accommodate Aadon's exploration, feeling like a cat, petted to within an inch of his life.

When Aadon began to shove at the jeans, Jesse planted his feet on the bed. "No, don't."

Aadon froze, staring down at him, and Jesse's heart pounded with excitement at the fierce look on his face.

"Leave them," Jesse insisted.

Aadon's eyes narrowed slightly, but his hand moved away from Jess's ankle up toward his raised knee.

"It's not a scene if they're not bonds," Jesse reasoned. "I can kick them off if I want."

Aadon's hand continued to Jesse's inner thigh, and Jesse's stomach clenched in anticipation. He let his knees fall open, pulse quickening at the heat emanating from that traveling palm as it floated down toward his privates. Long fingers caressed his sac, slipped down to tease at the sensitive spot behind, and Jesse let his head fall back onto the pillow.

Carefully, Aadon manipulated Jesse's body until he found Jesse's hole with his fingers, and the tiny sounds of pleasure Jesse let slip drew Aadon ever closer toward the conclusion Jesse was angling for. "You really want this," he whispered, looking down into Jesse's face and watching the pleasure wash over his features. His eyes were closed, but Aadon didn't have to see into them to know Jesse was enjoying this. He was so relaxed, his skin flushed, his lips parted in a sexy half smile as he panted and squirmed.

"Whip it out and put it in, huh?"

"Yeah."

Aadon applied more pressure at Jesse's entrance. "Not because you like it rough, though." He leaned to brush kisses over Jesse's heated torso. "Because you love the fact I'm so close just watching you I won't have time to get all my clothes off before I lose it."

Jesse's eyes flew open, and he grinned up at him. "Really?"

"You know I am."

"Then what are you waiting for?"

"You to roll over and get your ass in the air." He said it in the best commanding voice he could muster, but the effect was ruined by his inability to actually breathe. It came out sounding like he was on the edge of coming in his pants.

Jesse's grin widened. "Yes, sir." He rolled and pulled his knees up, lowering his front half to his elbows this time as he peered over at Aadon. "Get your junk out, let's go."

Aadon was only partly joking about his own impatience. He got off the bed and hurriedly retrieved lube and condoms from Jesse's backpack, tossing them on the bed beside Jesse's knee. When he rounded the bed for a view of Jesse from behind, his heart about stopped.

From the soles of his feet peeking from the crumpled tangle of denim, to his wide-spread knees, to the delicate anatomy displayed between his thighs, ready for Aadon's taking, there was nothing weak or hesitant about Jesse's submission.

Aadon's cock pressed for escape from its own denim prison, and he flicked the buttons open down the front of his jeans. He wasn't going to insult Jesse by asking again if he was sure. It was obvious he'd thought this through, and Aadon realized the fragility Jesse had once displayed was absent. He might be vulnerable now, but only because he allowed himself to be and trusted Aadon to take care of him.

Aadon crawled up on the bed and grabbed the lube. "You're beautiful, Jesse."

Jesse smiled to himself and lowered his forehead onto his arms. In that moment, he knew without doubt, the difference between what he'd known and what he now had. That Aadon could see the beauty in his brokenness where Anthony had sought only to destroy told him he'd made the right choice. Warm, lubed fingers pressed at his opening, and he closed his eyes, concentrating on the gentle touch, the methodical way Aadon opened him up and got him ready. He was gentle and thorough, and Jesse couldn't find it in his heart to complain at the delay because this was what Aadon needed: to establish his hold, his dominance in all the things Anthony had never been.

He wasn't teasing or holding back. He was loving Jesse in ways that were new and far more intimate than just fucking. Far more real than anything Anthony had ever given him. The careful preparation didn't last forever, though, and Jesse sighed heavily when Aadon's fingers withdrew.

"Be patient," Aadon admonished softly.

Jesse heard the condom packet tear and lifted himself enough to look back and see Aadon slip the bit of protection over himself.

"You ready for this?" Aadon asked, skimming a hand over Jesse's hip and down his thigh.

Jesse nodded. "I know it's big. I want this,"

Aadon's large frame descended, his chest contacting Jesse's sweat-slicked back as he draped himself over him. With his lips close to Jesse's ear and his hands carefully steadying him, Aadon whispered, "Me too. So much," in Jesse's ear.

A soft sigh stretched into a long, low moan as Aadon finally penetrated, the motion of taking Jesse an equally long, slow push.

"Like that." Jesse sighed as Aadon's groin came to rest against his ass, and he felt the fullness and pressure, the cold press of buttons and roughness of denim against the backs of his thighs. "So good."

"You are," Aadon agreed, stilling his movement to calm the wild throb of his own cock and the insistent beat of his heart. He was afraid to move, afraid the smallest motion would tip him over the edge and make this the shortest lovemaking session in history.

Jesse's fingers crab-walked across the bedspread, stopping on either side of his head to fist it up into tight bunches, and Aadon hitched in a steadying breath to get himself under control.

"Okay?" he asked.

Jesse nodded. His hands jerked, fingers splaying and tightening again, and Aadon reached to close his bigger hand over one of Jesse's. "Hold still, Jesse. Don't you move. This is my show, you got that?"

Jesse whimpered and nodded, biting his lower lip, fighting to control the desire to push himself back and up against Aadon's body. He'd forgotten, so far back, beyond ever meeting Anthony, when sex had actually felt good and satisfying. Aadon was reeducating him, and he wanted nothing more than to fall into the lesson with everything he had, but he swallowed his impulse and held himself trembling still, waiting.

"Good," Aadon praised, closing his fingers around Jesse's. "Very good." He pulled back, hauling himself upright where he could balance on his knees and use his other hand on Jesse's body, stroking and holding him still as he pulled most of the way out. He might have done it as slowly as he did to prolong the contact, the act, as long as either of them could stand it. He might have drawn it out so he could hear the silky, whimpering sounds spinning from Jesse's lips and feel the way his body responded with a shivering, tremulous struggle against his need. Maybe it was all of that, and more. Because the reverse was equally inspiring, when he pushed back in, and Jesse fought his own desire to thrust back and meet him.

"You want it so bad," Aadon said gently.

Jesse nodded, head dropping to the comforter between his clenched hands, back arching up into the light caress of Aadon's fingers down his spine.

"So do I."

"Like torture," Jesse muttered, every line of him tense and trembling. "You're torturing me."

"And me."

"So cruel." Even to Jesse's ears, the words sounded a lot less substantial in tone than in content. He'd never had as much trouble following Anthony's directions as he was Aadon's. Anthony would hurt him if he disobeyed. Aadon would not. He remained still, as much as his body, mind, and soul wanted desperately to mesh with Aadon's. He followed direction because

Aadon wanted him to. Because the reward of that gentle touch, gentle voice, sweet slide of cock into his body was so much more than worth it.

"Do you know how hard it is to go this slow?" Aadon asked, trying not to sound desperate.

"Then why?"

"Because I want it to sink in." Aadon petted down Jesse's spine again.

"It's in," Jesse reminded him with a faint wiggle of his behind.

Aadon tapped his ass cheek lightly and chuckled. "Not that." He bent and kissed Jesse's exposed back. "This." He kissed further up. "And this." More kisses, more comments. "All of this. I want you to understand what it really is."

Jesse nodded. "I get it."

"And you want more?"

"Yes."

"Please?" Aadon stopped his kissing, stopped the slide of his cock into Jesse and lifted his head so his chin rested on Jesse's back. "Did I hear you say please? I don't think I did."

Now Jesse chuckled, more like a giggle, actually. "Aadon, please. Please, please. Please give me more."

"Ahh." Aadon let the word slide out while he slid in as far as he could. "Now that is music to my ears." He lifted himself up again and placed a hand on either side of Jesse's hips where he had a firm grip. From there, he sat back, pulling Jesse with him into his lap. "Sit up." He kissed where he could reach as he spoke. "You want more? You take what you want, Jesse. Anything you want. This is all you." He slid his hands around, one up Jesse's torso to glide over a nipple, the other to his cock. "I'm all yours."

Legs and feet trapped between Aadon's thick thighs, Jesse had to lean forward on hands and knees to move himself, but with Aadon's help, he found a position that let him maneuver his ass enough to grind on Aadon's cock.

"I take it all back," he panted, as he reveled in the feel of Aadon inside him. "You can talk." He groaned as Aadon thrust up to meet his lowering ass, and his cock dug in deep. "You could probably talk an orgasm out of me, no hands necessary."

Aadon grinned, lips pressed to Jesse's shoulder blade. "A challenge. I'll have to try that one day."

"Not today." Jesse clamped his lips shut and closed his eyes as he pumped, losing himself for a moment in the rhythm. "Today, just do this. Me. Like this. Just...." His words dropped off as his pace increased, and anything else he tried to say came out only in soft pants and clipped, muttered curses. Aadon's fist worked him in perfect time to the rest of their movement, and it was only a few heartbeats before his balls drew in tight, and that fire lit through him, starting low and hot and sparking a chain reaction up his spine.

Aadon pushed, a hand in the center of his back, shoving him toward the mattress, driving into him and shouting as his cock hammered over Jesse's gland.

It was over. Jesse's orgasm blinded him, deafened him, turned him inside out and numb, and he sagged, only to return to himself in the next heartbeat to feel Aadon wrapped around him and shuddering against him, whispering his name.

In that moment, with the feel of Aadon wrapped around him, pressed against him, inside him—everything—Jesse knew peace. The crush of wrinkled T-shirt against his back and the bite of denim and buttons against his legs registered in his brain as a perfect counterpart to the splay of hands against his chest, the hard clamp of muscled arms, and bare skin holding his own arms against his sides. Once again, Aadon's orgasm had hit him hard and turned him fierce and tight. Jesse rocked ever so slightly, forward and back, and listened to the bigger man breathe, ragged gasps punctuated with labored swallowing.

The sticky heat of his own come on his bent thighs served to prove answer to Aadon's next whispered question: "Okay?"

"Perfect." Jesse wiggled one hand up to lay over Aadon's. "You?"

No answer. Just the tight, tight hold and Aadon's weight crushing him into a ball.

"Aadon?"

Aadon shifted them both, his strength no contest for Jesse's lethargic, sloppy afterglow. Before he knew it, Aadon had them on their sides, basically in the same position, his arms still wrapped around Jesse, but his lips now a hairsbreadth from his ear.

"Everything I ever wanted, Jesse," Aadon whispered. "The first time we were together, I knew it, and it terrified us both."

"It still scares you," Jesse guessed, bringing his hands up to clasp Aadon's against his chest. "I can feel it, the way you're holding on so tight, trembling, breathing like you expect someone is going to suck all the air out of the room any moment."

Shifting, forcing Aadon to release him, or at least loosen his grip so he could move, Jesse rolled toward him, onto his back so he could look into Aadon's face. It also meant releasing Aadon's softening cock from his body, so he reached to make sure the condom stayed safely in place until it was free and he could toss it over the side of the bed.

Aadon stared down at him, his eyes far away. Jesse touched his cheek. "Hey."

A vacant smile ghosted over Aadon's face, a shadow unable to hold against whatever was going on inside.

Jesse stroked fingers over Aadon's stubble and lifted his head to plant a kiss on his slack lips. "C'mon back here, Aadon. Nothing to be scared of."

"Not scared." Aadon sighed, and finally, his gaze focused on Jesse's face. "Oh hell, okay. Maybe a little." Now his hand was cupping Jesse's face, and for a few moments, gazes locked, they could silently agree to share that little bit of fear, of euphoria in knowing they'd found something terrifying and brilliant that neither of them wanted to let go.

Chapter
Twenty-One

RICKY knew they were coming because Dr. Carol called Aadon's cell to tell him Ricky had seen them from the common room's window, walking hand in hand up the path toward the visitor's garden. So when they saw him strolling out the French doors from the lower dining hall into the moonlit garden, Jesse could feel Aadon's shock through his hard clenching fingers and hear his joy in the sharp intake of breath.

"Ricky!" Aadon stood and was halfway to hugging his brother before he thought about it. Even before he let go of Jesse's hand.

"Hey, A." Ricky stopped just short of the offered embrace, stuffed one hand into a pocket and used the other to rub through his hair. He jutted his chin at Jesse. "He the one?"

Jesse tried not to glow at that fortuitous phrase.

"The one." Aadon chuckled. "Yeah, Ricky. He's the one. Ricky, this is my boyfriend, Jesse. Jesse, my older brother, Ricky."

Jesse nodded, met Ricky's fleeting gaze. "I've heard a lot about you," he offered. "You guys are so lucky, having a brother. In my family, there's just me."

"Heh." Ricky's lip twisted up, and the hand in his hair tugged at the blond strands a bit as he shrugged. "Lucky me. Work for A."

Jesse let his smile widen. "Not to hear him talk. Not with all the great things he tells me."

"Shitty things, too, huh?" Ricky twitched, jamming his balled up fist deeper into his pocket, dragging the too-loose jeans down past his hip. Jesse noticed someone, a middle-aged woman he assumed was Dr. Carol had approached from inside and now stood almost next to Ricky.

Jesse glanced from Ricky to her and to Aadon, but settled his gaze back on Ricky. "Some that happened to you," Jesse agreed. "Sort of...." He licked his lips and felt almost like doing as Ricky was and ducking his head, hiding his trembling hand in his pocket, as deep as it would go, as if that would stop the shaking or take away the rolling sick in his gut. "Sort of the same things that happened to me, so I guess he thought I'd understand, you know?"

Ricky's hand dropped from his hair to his side. His gaze traveled from Jesse to his brother, a question in his eyes. He even glanced at the doctor, who Jesse had thought he didn't know was there. Finally, his questioning look settled on Jesse again. "Does... do... you." He cleared his throat and took a step forward, pale eyes intent and focused. "You got better?"

"Umm." Jesse glanced to Aadon, to Dr. Carol for guidance, but they both just watched him. No way could either of them answer that question for him. "No." He felt Aadon's hand in his slip and hung on tighter. "And yes, kind of. But... some of it...." He shrugged. "I'm still trying to figure out if there is better, you know? Or just different." Now he looked fully at Aadon and brought their clasped hands to his lips. "But I have Aadon too." He turned back to Ricky with a small shrug. "If you'll share him."

Ricky's grin rivaled the brightness of the near-full moon, and he nodded. "Yeah. That'd be good."

JAIME SAMMS has been writing her stories between men long enough to know better, but not nearly long enough to have told all the tales she has to tell. She splits her time between a day job that pays the bills and her writing that feeds her soul. She's also a mom with a saint of a husband, who keeps the kids fed and clothed and home schooled and herself on a schedule that keeps her sane. She also reviews stories between men for the Dark Diva Reviews, http://ddrreviews.blogspot.com/, and yaoi novels for Kuriousity, http://www.kuri-ousity.com/. The three cats in residence seem to approve of this arrangement enough to warm her toes at night and keep up a supply of mice from the backyard they think the family needs for survival. Who are we to argue?

Visit her web site: http://www.jaime-samms.net, her blog: http://jaimesamms.blogspot.com, and her LiveJournal: http://dontkickmycane.livejournal.com/

www.ingramcontent.com/pod-product-compliance
Lightning Source LLC
Chambersburg PA
CBHW071310250626
47159CB00004B/1376